MISCHIEVOUS MEMORIES

Theodosia remembered their first kiss. Marcus had turned her to face him. There had been a question in his eyes: Are you ready now? Her own gaze must have given him the answer he wished, for he drew her toward him and kissed her. His lips were tender on hers but it was not simply a passing touch. She had no desire to draw away from him, but she had not previously experienced the chaos which gripped her, and she was shaken. When he had at last desisted, she found that her hands were on his shoulders and had no idea how they had gotten there.

That kiss had been as innocent as they. But Marcus was no longer a raw romantic youth but a sensually seasoned man. Theodosia was no longer a fluttering girl but a woman with a fiercely hungering heart. And if they kissed again, it would be very different—and far more dangerous. . . .

IN MY LADY'S CHAMBER

by

Laura Matthews

A SIGNET BOOK

SIGNET
Published by the Penguin Group
Penguin Books USA Inc., 375 Hudson Street,
New York, New York 10014, U.S.A.
Penguin Books Ltd, 27 Wrights Lane,
London W8 5TZ, England
Penguin Books Australia Ltd, Ringwood,
Victoria, Australia
Penguin Books Canada Ltd, 10 Alcorn Avenue,
Toronto, Ontario, Canada M4V 3B2
Penguin Books (N.Z.) Ltd, 182---190 Wairau Road,
Auckland 10, New Zealand

Penguin Books Ltd, Registered Offices:
Harmondsworth, Middlesex, England

Published by Signet, an imprint of New American Library,
a division of Penguin Books USA Inc. Previously published as
In My Lady's Chamber by Elizabeth Neff Walker.

First Signet Printing, July, 1993
10 9 8 7 6 5 4 3 2 1

IN MY LADY'S CHAMBER

Chapter One

"You must know, my dear Miss Tremere, that I am more than pleased with your care and guidance of the children, and I do not for a moment wish you to think that I hold you to blame for the lowness of their spirits." Lady Eastwick drew the shawl closer about her shoulders and a momentary sadness lined her attractive face. "We all feel a great loss at Katey's death, of course, but that is months ago and I cannot help but worry at the others' continued melancholy. It is time they put aside their grief and went on with their lives."

The young woman who sat opposite her nodded composedly as she tied a knot in her embroidery thread. "Yes, I've felt much the same, Lady Eastwick. At first I wished to see them express their grief openly, but enough time has passed that the wound should be healing now. I think perhaps they were awaiting Lord Eastwick's letter, you know."

Her companion shifted the candle away from her so that the suspicion of moisture in her eyes would not be noticed. When she spoke, there was a faint quaver to her voice. "Poor Eastwick. To learn of his youngest child's death in a letter! And he was so very fond of her—as he is of all of them, of course. We have lost two others, but he was here then, and they were infants, not surviving the first few weeks of life. It's not the same with a child of three. And dear Eastwick in America with hardly an acquaintance to condole with him! At least I had you, and Edward and Thomas and Charlotte and Eleanor and John and Amy to share my heartbreak." She stared unseeing at the windows, their panes of glass reflecting the dimly lit room against the black of the summer evening without, and sighed. "I don't have to tell you what a comfort you have been to me, Miss Tremere. Edward has tried to stand in his father's stead but..."

"There has been a great deal of responsibility for one his age," Miss Tremere remarked matter-of-factly as she set a stitch. The firelight caught the contours of her face as she bent over her work, glowing on the high forehead and the wide brown eyes. A serene face it was which neither proclaimed nor denied the four and twenty years she had acquired but a face in which both beauty and character were expressed most forcefully. The full mouth wore a half smile now, and there was a twinkle in the eyes. "He has found it difficult to juggle the roles of loving brother and acting head of family. Although he was as distressed as anyone else at Katey's death, he wanted to appear a tower of strength, and has, I fear, left his sisters and brothers entirely out of charity with him."

"Humph! It perplexes me to understand how he's turned out so stuffy. Lord knows there isn't a stodgy bone in his father's body, nor in any of the rest of the family, except possibly.... Well, that's no matter. Thank God Eastwick will be home in the autumn for Edward's coming of age. I do miss him dreadfully, though I fully realize the importance of his work. Do you really believe all the children have been awaiting his letter?"

"I think it unsettled them, knowing that Lord Eastwick wasn't here to share their sorrow. Now they've heard from him, and have his own expressions of loss, they will be more ready to leave the past behind. On the other hand, they had acquired some distance from that dreadful time, and now it is made fresh again for them. What they need is a distraction, an absorbing, continuing project to stimulate their interest. We've taken picnic lunches and visited various historic and beauty spots in the neighborhood, but I cannot feel our expeditions have been altogether successful. During the last week I've been developing an idea. You may think it a bit farfetched."

A log fell in the grate and Miss Tremere rose to poke it farther back. The night was not cool enough to require adding any more wood since the ladies ordinarily retired before eleven. As it was, they were sitting later than usual to discuss this matter of importance to them both. Lady Eastwick surveyed her companion with interest.

"Farfetched? My dear Miss Tremere, I am quite sure any scheme you could promote would be most welcome. I have the utmost faith in your ingenuity."

The governess remained standing by the mantel, the poker pointed to the inscription thereon. "Every fireplace at Charton Court has this same inscription on the mantel, and over the years I've heard the children speculate on what it has to do with the family 'mystery,' as they call it. Correct me if I've misunderstood, but I believe the essence of the story to be that some long-gone Heythrop ancestor had in his keeping a treasure of sorts, either family or national, which was symbolized by this inscription. Now, I realize that through the years also every generation of Heythrops has made a search with absolutely no success. Nonetheless, I propose a search of our own, aided perhaps by a few—ah, shall we say manufactured—clues. I could weave the plot into our history lessons as well as our literary forays. It would be necessary, I feel, to provide some sort of reward at the end of our venture—an old flagon or altar plate, for instance, to be discovered at the conclusion. I feel sure that with a little planning we could make quite a summer's worth of entertainment out of it."

"A treasure hunt?" Lady Eastwick asked faintly.

"Precisely. Now I do see the drawback, which is that

9

we would be hoodwinking the children somewhat, leading them to believe that they were on the trail of the real mystery, as we would start from that point. But I think it would be absolutely necessary at the start to gain their enthusiasm by beginning with something which already holds a fascination for them. I would make it clear as we progressed that we might be straying from our original purpose, but I don't think they would care by that time. Once the spirit is captured, the momentum will roll them along, and if the prize is a bit of a disappointment, well, there will still be a prize."

Lady Eastwick sat contemplating the proposal for some time, weighing its advantages and disadvantages, liking it better the more she thought about it. There was, in the end, only one consideration which made her hesitate. "Edward won't like it."

"No, Lord Heythrop wouldn't approve, to be sure." Miss Tremere smiled her calm, reassuring smile. "I propose we don't include him in our plans."

Her employer gave a quickly stifled laugh. "But he's bound to hear of it."

"From the children, yes. And if he should complain to you of their frivolity (and mine) in such a pursuit, I trust you could convince him of the benefits of such a diversion." Miss Tremere pursed her lips thoughtfully. "But only in extreme necessity would I divulge the whole to him. He takes his family and his heritage most seriously. He might feel that we were making light of his very traditions if he saw them distorted into a...treasure hunt."

"I fear you're right," Lady Eastwick mused, absently toying with a little gold locket which contained her husband's likeness in miniature. "And yet I don't think Eastwick would disapprove. In fact, I think he would congratulate you on a most propitious scheme. It will make a great deal of work for you."

The wide brown eyes danced. "I shall thoroughly enjoy it. And consider it a challenge to see how long we can keep your first-born from guessing the truth.

John and Thomas are still too much the schoolboys to be more than intrigued by a mystery of any sort, I gather, and the girls confessed to me when first I came here three years ago that they intended to find the treasure themselves, just to prove that all the *men* (I shan't tell you what adjective they used) who had searched for it previously had been outwitted by the first females to grace your family for generations. I dare say they would prefer it if Thomas and John were still at school, but for our purposes it is better that they're here on their summer holidays."

"Decidedly. I have hated to think of them away at Eton when they were feeling so wretched, and at such a time I can't believe the girls will mind sharing the adventure. Now, what is to be my part in this?"

Miss Tremere picked up a leather-bound journal in which she kept a variety of useful notations, a record she had started, she realized, when she was Charlotte's age. Her careful copy of the inscription from the fireplace was there, separated from her lesson plans for the girls' schooling by a leather bookmark she had been given long ago. As always she touched the leather reminiscently. It had been given to her by Marcus Williams, Viscount Steyne, some six years previously on the occasion of her eighteenth birthday. The journal, too, contained numerous entries from those days, though she rarely referred to them now.

There had been a time when she read those passages with provoking frequency. No more. Miss Tremere had, of necessity, set aside her girlish dreams of romance, and found her life as governess to the Heythrop girls eminently comfortable. Fantasy was for children—and for adults determined to spark their young imaginations in a worthy cause, she reminded herself with a faint smile. She no longer dwelled on what might have been. The present, the future were what she had to work with. Miss Tremere looked up from the journal and addressed her companion.

"There are two things you could do for me if you would, Lady Eastwick. Most important is the treasure itself. As I see how the hunt progresses and determine on a location for the 'find,' I will have to have something to put there. I doubt it need be particularly valuable, so long as it is sufficiently old."

"My sister is in London this summer. Surely she can find something there for us which will serve our purpose. You have only to let me know what it is you wish. And the other?"

Theodosia closed the journal. "I will need to know as much of the 'legend' as you can recall."

"I fear I'm sadly lacking in curiosity, Miss Tremere, and haven't paid a great deal of attention to it. When I came here as a bride Eastwick told me of how he had searched as a child; they all had. And of course I can remember him sitting with our children, passing on the tale. Nothing ever had Thomas so wide-eyed, I promise you, or Edward so animated. I can't imagine how Edward has become so prosaic! But that is aside from the point. Eastwick did once show me an old document which purported to tell the whole story, but it's a little difficult to read, being faded and in a rather cramped hand. Now where was that kept, I wonder? Certainly not in Eastwick's bedchamber."

Miss Tremere waited patiently while her employer searched her mind for a recollection of the circumstances. Lady Eastwick was at her most attractive when puzzling over some elusive detail. Her fragility was belied by the large family she had produced, and her whimsicality by the way she unerringly set about solving any dilemma on the most practical of footings. If she had taken to wearing caps, it was because of her position, and not because her glossy black hair had any trace of gray. The delicate features were now adorably puckered with her efforts—quirked brows and a lip caught between fine white teeth.

"I remember he was showing me a survey map of our area, a very old one. Edward had ridden off and come home very late that day. He must have been only twelve then, and we were considerably alarmed. Apparently he had taken a fall some distance off and the horse had strayed. Fortunately the beast didn't take it into his head to return to the stables! It was after we had gotten Edward to bed that Eastwick showed me a map—not the one I just mentioned, but a more recent one. Edward must have been beyond Monksilver! That's why Eastwick showed me the map, you see—to try to determine where it was the boy had gotten himself to! And, really, it is difficult to believe but he had gone through Heddon Oak and Stogumber and right through Monksilver up to Bird's Hill! Imagine!"

Miss Tremere murmured a suitable exclamation of astonishment and awaited further developments.

"Now I remember. We were in the archive room. That's where Eastwick keeps all the old maps and out-dated family papers and such. After he had shown me the newer map, he remembered the old one and thought it might be of interest to me. I can't think why! I have no sense of direction at all, and he had to go over Edward's probable route very carefully for me even to follow what he was saying. But there, he's very patient with me, and he knows it's highly unlikely I shall ever have to guide myself with a map. I was fascinated, however, by a great series of markings on the old map and he explained that they were from a search for the treasure—oh, eons ago. And then he showed me the document containing the story of the family mystery. So that's where it will be—in the archive room."

"Excellent!" Miss Tremere congratulated her, with only the very slightest twitching of her lips. "Shall we look for it now, or are you ready for your bed?"

"It won't take a moment. I can clearly see where he put it now, in my mind's eyes, you know. It's such a *large* house, and I dare say quite unmodern in some respects, but I have a fondness for it just the same. Even the archive room, which is depressingly full of dusty old documents and crumbling papers. But you get *used* to a house, don't you, and feel very comfortable with it. We'll need our candles to go into the East Wing."

Despite the additions of various generations of Heythrops to Charton Court, it maintained a distinctly Tudor atmosphere which might have been daunting to a visitor, but Lady Eastwick and Miss Tremere were familiar with the rambling old pile; at least as familiar as one can be with an almost unending succession of rooms and odd nooks and crannies. Not that Charton Court provided no possibilities for exploration: far from it. A medieval manor house had been largely, but not entirely, torn down to make way for the present house, which consisted of four wings around the internal courtyard and the big hall. A successor to this ambitious builder had added a chapel, an entrance porch and towers at the four angles, as well as bay windows, and no succeeding generation had escaped the desire to improve and extend, though they did so with a rare sensitivity to its original character. No modern convenience was bypassed (there were a total of fourteen water closets) and chimneys were rebuilt as they began to cause problems, but withal the house exuded an almost palpable air of antiquity and romance.

The idea of a treasure hunt would probably not have occurred to Miss Tremere had she not daily found herself in a suite of rooms such as she did. Her bedchamber contained an enormous four-poster bed, richly carved by a talented artisan of the late fifteenth century, and on each of the walls were tapestries depicting medieval hunting scenes, while above, the ceiling plasterwork incorporated the monograms of several long-dead monarchs. The Tudor closet which attached to this room, and where she had her desk, had a leaded glass, Gothic window and a cantelevered beamed ceiling. There was also, most fascinating of all, in addition to the mammoth oak portal leading into the room, a minute door which only a child could enter upright—and which led straight into...a blank wall. Such occurrences were not rare at Charton Court, but they were provocative.

Their candles threw grotesque shapes on the walls and flickered in the draughty corridor as they passed door after door toward the far end of the wing. When Lady Eastwick eventually paused, she drew a ring of keys from her reticule, and though it could not have been recently that she visited the room, immediately chose the one which clicked in the well-oiled lock. "Eastwick keeps all the rooms which are not in use locked. We never locked anything where I grew up in Cumberland, but then strangers were more noticeable there." She moved at once toward an old oak chest, setting her candle down on the shelf beside it. "The bottom drawer, I think. Yes, here is the map and...no, that's not it. Ah, I have it. You will want both maps, I suppose."

The document she produced was wrapped in a leather tube and proved even more fragile than she had suggested. The parchment was yellowed and had a tendency to crumble at the edges when extracted from its case. Miss Tremere gingerly spread it out on the slanted surface of a walnut writing desk, holding her candle so as to get the best light and yet not allow any hot wax to drip on the sheet. "Hmm, I think I shall be able to decipher it in daylight. I'd not care to ruin my eyes working at it by candlelight! And if I'm successful, I shall make a copy, as exact as I am able, so that future generations will not need to depend on the original, which is likely to disintegrate one of these days. Now, as to the map, did you think that it showed the search made by the writer of the document?"

Lady Eastwick considered this point with her customary quaint distortion of face. "I can't be sure. It doesn't look as old, does it?"

"No, and one would think a map would be a great deal more worn than the document. No matter. Perhaps there will be a clue as to date on one or both of them. I mustn't keep you from bed, Lady Eastwick. Is it all right for me to take them to my room?"

"Oh, certainly. I intended you should. You wouldn't want to have to come to the archive room to do your deciphering; it's far too musty here."

Miss Tremere had rolled up the parchment document and slipped it carefully into the leather tube when the door was flung open with a resulting crash, and Lord

Heythrop stood there in his dressing gown, armed with a poker. His countenance rapidly disintegrated from towering rage to astonishment to a painful sheepishness. "I couldn't imagine who would be in the archive room at this hour of the night," he blurted, unsuccessfully attempting to hide the poker behind his back. Avoiding Miss Tremere's calm gaze, he spoke rather sternly to his mother. "It's gone eleven, Mama, and you should be in bed."

With an expressive glance at her companion, Lady Eastwick replied gently, "I was just showing Miss Tremere some maps and old papers, Edward. She is going to take them to her room."

His frown was a study in baffled indecision. "Do you think Papa would approve of their being removed from here?"

"I'm sure he would." She took his arm, careful to choose the one not holding the poker, and urged him toward the door. "You shall see me to my room, dear, after we've locked the door."

While Lady Eastwick made a great show of not being able to find the right key, Miss Tremere slipped away down the corridor, as she felt sure her employer intended her to do. Obviously Lord Heythrop had every intention of pursuing his inquiries into such an unprecedented action on his mother's part, and Lady Eastwick was in a better position than the governess to deflect his curiosity. Guided by her thorough knowledge of the layout of the house, Miss Tremere glided swiftly and silently through the corridors and up the main staircase to the first floor, where her suite was located in the West Wing, being closest to the nursery and schoolroom on the floor above. A fire burned low on the hearth and she smothered a yawn as she placed her newly acquired materials on the nightstand.

The maid she shared with the girls had left her nightdress on the bed and set the warming pan by the fire. Really, she thought, as she released her long brown hair from the pins which held it atop her head, there could be nothing more pleasant than being a member of the Heythrop household, practically treated as one of the family and having something useful to do in addition. Well, almost nothing as pleasant. One could have been mistress of one's own household....

Her thoughts were drawn up abruptly and she stood by the fire to remove her beige round dress, its plainness alleviated by a plaiting of peach-colored satin ribbon which the girls had urged her to buy in the village. As she slipped the flannel nightdress over her head, curiosity about the documents drew her over to the stand and she could not resist beginning to read the account of the treasure. Puzzled, she thumbed through the sheets, a small frown gathering on her forehead. A hesitant knock at her door startled her.

"Who is it?"

There was a slight pause. "Edward."

"Just a moment, please." Miss Tremere hastily donned a dressing gown which was folded over a ladder-back chair near the wash-hand stand, but she did not retrieve her candle to take with her to the door.

Lord Heythrop stood rather awkwardly in the hall, as though he had thought better of his mission but could find no way now to retreat. He had disposed of the poker but the candle he carried threw its meager light on her released tresses and night clothing. "I beg your pardon! I never thought you'd have....That is, it's been only a few minutes....I won't disturb you."

"If it is a matter of importance...."

"No, no, nothing which cannot wait until the morning, I assure you." In an effort to regain his composure, Lord Heythrop tugged at his cravat, managing only to ruin the lay of its folds. Desperately he assumed the stiff stance which his brothers and sisters had come to know so well since their father's departure for America, and said in a toneless voice, "My family keeps rather voluminous records of previous generations in the archive room. As a rule there is nothing particularly personal or private about these papers, but you can understand that having a complete set of records—as complete as it is—proved invaluable to each succeeding generation of Heythrops. There are records of births and deaths, old account books, family Bibles, any number of things. Therefore it has always been the practice at Charton Court never to remove anything from that room, on the slight chance that an item might be mislaid. I'm sure you can understand the efficacy of such a policy."

"Certainly."

When she said nothing further, he cleared his throat. "The fact of the matter is, Miss Tremere, that my mother should not have allowed anything to leave the room. I don't blame you! You could not have been aware of that unwritten rule. Perhaps my mother is not aware of it. But I am entrusted with the safekeeping of all that is in Charton Court in my father's absence, and I should be remiss in my duties if I permitted such a breach of security."

"Yes, I do see that," Theodosia mused, regarding him gravely. "And I feel that I should perhaps just tell you that the papers I brought to my room are not complete."

Startled, he asked, "What do you mean?"

"I took away the ninth earl's account of the treasure and it states most definitely that there is attached a letter from the first earl which is supposed to provide a clue as to the location and meaning of the mystery. There is nothing whatsoever attached to his account!"

Poor Edward was struck dumb. A dozen thoughts ran through his mind, not the least of them being the question of why Miss Tremere should have taken such papers from the archive room, but what he at length blurted was: "You must be mistaken."

"I assure you I am not. The ninth earl's account is apparently complete, though I have not finished reading it. Lady Eastwick also had me take an old map and a more current one to study. They seem quite in order. What is missing is the first earl's letter."

"That's impossible," he stated bluntly, his brows lowering with annoyance. "I myself have read the first earl's letter. Father showed it to me years ago. It was a poem of sorts, which no one in the family had been able to unravel as an explanation of where the treasure was."

Miss Tremere silently walked to the stand, picked up the papers and brought them to him. "As you can see, it is not here, Lord Heythrop."

Edward went through the papers three times. His chagrin, his frustration, found outlet in a not entirely illogical way. Belligerent, he demanded, "Tell me, Miss Tremere, why were you reading these papers about the treasure in the first place?"

Casting an unconcealed glance at her dressing gown, Miss Tremere suggested, "Perhaps we could discuss that in the morning, Lord Heythrop."

"Of course!" Edward backed away from her, apologetic, but still with an effort to maintain control of the situation. "If you will come to my office...my father's office...in the morning, we can speak there."

"Very well, Lord Heythrop. I shall wait on you in the morning."

As she turned back into the room he murmured, "Good night, Miss Tremere."

"Good night, Lord Heythrop." She closed the door gently, a rueful smile playing about her lips. After a quick pass of the warming pan between the sheets, she climbed into the bed and promptly fell asleep.

Chapter Two

Owing to the early hours they kept, the Charton
Court household were also early risers. By her own
request, Theodosia Tremere had her morning chocolate
brought to her room shortly after seven, where she
allowed herself the luxury of sipping it slowly in bed
while she made notes in her journal of her plans for the
day in instructing her charges. Though turned seventeen, Charlotte was still considered a member of the
schoolroom, a circumstance which caused her no annoyance since she was fond of Miss Tremere. At thirteen Eleanor showed little promise of scholarship, but
her ability in watercolors and any form of needlework
was admirable. Surprisingly, it was Amy, at the tender
age of seven, who required Theodosia's most particular
care. The child had a quickness of mind and a reten-
tiveness of memory the like of which Theodosia (as well
as Amy's family) had never seen.

Her notes completed, Theodosia put aside her journal. Although the younger boys were home from Eton
and wandered in and out of the schoolroom at will, they
were not ostensibly included in her lessons. It was summer, after all, and the poor, hard-working male schol-
ars needed this break from their grueling schedule. Or
so they said. Theodosia found little difficulty in gaining

their interest in contemporary literature, a subject wholly neglected by their curriculum. Afternoons would often find all five children sprawled in various positions of disarray about the sun-drenched topiary and gardens, indulging in their favorite pastimes of reading or drawing; and if they found themselves reading something Miss Tremere had suggested—well, by Jove, she knew just what a fellow would enjoy.

In honor of the start of her scheme, Theodosia donned a sky-blue jaconet walking dress with braided collar and cuffs before retrieving the map and leather tube from its overnight resting place. She took them into the beamed closet to work on, leaving the door open to her bedchamber so she might hear if one of her charges came looking for her. There was plenty of time to transcribe the document before Lord Heythrop would expect her at his (father's) office. Poor Edward, so determined to uphold the family responsibilities in lieu of Lord Eastwick, and what a wearisome task he was making of it! Theodosia allowed herself one wistful glance out the window at the sunny summer morning before setting to her task. She had only just begun when she was interrupted by a knock at her door, and she closed and locked the desk before rising to answer it. The oldest of the three sisters stood smiling in the hall, her black curls charmingly framing an angelic face.

"Are you not coming to breakfast now, Miss Tremere? Amy is eager to show you the new kittens. Miss Whiskers littered last night."

"Did she? In the barn, I hope. Or did Amy have her hidden under her bed?" Theodosia closed the door and walked down the hall with Charlotte, not at all impatient at being disturbed in her task.

"Well, Amy did have her in her room, but Edward heard Miss Whiskers' mews and insisted that she be taken out to the barn." Charlotte was indignant.

"I'm sure Miss Whiskers didn't mind in the least, my dear. She probably had a spot picked out there for the purpose and would have felt unsettled to use Amy's room."

"But we didn't get to see her have the kittens!" Charlotte protested. "Edward wouldn't let us stay there with her."

"Most unfortunate," Theodosia admitted, "but the barn is drafty and I doubt Lady Eastwick would have appreciated your all coming down with colds."

"We *told* Edward we would wrap ourselves up well! He wouldn't listen!"

"He was only thinking of your welfare."

"Humph! That's what he always says, and it is no such thing. He simply likes to lord it over all of us. I pity the poor girl he marries."

"Nonsense," Theodosia rejoined, but with merry eyes. "Once Lord Eastwick returns and your brother is unburdened of some of his responsibilities (and there are many of them, Charlotte), you will find him a great deal easier to live with."

Since they were just entering the Breakfast Parlor, Charlotte said only, "I certainly hope so."

Assembled at the shining mahogany table were all of the other resident Heythrops except the eldest son. Eleanor, dressed in a delightful creation of her own design, was conversing quietly with her mother, while the two boys, Thomas and John, were teasing Amy about the kittens. Sentences broke off abruptly as a chorus of "Good morning, Miss Tremere" greeted her arrival, and the boys politely rose and vied for the honor of seating her between them.

"It's a perfect day for a ride," Thomas suggested, "and I've a mind to show you the castle remains near Bincombe, if you'd like."

"Oh, she's seen them a thousand times, I'll bet," John retorted disparagingly. "Much more the sort of day to take a walk to the Home Farm and have a syllabub in the dairy."

"Well," Amy interposed, "for certain the *first* thing she will wish to do is see the kittens. Oh, Miss Tremere, there are six of them! The most adorable little things you've ever seen."

"They look like rats," Thomas muttered.

Theodosia took a sip of the scalding coffee and surveyed each of the children in turn. When she spoke, it was in tones of doom. "I am summoned to Lord Heythrop's office."

Her pronouncement fell on shocked ears. "Oh, no!" "What can *you* possibly have done to incur Edward's wrath!" "You see, I told you! He likes nothing more than to lord it over *everyone!*" "Mama, surely you won't let Edward come the heavy with Miss Tremere!" "Really, it's too, too bad of him! You were to see the kittens straight away."

Lady Eastwick glanced quizzically at the governess and shook her head. "Now, children, I am sure Edward hasn't the least intention of scolding our Miss Tremere. More likely he has some question of an academic nature which he feels she may sort out for him. He was never more than passable in geography, as I recall."

Although skeptical, the children made an effort to brace Theodosia's spirits. "That will be it," Charlotte asserted. "Edward will want to know something about America and where Papa wrote he would be traveling."

"I shall be happy to help him if I can." Assuming a brighter countenance, Theodosia helped herself from the plate of kippers being held by the underfootman, who looked quite as anxious as the children. "Perhaps we should send off to London for a more current map of the New World, Lady Eastwick. Only the very largest towns show on ours, and Lord Eastwick finds himself in some rather obscure places."

"An excellent idea. Eleanor, you will find Cary's direction in the *New Itinerary,* I believe. If you will bring it to me in the Front Parlor, I shall write to him this morning. He is bound to have maps of America as well as England, I dare say, and if not, he will know where to get them. Come, children. Leave Miss Tremere to finish her breakfast in peace."

Only Charlotte remained behind, not having finished her toast in her concern over the governess being called to Edward's office. "He's not likely to raise a great fuss, you know. He likes you."

"I'm relieved to hear it. But you mustn't fret, my dear. I promise you I'm not quaking in my shoes, though you mustn't think me any the less respectful of your brother. His is not an easy position. Still," she said briskly, "I am sure he and I shall overcome any little problem which may be plaguing him. You don't think he holds me responsible for Miss Whiskers, do you?"

Charlotte laughed at the mock-alarm in Miss Tremere's eyes. "I would that I could jest about his crotchets. The other day he told me I was seeing entirely too much of Carlton Winstanley. Honestly! The poor fellow is only home on leave for a month and has been over but twice! To take tea with the entire family! I haven't seen him alone at all."

A wistful note had crept into her voice and Theodosia smiled across the table at her. "He will be at Wildcroft Grange for another two weeks. I'm sure we'll see him again."

"Yes, and Edward will *speak* to me again. Really, I think he's jealous of Mr. Winstanley and his naval career. They used to be the very best of friends, you know, but Edward won't even listen to all Mr. Winstanley's adventures."

"Lord Heythrop is possibly thinking of his father's mission in America, Charlotte. When the earl is endeavoring to avoid a military conflict with the Americans, it hardly becomes his son to glory in the British naval ploys there."

Charlotte tossed her black ringlets disbelievingly. "I don't think so. Edward just wishes that he were off somewhere being brave and serving his country like Mr. Winstanley is, or trying to maintain the peace like Papa. He doesn't like playing nursemaid to his family—and he doesn't do it very well!"

"You aren't making it any easier for him," Theodosia said gently. "Now don't take a pet, my dear; I know you have had a great deal to put up with. When all is said and done, though, Lord Heythrop does have more to handle than one his age ordinarily would, what with times being rather difficult right now. It seems to me that you and your sisters and brothers would make things easier for yourselves by trying to accommodate your eldest brother instead of fighting him on every little point. You only set up his back that way."

"He used to be one of us. He used to *care*."

"He still does care."

"No, he doesn't," Charlotte protested, a catch in her voice. "When Katey...died he didn't shed a tear."

"Of course he did, only not where you could see him. In front of the family he wanted to appear sure and steady, someone you could lean on. Charlotte, he thought that was the way he was supposed to behave, the way his father would have behaved."

"Papa wouldn't have been so rigid. There were tear stains on his letter."

"I know. But you must believe that Lord Heythrop thought he was acting for the best. Perhaps I shouldn't tell you this, but I feel I must: I was the one who brought him the news. Your mother couldn't bear to do so at the time, and Lord Heythrop had fallen asleep in a chair in the library after sitting up all night with Katey. Charlotte, he wept as though his heart were broken when I told him." She studied the girl's astonished face, and cautioned, "Now don't mention it to him. I could tell he thought he was acting...unmanly. Gentlemen have a very strange emotional code. Far be it from me to understand it! Some of them think nothing of weeping buckets, and others wouldn't be caught with so much as a trace of moisture in their eyes."

Her charge sat for some time considering this enlightening information, and slowly inclined her head. "I'll try to be more accommodating to him, Miss Tremere."

"Good. Now I really must go to him. I'll join you in the schoolroom in awhile."

The door to Lord Heythrop's office stood open and Theodosia could see him seated at the enormous leather-topped desk busily checking through the accounts. Despite his apparent concentration, however, at the sound of footsteps he looked up and immediately rose when she stood in the doorway.

"Ah, Miss Tremere. Won't you come in—and close the door if you would. One of the children is bound to let curiosity get the better of manners." He waved to a chair opposite the desk but did not seat himself when she did. Folding his hands behind his back he wandered undecidedly about the room, his boots sounding loud on the polished oak planks. Theodosia waited patiently for him to speak.

At length he said, "I don't wish to seem an inquisitor, Miss Tremere, but as I explained to you last night the documents in the archive room are basically of a family nature. The treasure especially has been a closely guarded secret and I cannot for the life of me see why you would be reading the papers regarding it."

Theodosia sighed. So much for her plans to avoid telling him what they were doing. "Lady Eastwick and I have been concerned with the children's low spirits, Lord Heythrop. I suggested that we might interest them in a project to take their minds off their sad loss, and what I had proposed was a hunt for your family treasure."

It was almost beyond Edward's comprehension that his own mother could have agreed to such a sacrilege as to allow an outsider, practically a stranger, to delve into the family mystery. In the centuries that had preceded his own existence, he felt sure that never had anyone but a family member been made privy to the sacred intelligence that there even *was* a treasure. And here was a governess—a governess, by God!—perusing at will every clue to its meaning and location. Not only that, but she had already mislaid the most vital clue!

"I fear my mother was a bit misguided to acquiesce in such a scheme, Miss Tremere," he intoned stiffly. "The Heythrop treasure is not a matter to be handled lightly and by...someone outside the family. My father would be justifiably irritated to hear of it."

"Lady Eastwick thought otherwise. She felt that the earl would welcome a diversion for the children, and as so many generations have proved unsuccessful, there is little chance that we would actually find it. I could, of course, devise some simpler means of occupying the youngsters' minds, but when there is already a very strong temptation in the family tradition which will catch their imaginations, it seems pointless to ignore it. Since I first came here, I have heard of the mystery off and on and I would find it a useful tool to restore everyone's spirits." She smiled calmly at him. "I am not likely to spread any word or make off with the valuables, Lord Heythrop. Lady Eastwick is prepared to trust to my discretion."

His face suffused with color under her steady regard. "Well, but.... Of course, I am sure.... I can understand how you came to be intrigued by our mystery...."

"Frankly, Lord Heythrop, I am inclined to regard it as rather a legend. We are too remote in time from the last possessor of the treasure to adequately put any interpretation on the few clues available. Still, I foresee a rather merry treasure hunt which will occupy the summer months. Do you not feel any concern for the lowness your brothers and sisters are experiencing?"

"Yes, certainly I do, but there must be other ways to cheer them."

"None quite so effective, I think. I have already pursued a relentless course of entertainments fit for their ages, with less success than I had hoped. If you have some suggestion, I would welcome hearing it."

Her very competence made him feel unsure of himself. Sitting at her ease, her hands folded gracefully in her lap, he could think of nothing to suggest to her but more studies, which he knew to be impractical and exactly the opposite of what the younger ones needed. Miss Tremere had a most unusual effect on Edward, and one he did not wish to explore at any depth. It was not merely the soothing influence she had on all about her, nor the subtle but delightful sense of humor she had exhibited on numerous occasions; there was that problem of his seeing her as a woman.

Time and again he had reminded himself that she

was a governess in his house (his father's house), that to consider her in any other light was reprehensible. But in his eagerness to fulfill his responsibilities, Edward had cut himself off from the normal social intercourse of the neighborhood, and seeing Miss Tremere daily was a powerful tonic to one of his disposition. Maintaining a rigid control over his emotions (if not always his temper) for the sake of the position he was attempting to fill, he found in her a wholly sympathetic blend of composure, intelligence and beauty.

Lowering his eyes from her gaze to study the high polish on his top boots, he shrugged. "They'll adjust in time."

"It has already been several months, Lord Heythrop. Looking for the treasure seems a perfectly harmless way of diverting them. Lady Eastwick remembers how fascinated you all were when Lord Eastwick told you of it as children. I envision expeditions to Bicknoller, searches of Charton Court and its surrounds, an investigation of the parish records of both areas, a thorough study of family history. But we will need the missing letter."

Long since Edward had forgotten the lost item, but he was recalled to his former suspicion, regardless of knowing deep inside himself that Miss Tremere was not guilty of negligence. "Possibly it has fallen somewhere in your room, ma'am."

"No, I didn't open the leather tube until just before you arrived and it was not there. There is no chance of its having come away from the other papers in my suite, or even on the route from the archive room. My quick scan of the papers last night did not indicate any older paper in another hand, so I would feel confident in saying it was not with them at all."

"I don't see how that can be," he protested, running long, thin fingers through his neatly brushed black locks. "Mother surely would not have taken it; she's not the least interested in the mystery."

"No, and it took her some time to remember where the papers were. She'd only seen them once before, apparently. And I don't imagine your father would have removed it from the archive room, considering the unwritten law that everything remain there."

Edward had the grace to flush at this rejoinder, realizing full well that Miss Tremere considered that he exaggerated slightly as to the strength of this policy, which he did. Nonetheless, he was convinced that it was not his father who had taken the letter, and he dropped onto the large oak chair behind the desk in an attitude of abstraction. "I can't swear that it was here when Father left for America; I had no reason to check the papers then. I doubt he did, either. And it makes no sense for someone to have stolen it and not the other papers."

"More likely it was a family member who wished an opportunity to study it more carefully. Still, the archive room is kept locked and the children could not have gotten in without asking you or your mother for the key. I presume none of them approached you."

"I would hardly have allowed them to scrounge around there unaccompanied!" A thought struck him and his brows drew together in an angry line as he abruptly rose to his feet. "If you will excuse me, I must have a word with my mother."

Fortuitously, Lady Eastwick was just in the motion of tapping at the door when her son threw it open. She felt that Miss Tremere had been with her son a sufficient time to require her intervention, and when she saw his scowl she exclaimed, "For heaven's sake, Edward, you haven't gone and lost your temper with Miss Tremere, have you?"

Ignoring her question, he posed one of his own. "Mother, did you let Uncle James in the archive room when he was down for Katey's funeral?"

Lady Eastwick glanced from him to Theodosia, and satisfied that the governess showed no sign of distress, back to her son again. "Yes, dear. He wished to see some records relating to his birth or his godparents or some such thing."

"Did you give him the key, or did you go with him?"

"I gave him the key, of course. Why shouldn't I?"

"Because he's gone and taken one of the papers relating to the treasure," her son growled.

Mystified, Lady Eastwick turned to Theodosia for enlightenment, since her son made no effort to explain. The governess attempted to bring some reason to the rapidly deteriorating situation.

"The first earl's letter wasn't attached to the other papers as it should have been, but I'm sure there is no way of knowing how it came to be missing. Just because Mr. James Heythrop visited the archive room doesn't indicate that he took it."

"Well, of course not! Edward, how could you suggest such a thing?"

"Because he's a loose screw if ever I saw one." His face set stubbornly. "You needn't remind me that he's father's youngest brother. I am well aware of it and rue the relationship. Father informed me before he left that he had provided Uncle James with an allowance sufficient to see him through to the fall—and a very generous one it was!—and yet my dear uncle approached me for money while he was here. And that was only half a year after Father left! You may be sure he has a mind to find the treasure on his own and sell it to settle his gambling debts."

"Edward! I really am ashamed to listen to such talk. And before Miss Tremere. I thought you had more family feeling than to do such a thing."

Theodosia stood unperturbed by the contretemps but Lord Heythrop hastened to undo any damage he might have caused. "I'm sorry, Mama! Miss Tremere, you must make light of my words. I fear I am distracted at thinking the letter lost. But it is possible that Uncle James has inadvertently taken it with him, and I shall write to check."

Feeling there was little likelihood of dissuading him, Lady Eastwick cast him an exasperated frown and drew Theodosia from the room. "You may be sure his letter will not be a model of tact, either," she grumbled. "Not that he may not have hit on the truth. I'm reluctant to say so, but James is not quite the thing. Well, you met him when he was here in March. He's a beau, of course, and can exhibit the most winning manner, but he *will* play too deeply and lead the most reckless life. Eastwick has long since despaired of him. The estate at Bicknoller should be quite sufficient to provide him with the means of living elegantly, if not luxuriously, but he won't have a thing to do with it but collect the rents. And he has allowed it to run down most frightfully. There isn't the least reason for Eastwick to make him an allowance. You mustn't think that I resent the loss of money; what I resent is seeing it change hands over a game of faro or bassett."

"Gambling is a hazardous pastime."

"Indeed. Forgive me for washing the family's dirty linen before you, Miss Tremere. I think of James as little as possible because he is such a thorn in Eastwick's side. I almost.... Well, I almost cautioned you when he was down last time. He has quite an eye for the ladies and I could see that he was making up to you, but you seemed to have no difficulty handling him."

Theodosia grinned. "I had to use my hat pin a few times, and keep my door locked."

"Did you? I'm so sorry. You should have told me. I would have spoken to him, though I doubt it would have had much effect."

"I was able to avoid him most of the time. He hadn't been here before since I came."

"He considers London the only civilized spot in the entire country." Lady Eastwick sighed. "Don't think he came here to condole with us for poor Katey. It simply provided him an opportunity to try to get extra money from Edward."

"So you really do think he may have taken the first earl's letter? Why would he not simply have made a copy of it?" Theodosia's brows rose questioningly.

"He's an arrogant devil. Why should he bother to go to all the effort of making a copy when he can simply lift the original? He's probably crumpled it to pieces by now."

"I do hope not. Lord Heythrop was not at all anxious for the children to search for the treasure with me, but I don't think he actually forbade it."

"If he had, I would override him in this case, my dear Miss Tremere. I think it an excellent scheme and hope you will proceed as we planned."

They had paused at the foot of the stairs and Theodosia nodded. "I'm glad. When I've finished copying the ninth earl's letter, I'll take the copy with me to the schoolroom, but I'll need to go over the old map with the children. Then I can return everything to the archive room. Hmm. Since we haven't the major clue right now, and before I think of manufacturing any, I had best have the children find what they can among the old documents. I don't mean to have them go through everything again, but the old account records, which show when the various buildings were put up and additions and changes made, could be of invaluable assistance. And it would give the children a better knowledge of their home and their heritage. Do you think Lord Heythrop would object to my allowing them to go through the records?"

"Of course he will," Lady Eastwick chuckled, "but pay no heed to him. As Heythrops they each have the right to do so. He'll only worry that they will lose or destroy something, and I know you will supervise them closely." She withdrew the ring of keys and detached that for the archive room, handing it to Theodosia. "You'll not want to come to me each time you need to get in there. Just keep this with you."

Theodosia was aware that Lady Eastwick did not make the gesture lightly. Her role as chatelaine was important to her and she regarded it as a responsibility only slightly less significant than her role as wife and mother, seeing it as an extension of both. If she felt any chagrin that James Heythrop had possibly walked off with a family paper in abuse of the faith she had placed in him in lending him the key, she did not show it, and she would not permit that mishap to cloud her trust in the governess. Accepting the key with a grateful smile,

Theodosia said, "Thank you, Lady Eastwick. I'll take special care of it and direct all the children's activities in the archive room."

"I know you will, dear."

Chapter Three

The Honorable James Heythrop was not aware
that anyone had entered the room when he muttered,
"Damned young puppy!" Edward's letter, as his mother
had foreseen, was not a model of tact, and James, despite the fact that he was in possession of the paper
requested, was in no mood to tolerate his youthful
nephew's stern reminders of the sanctity of any documents relating to the Heythrop legend.

"Some problem, James?" his visitor inquired lazily.

"Steyne! I didn't hear you come in." He rose hastily
to his feet and thrust the offending letter onto a stack
of duns.

"Your porter said you were expecting me."

"I am. I am. Have a seat. I appreciate your coming.
You never seem to be at home when I call and I have
a matter of importance to discuss with you." He
watched the taller man dispose himself leisurely in the
bergère chair with its massive armrests carved as
winged chimaera. Every item of furniture in the room
was as boldly designed as the chair, and almost every
item was unpaid for, since most of them were new.
James had found it expedient to make an impression
on Viscount Steyne. Never one to quibble over invest-
ing a few pounds when there was a fortune to be won,

James with his gambler's mentality had refurbished the rooms he let in Deanery Street, and if he hadn't bothered to pay for the furniture, so much the better.

His visitor draped one long leg over the other, regarding James with speculative eyes. "I don't believe I hold any of your notes, James. Am I mistaken?"

Biting back an exclamation of annoyance, the older man gave a negligent shrug. "Of course you don't, Steyne. I've had quite a run of luck, and it's convinced me as nothing else could, that it's time to put the gaming tables behind me. Losing always spurs one on, but winning has quite the opposite effect with me. Or perhaps it is something else which has changed my outlook." He studied the closed face opposite him, but could gather no hint of whether the viscount took his meaning.

James had never understood why Steyne received the attention he did from the ladies. There was nothing even remotely handsome about the rugged face, the cool brown eyes, the firm, cleft chin. Or at least, nothing to compare with his own extraordinary looks. James had the coal-black hair of the Heythrops, the symmetrical blend of features which had earned them the reputation of being one of the handsomest families in England and a well-made person, which was the envy of most of his contemporaries. At eight and thirty most of his friends were possessed of paunches and had frequently occurring bouts of colic, if not gout, which were only to be expected from their daily overindulgence. James was only of medium height, but his wiry frame looked and performed as youthfully as it had twenty years ago, or so he imagined. Not for him the heavy meals and bottles of port consumed thoughtlessly while amusing the ladies or playing faro. He had found early on that both were enough to drug a man into less than his usual wits, and James was not one to give the advantage to an opponent. He lived by his wits.

Of course, Steyne hadn't gone to seed, either. He was nearly a half-dozen years younger than James, and like himself had never married. There were any number of ladies who had tried to fix Steyne's interest, with their parents' concurrence; that at least was quite different than James. When James had first come on the town there had been the expected flutter of maidenly hearts, but time had shown prudent parents that he was not a worthy match for their darlings, and James had been as content to leave it that way. There had been an opera dancer and then an actress, a girl from a fashionable modiste's shop, any number of them. He had lost count long ago. But today he was embarked on a different road altogether, and Steyne was likely to prove the tollgate keeper.

The viscount had made no response to his remark and James had really not expected that he would. With a rueful grin he confessed, "I'm afraid I never expected it to happen. After all, I've led a perfectly contented life until now. Saw no reason to take the big step and saddle myself with a lot of responsibilities. But all that has changed."

His guest raised one expressive eyebrow, unimpressed with James' boyish disclosures. "Precisely what has changed, James?"

There was no mistaking the underlying cynicism of the question. Well, James had known it wouldn't be easy. You did not lightly pit yourself against such an opponent but James had a trump card which he intended to use at exactly the right moment. "Everything." He made a gesture of surrender. "I needn't tell you how admirable your sister is, or that she outshines any of the children making their come-outs each year. My heart has never stood in any danger from the debutantes; I thought it stood in danger from no one. I remember Ruth at eighteen—captivating, clever, beautiful—but not for me. What was I then—twenty? I saw Morrison snap her up, and had no regrets. If I had known then what is plain to every eye now.... Not only has her beauty weathered, but her sense and her nonsense. She's the most capable, charming, delightful woman I've ever met. And to be widowed at her age cannot have been an easy matter to one of her sensibility. Much as I hate to admit it, though, I'm frankly grateful. I want to marry her, Steyne."

"You can't be serious."

Even this James had expected, and he forced himself to laugh. "I know. I've said the same to myself: You've led a ramshackle life, James my boy, and it must be age creeping up on you to have such a turn of heart. But I *am* older, Steyne, and I'm tired of the fruitless pursuit of novelty. God knows I've had my share of pleasures, and sowed my oats a great deal longer than most. The harvest looks a little ragged, I realize, but I'm presentable, have a tidy little estate in Somerset and an income from my brother."

"I haven't known you a day when you weren't in dun territory," Steyne retorted. "You can't seriously believe you can change overnight. And I don't believe Ruth could accustom herself to having bailiffs at the door."

As yet unspoken was the thought James knew to be in Steyne's mind: that a ne'er-do-well like himself must be considering marrying Ruth for her money, and that with his gambling propensities, her money, in spite of its immense amount, would likely soon be dissipated. James rather admired the cool way in which Steyne was handling the situation, but he had no compunction in pushing his own advantage. "There won't be any more bailiffs, my dear Steyne. I have my own affairs well in hand, and I flatter myself I can keep them that way. Your sister, I feel sure, can manage a household economically if need be, and she would have her choice of living in the country or in town."

"Really." For the first time, Steyne smiled. "Did you have in mind to install her here?"

"Certainly not," James snapped, then reminded himself to keep a better hold on his temper. "I would take a house in one of the more fashionable squares."

"Let it, you mean, or buy it?"

"Whichever suited your sister."

The inexpressive face remained unreadable; the eyes hooded. Slowly, cautiously, Steyne spoke. "I presume you have some reason to believe my sister would listen to an offer from you."

James would have preferred to introduce the subject himself, but the opening would do. "I blush to say so, but, yes, some small indication. I have seen a great deal of Ruth this past season, escorted her several times, and I have some hope that she returns my regard. She is, of course, of an age where she doesn't need your approval, or anyone else's, but I didn't wish to approach her without informing you. There were no children from her previous marriage, so she owes no allegiance to her in-laws. I would welcome your consent, because I feel sure Ruth would hesitate to marry without it."

The subtle innuendo with which this last was spoken surprised Steyne. Obviously James did not believe it. The words were belied by his confident air: He reeked of self-assurance. Can my sister possibly have been taken in by this jackanapes, Steyne wondered, while maintaining the calm exterior he had preserved through the various provocations of the interview. Surely Ruth has too much sense to be cozened by a few flattering words. True, there were not many men available for her to remarry other than the fortune hunters like James Heythrop, and it would be a great pity for her to spend the rest of her life alone—but this ass! A hardened gambler, a profligate womanizer, a selfish, conceited sportsman, to say nothing of his having the moral fiber of a toad! Lord Steyne had a remarkably low opinion of the man—and yet he allowed no emotion to show.

"I'm afraid I would have to know a bit more about your prospects before I could see my way clear to countenancing the match."

James relaxed with an almost audible sigh. He had expected more opposition, but it was well-known that Steyne was fond of his sister and would want her to marry for happiness. And even a younger son of an earl was a step up from Morrison, no matter how prominent he had been in political circles. "Just so. Can't say I blame you. This letter I've had," he remarked as he flicked it with an indolent finger, "will necessitate my going into Somerset. You know my brother's in America and his family calls on me for advice from time to time. I went down when his daughter died in the spring, a sad affair. Still, he has six other children. Ah, and that's a matter I wished to mention as well. You may accept my word that it doesn't bother me that Ruth can't have children."

I'll bet it doesn't, Steyne fumed inwardly, clenching his teeth. "I see."

"I know it would put off other men, but I've never felt the necessity of producing an heir."

Small wonder, his visitor thought.

"What I suggest is that you come with me to Somerset. It would give you a chance to see my estate at Bicknoller. You'd have a better conception of my income after a look at the place and the books." James had no doubt that everything was in order as far as the books were concerned. He'd taken a cursory glance at them when he was down in the spring, and they showed a very handsome profit. The income from the estate was not the reason he was forever at point non plus. Even Eastwick had no idea, he felt sure, how he managed (with the aid of a devil of an estate manager) to squeeze every last penny from the estate and his tenant-farmers. If he had, Eastwick would probably have discontinued the allowance as unnecessary, but there would be no question of that if James took a wife. And if he took the right one, there would be very little reason to worry about money and tradesmen's bills for a long time to come. And James, if he had not precisely decided to change his way of life, had certainly tired of the perpetual nuisance of duns.

There was, also, the possibility that he had discovered the clue to the Heythrop treasure, but he had no intention of hanging all his hopes on that. His reading of the first earl's verses might or might not be right; in either case it would be useful to have Steyne along on the journey to distract attention from his intended search. Lady Eastwick would consider it her responsibility to entertain the viscount, and that little prig Edward would undoubtedly latch on to such a Corinthian as Steyne. All around, the plan had advantages.

"I'll consider your Somerset offer, though I have several engagements I'd be loath to break in the next few days. When did you contemplate leaving?" Steyne watched as James hastily revised his schedule to accommodate the viscount's whims. No wonder the man had such poor luck at the tables; off guard, his face could be read like a book.

"Next week. I can't get away until then."

"I'll let you know tomorrow or the next day."

To all appearances Steyne took his leave as composedly as he had arrived, but he drew in a deep breath when he stood outside the house in Deanery Street. James' lodgings were in a perfectly respectable house, his landlady an older woman of reduced means. His talk of taking a house in one of the squares was laughable; he counted on moving into Ruth's house in Mount Row beyond a shadow of doubt. Did he think Steyne was so slow as not to have seen the stack of duns on top of which he placed his nephew's letter? The man was an incorrigible gambler and spendthrift, the scourge of his family and lacking any close friends. His position opened any club door, of course, and he had a certain ability in sporting activities, but there was an end to his virtues.

Despite the heat, Steyne gave his tiger instructions to take the curricle back to his house in Piccadilly, chosing instead to walk to his sister's while he contemplated what James had told him. It was true that Ruth, widowed for well over a year now, appeared in company to be her normal self, but Steyne had witnessed in private moments a despondency which alarmed him. She was still feeling her loss severely, struggling to come to terms with it and determined to carry on as she thought others expected her to. Did she think she was expected to remarry? Was she listening to the old cats with their litany of "A woman should be married; a woman needs a man's support; a woman alone is unacceptable to society"? In the past months he'd heard all the clichés offered to her, but surely she could not have lost her balance to such an extent that she would consider James!

His rapid stride set the tassels on his Hessians swinging wildly but disturbed the perfect set of the bottle-green coat and dove-colored pantaloons not a whit. The white cravat and gold buttons sparkled in the sunlight but he was too preoccupied to give a thought to his appearance. Brummell would doubtless register horror at the pace he set, and the possibility that his cravat would wilt from his exertions, but Steyne himself cared little for such matters. He submitted himself patiently each morning and evening to his valet's careful ministrations, and then heeded Brummell's useful piece of advice: to ignore his appearance until time to change again. Of course, Brummell exerted himself as little as possible to maintain the perfect effect he had achieved, whereas Steyne promptly forgot what he was wearing. With his eyes closed, he would probably have been unable to tell you which of his coats he had allowed his valet to ease him into that morning, or which of the equally inoffensive pairs of pantaloons he had donned. Yet the end result was the same. Owing to Housett's unparalleled skill and infinite patience, Steyne was always turned out quite unexceptionably, even admirably.

The house in Mount Row where he eventually came to a halt was a classical stone building, unpretentious but stately, in which his sister had taken up residence after her year's mourning. Until then she had stayed in Shropshire, and Steyne had frequently journeyed to the country to be with her. It was at his urging that she had come to town, and he was not at all sure now that it had been wise. In the country there had been some neighboring families whose concern for her had been decidedly more beneficial than the callous, superficial consolation of her society friends. She refused to be a damper or a burden on social occasions, and the supreme effort she made to appear constantly cheerful had taken its toll. Perhaps there was no lessening of her beauty, but the spontaneous quality she had always possessed was now lacking, and to Steyne she appeared pale and drawn compared with the robust health she had enjoyed in the country.

Mrs. Morrison was seated at the piano-forte in the silk-hung drawing room, quietly playing a melancholy country tune. Steyne had not had himself announced and he stood observing her for some minutes, noting especially the lone tear which had slipped out and marked a path down her cheek. Her light brown hair was drawn up in a rather frivolous knot, a style which her dearest friend had insisted was all the rage, and the deep brown eyes were moist with unshed tears. As she finished the piece, she happened to glance up and see him. "Marc! Why didn't you speak? Forgive me for leaving you standing there."

Hastily she pressed a handkerchief to her eyes, trying to make it look as though she were dabbing her nose, and rose to greet him with outstretched hands. "What brings you out so early?"

"You do, my dear. Have you time to talk?"

"Certainly. Take the Wig chair, Marc, and I'll ring for tea. There should be some plum cake. Do you fancy that?"

"Please." He waited until she had seated herself opposite him, but even then he found it difficult to come to the point of his visit. To erase the impression of sorrow she had masked her face with a cheerful smile and inquisitive eyes but her hands twisted restlessly in her lap. Finally he said bluntly, "Ruth, I've just been with James Heythrop."

If he had expected a maidenly blush or some indication of her attachment to the fellow, he was startled by her flashing eyes and the rare hard note in her voice as she asked, "What did he say about me?"

"Basically that he had a great admiration for you and wished to marry you. And that he felt you reciprocated his regard."

"Is that all?"

"Dear Lord, I would have thought that enough," he returned faintly. "He did, of course, assure me of the strength of his financial position."

"He doesn't *have* a financial position," Ruth retorted. "You know that, Marc. If he wanted to marry me, it would be for my money."

They were interrupted while Ruth gave instructions to the footman who had appeared to her summons, but Steyne spoke the moment the door closed. "You don't sound as though you would welcome an offer from him."

"Do you think I've lost my mind?" Suddenly she put her head in her hands and whispered between her fingers, "Maybe I have. I've behaved very foolishly with him. I don't suppose you would understand, Marc, but I've been so desperately lonely."

Steyne felt a twitch of apprehension and came to lay a hand on her shoulder. "I know you have, my love, but I can't think James is the one to alleviate your loneliness. There is certainly no comparison between him and Stephen Morrison."

"Oh, I know it. Marc, I'm thirty-six years old. There are no men around like Stephen. And I can't understand why I am going to all these parties and smiling and talking and acting as though I were having a lovely time. I hate it. Without Stephen it seems empty and useless. No one even has a sensible thing to say about politics. When Stephen was in the House the people who came to us were interested, concerned. Now all they talk about is Prinny's entertainment last month. My God, it was wretched. Such a show and a waste of money. I feel so removed from everyone else."

"Yes, I can see that." He stroked her bowed head and said gently, "Tell me about James."

Ruth took the opportunity provided by the entry of the footman with the tea tray to rise and walk to the windows. She stood with her back to her brother. "After a few weeks in town I began to feel that I was an imposition to you and my married friends, tagging along without an escort. I've known James for years, of course, and when he offered to escort me about, I thought it a satisfactory solution. Everyone knew he had no interest in marrying and a string of light-skirts to keep him busy. He wasn't my only escort, of course. Old Mr. Hawkesbury and young Notgrove often took me places, too, and occasionally Lord Enstone.

"They were all very...correct. When young Notgrove appeared to be developing a most inappropriate *tendre,* I dropped him from my train as gently as possible. One evening, on the way home from the Yarntons, I was with James and feeling low. He's like a rat; he can smell vulnerability." Ruth swallowed painfully. "I have missed the physical...closeness of marriage, and I allowed him some freedom with my person. Marc, I was just so tired of putting on a front, and I didn't care what James thought of me. I don't have a very high opinion of *him.*"

Her back was still to him and he clenched the arms of his chair. "You will have to be more specific, Ruth. I'm sorry, but it is essential that I know. Did you go to bed with him?"

"No...No. Not then, not since. But I have acted very imprudently on several occasions. Once I invited him in and we might have....I couldn't take him to my room—the servants, the memories of Stephen. I wanted to, and he knew it. As I said, all the others had been very correct, and I began to allow James to escort me more and more simply so that I could have that contact. It was foolish of me, heaven knows, but I've felt so unhappy and for a while I could forget. I had no intention of marrying him, and never thought that he might entertain the idea of making me his wife." She sighed. "I suppose I should have. The man has absolutely no scruples."

So that's why he felt so sure she would marry him, Steyne thought, allowing himself to relax ever so slightly. This was not necessarily the end of the matter, however. James could not be trusted to take the shattering of his dream with equanimity, and Steyne shuddered to think of the chaos, the ruin he could cause with a few well-chosen remarks in company. Poor Ruth. Though he deplored her choice of companion, he could sympathize with her need for solace, be it only physical. And ladies hadn't the freedom of choice and action that gentlemen had. He poured out two cups of tea.

"Come and have some of the plum cake. It's delicious." He met her eyes, stricken, lost, as she turned to him. "Come, Ruth. You haven't done anything so dreadful but we'll need to discuss strategy. James has invited me to go into Somerset with him to see his estate, and I think it might be a wise idea if I did."

"Whatever for? Marc, I wouldn't marry him if he were the last man on Earth!"

"I should hope not, my dear. He is in a position to do some damage to your reputation, though, and I think it would be best if he felt the refusal was entirely my doing. If, after I have seen his estate, he should attempt to let an unsavory word drop, it will easily be countered by my having investigated his financial standing. Do you follow me?"

"Yes. I'm sorry to cause you such trouble, Marc."

He reached out and pressed her hand. "Don't be. I wish I could do more for you. I hate to see you unhappy. Perhaps you should return to the country after this is settled. You could visit Aunt Margaret, but I wouldn't advise it. In August I plan to go to Kingswood for several months. Come with me."

"Thank you. I'll consider it." She smiled tremulously. "How very confusing life is."

Life, for Lord Steyne, had never seemed the least confusing. No, that was not perfectly true, but for the most part he felt he had a strong influence over the events and personages surrounding him, and a confidence in his own ability to control his affairs. At one period that had not been the case, of course, but he had survived that disappointment to become a wiser if possibly more cynical gentleman. One could not, after all, plot the direction of one's life with certainty when the necessity to take into account a woman's whimsicality intruded itself.

His wry smile emerged as he took leave of his sister. "Yes, my dear, there are times when everything seems indescribably bleak, but, believe me, they improve. No confusion, no hurt, no disappointment, lasts forever."

Chapter Four

James Heythrop was gratified to receive Lord Steyne's message that he would be willing to accompany him into Somerset. There was no mention of the reason for their expedition, and no comment on the possibility of a marriage between James and Ruth Morrison. But James was confident that Steyne must by now have spoken with his sister, and that the acceptance of the invitation was as good as a promise that the two of them would marry. Not that Steyne would necessarily view the proceedings with pleasure. James knew him better. It would cause the viscount vexation, if nothing worse, to see his sister wed to a man he considered a loose screw and a jackanapes.

James had no delusions about Steyne's opinion, or even that he had convinced the younger man of his intentions to reform his way of life, but Steyne was unlikely to chance a feud with his sister, considering Ruth was his senior and a mature woman. Very mature, James decided smugly as he sealed a note addressed to Lady Eastwick. He would not honor that puppy Edward with the courtesy of a reply. And since his own arrival was the only matter of importance to him, he mentioned simply that he was bringing a companion. Let them stew wondering if it would be a female companion. They had made such an ungodly fuss the time he had brought a female that he found it amusing to leave the possibility up to conjecture.

All things considered, James was in an unusually cheerful mood during the days preceeding their departure. He called but once in Mount Row, as purely a matter of form, but he was not unduly cast down when he was informed that Ruth was not at home. A Mrs. Calderwith in Arlington Street was always at home to him, and he took himself there without delay.

James had intended to take his traveling carriage into Somerset, but he was more than pleased to learn that Steyne expected to carry the two men in his own. Having accepted this boon, he made no effort to defray any of the expenses involved in posting charges. They spent one night at the Haunch of Venison in Salisbury, where James could see no possible means of avoiding his own expense, so he paid for his room and meals without demur, noting only that Steyne was rather open-handed with his gratuities.

After Salisbury they left the mail coach route to make their way across country on poorly surfaced roads which called forth James' frequent aspersions as far as Taunton, and afterward, his oaths.

"What the hell do they do with the money they collect from me for repairing the roads?" he grumbled as the carriage rumbled through yet another cavity, jostling him against the side. "I'd never set foot outside London...." he began, before realizing that he had told Steyne he would willingly live with his sister in the country if that were her choice.

But Steyne was apparently paying no attention to him. They were passing through Bishops Lydeard and the viscount was gazing out at the double-windowed belfry of the church tower. James found Steyne's habit of ignoring him slightly unnerving, though on this occasion it was just as well. Throughout the journey Steyne had alternately watched the passing landscape with a brooding expression, or read the book he carried with him, something in French which James was too uninterested in to ask about. Their conversation had been minimal, except during meals, when the viscount was invariably charming and fully open to discussing anything which came to James' mind.

One matter which James had not seen fit to discuss was where they would be staying. He knew that Steyne assumed they were bound for Fairlight, and in a manner of speaking they were, but as they approached the turnoff for Channock, he interrupted his companion's meditations. "You should tell the postboys to take this right coming up."

As always, Steyne was imperturbable. He let down the window and gave the necessary instruction, but when he had finished he turned to James. Though he said nothing, his very look was as good as a question.

"Umm, you must understand, my dear Steyne, that Fairlight has not been inhabited for some time. Everything's in holland covers, and the staff is of the smallest. When I journey into this part of the country I stay at Charton Court, my brother's seat. Quite natural, since I'm called to see to family business."

A slight tightening of the lips betrayed Steyne's annoyance. "All very well for *you*, James, but the same does not apply to me. I have some acquaintance with Eastwick; with his wife I have very little."

"You refine too much on it, old fellow. I've written to tell them I was bringing someone with me."

"Very thoughtful of you. Why didn't you tell me?"

James affected a look of surprise. "I felt sure you realized that we could not well stay at Fairlight."

"With the amount of notice you were able to give, what I assumed was that your household would prepare the place for your occupation."

Shifting uncomfortably on the seat, James attempted another tack. "You'll enjoy Charton Court. Lady Eastwick is a featherhead, but charming. Young Edward is a stiff sort of fellow, though well-meaning, I'm sure. The children won't bother you; they're reasonably well behaved. And they have a governess to keep them in line." James smiled rakishly. "Ah, the governess. A bit hasty with her hat pin, but worth it. Well past the first blush, but striking-looking nonetheless. This was before I became better acquainted with your sister, of course," he hastened to add at the dangerous light in Steyne's eyes.

His companion said nothing as they came to Channock and the postboys were instructed to deliver them to Charton Court. Accustomed to buildings of its size being in stone, Steyne was struck by the beauty of the red brick. There were battlemented towers at four corners, though the building was far from a square, with projections everywhere and a crazy jumble of chimneys on the rooftops. Steyne saw at least two drawbridges, now ornamental, over the dry moat, and over the entrance porch was an archway with the royal arms of England surmounted by a crown inscribed Dom Rex Henricus VII. A glimpse of a topiary and the setting of rolling hills completed the remarkable impression Charton Court made on Steyne's mind even before he entered the building. It is fortunate that first impressions are lasting, and that his was excellent, for when they were welcomed into the house by the butler, Fyfield, they were informed that not one member of the household was at home.

Steyne's expression was unreadable; James hastened into speech. "You must know that I always make a full two-day journey of it. Never reach here until almost dinner time. You were the one who wanted to be on the road at the light of dawn. Dare say my sister-in-law thought they'd be back in plenty of time for my arrival."

"Just so, sir," the butler murmured. "You are expected. My lady has had two rooms in the South Wing prepared."

Nettled by Steyne's lack of response to this information, James followed the butler without further comment. Their valises were brought from the post chaise by a pair of footmen who silently followed the procession up the stairs and through a series of corridors to the South Wing where James and his companion were given elegantly furnished rooms on opposite sides of the hall. Steyne was assured that a can of hot water would arrive momentarily for his ablutions, and he thankfully shut the door for some solitary reflection. The view from his window was out over the topiary to the sculpted lawns beyond, which meant that James had a room facing onto the courtyard. Understandable, Steyne thought irritably. Looking onto the courtyard would give James the constricted sort of atmosphere he doted on in London.

Arriving at a house as an uninvited guest was not Steyne's idea of a comfortable position in which to be, and that James had barreled him into it only served to heighten the annoyance he felt for his would-be brother-in-law. In fact, Steyne considered his position at Charton Court perfectly untenable. There was a tap at his door, and he turned to watch a strapping country girl enter and fill the wash-hand basin.

"Will there be anything else you'll be needing, sir?"

"Nothing, thank you."

Naturally they didn't even know who he was, he thought mournfully. Just like James not to mention who he was bringing in his letter, and not to introduce his companion to the butler when they arrived. If they had known, the girl would have called him "my lord." Steyne shook his head and proceeded to wash off the dust of the road. He had not even brought his valet, thinking that a few days at Fairlight would require nothing more strenuous than outfitting himself in country clothes, his favorite wear in any case.

Here it would be necessary to dress for dinner each evening, and though he had brought one decently formal outfit, he had brought only one, much to Housett's disgust. Steyne sighed as he exchanged his dusty, crumpled cravat for a fresh one whose folds, if acceptable, could never achieve the distinction that Housett managed to give them.

Depending on how one looked at it, the Charton Court party's visit to The Beeches—home of Mr. and

Mrs. Hedgerley—had been informative, uninformative, interesting, boring, delightful, a waste of time, etc. Lady Eastwick had been pleased to see her old friends and Theodosia and the children had done a bit of exploring since the Beeches was one of the spots marked on the old map, but aside from its being a lovely old manor house, they had made no discoveries of importance. Lady Eastwick, though thoroughly enjoying herself, finally rose and explained, "My husband's brother James is coming today and I should cut some flowers in honor of his arrival. I hope he'll be on time to dine. He forgets, I think, that we keep earlier hours in the country. I've warned our cook, though. James is to bring someone with him, but didn't mention whom."

In the carriage on the drive back to Charton Court Lady Eastwick confessed to Theodosia that James had once before brought a friend with him, and a very ramshackle fellow he had been. Oh, it was years ago but she still remembered the carelessness with which they had observed the hours at the Court.

"Never once on time for dinner, and as often as not eating at the inn. Cook was threatening to turn in his spoon. James was better when he was down in the spring. I had Edward speak to him. Well, you can understand at such a time I didn't wish to have the whole household upset on his behalf." Lady Eastwick lowered her voice so the children, chatting away opposite them, would not hear. "He has brought women, too, you know. Not to the Court, of course, after the first time, but to Fairlight. And then he expects me to invite them to dine! Really, he is the most unaccountable fellow. How could I do such a thing when the older children dine with us? Charlotte was only thirteen the last time, but she had been dining with us for a year, so grown up as she seemed. And even the younger ones are allowed to come for the last course once they can behave in polite company."

When Lady Eastwick was informed at the door that her brother-in-law had already arrived, her dismay was almost comical. "Before two? He's never gotten here before four. Oh, Lord, what must he think of us—all gone out visiting. Of course I know you have done everything to make him comfortable. Where is he, Fyfield?"

"In the Gold Parlor, milady."

Theodosia realized that her employer didn't wish to have all the children hovering about while she apologized for their absence, so the governess hustled them off in the direction of the schoolroom with a promise of tea and a story. Smiling her gratitude, Lady Eastwick squared her fragile shoulders and stepped forward to greet the least favorite of her husband's relations. As Fyfield opened the door for her, she realized that Edward had followed, in his role of host, and she now heard him exclaim, "Good God! Who would have thought?"

James' companion was no less of a surprise to her, though she managed to disguise her astonishment better than her son. It was true that she was barely acquainted with Lord Steyne, but she knew his sister well and would have recognized him anywhere. The ruggedly masculine face, the cleft chin, the knowledgeable brown eyes. Why in heaven's name had James not told her who he was bringing? And, what was more to the point, why would Lord Steyne have agreed to go *anywhere* with James?

When finally introductions were the least necessary, James seemed to remember that they were called for, and presented his companion with a decided flourish. Edward shook his hand gravely and Lady Eastwick extended a warm welcome.

"You are kind, ma'am," Steyne replied a little ruefully. "I had thought we were to stay at Fairlight, and had no intention of imposing on your hospitality."

"I've explained to Steyne," James interposed with one of the smiles that most irritated Edward, "that I always stay here, since Fairlight is in no condition to receive houseguests at a moment's notice."

As acting head of household, though, and because he had always admired Steyne from a distance, Edward promptly seconded his mother's welcome. "We're honored to have you, Lord Steyne. Is your room satisfactory? Mother has put you in the South Wing, hasn't she? If you would prefer a view of the hills, we can easily arrange that."

Lord Steyne declined this offer while James' lips curled in sardonic amusement. James had known that his nephew would toady to such a noted sportsman and distinguished peer. He had forgotten, however, that Lady Eastwick was a friend of Ruth Morrison's, but, listening to her anxious inquiries of the widow, he now saw this as an advantage. Everything was working out precisely as he could have wished.

The one offer Steyne was unable to refuse was the loan of Edward's valet to assist him in dressing for dinner. Valet was, in this instance, a rather grand title for the eager lad who appeared an hour before the appointed time for the meal. The boy showed not the least surprise that Steyne had only one set of dress clothing among the contents of the modest valise, and his services, though far from the expertise of Housett, were certainly useful in adjusting the tight-fitting coat to Steyne's broad shoulders. Knowing that Edward would need the boy, Steyne soon dismissed him with his thanks and stood staring out over the garden and lawns, reminded of Kingswood and feeling a sudden urge to be at home. There was nothing amiss in the Somerset landscape, but Kent and his own home were a deal more familiar to him. He couldn't fault the welcome he'd received, but it galled him that James had maneuvered him into Charton Court with such ease, and with his typical carelessness of anyone else's convenience.

Steyne was feeling restless. He had no wish to be the first downstairs and, unaccountably, memories of other visits to Somerset were crowding in on him. In an effort to stave off the past, which if not forgotten should have been, he wandered out into the hall and in the opposite direction from the main staircase. If memory served, the entrance porch had been only a story high and with luck one would be able to stand out on its battlemented rooftop for a view of the hills. As he approached the West Wing, he could hear voices, and he considered retracing his steps until he heard someone say:

"I'm sure, dear Charlotte, that your mother did not have *quite* that gown in mind when she urged you to dress especially well for the company." There was a warm chuckle in her voice when she said, "We are, after all, in the country, and our guests are only your uncle and a friend, not the Duke of York and his Duchess."

For the moment before they rounded the corner to enter his corridor, Steyne stood perfectly still, unable to believe what he heard. There could be no mistake, however, when Charlotte and Theodosia appeared before him. Despite the dimness of the hallway, and—what was it? six years?—he knew her instantly. "Doe?! What the devil are you doing here?"

Theodosia's footsteps faltered as she blinked at him uncertainly. "Lord Steyne? I might ask you the same." Gradually a smile widened on her lips and she moved forward with hand outstretched. "How astonishing to see you again. You must have come with James Heythrop. May I present Lady Charlotte Heythrop? Charlotte, Viscount Steyne."

Grudgingly Steyne switched his glance from Theodosia to the oldest of the Heythrop girls. A pretty child, frankly curious as to this meeting of former acquaintances. "Lady Charlotte." His bow necessitated he drop Theodosia's hand, which he had unconsciously retained.

A rather breathless silence all around was broken by Theodosia's asking, "Have you lost your way? We were just headed down to dinner, if you wish to accompany us."

"No. That is, I had planned to see the view from above the entrance porch, but I would be honored to escort you." He addressed himself to Theodosia. "You haven't answered my question."

"I live here, Lord Steyne," she replied, a laugh dancing in her eyes.

"You live here?" He did a hasty calculation as to whether it was possible she was married to Edward, but decided it was totally out of the question. Surely Edward was the oldest of them. He knew that she was not related to the Heythrops. Abandoning his attempt to figure it out, he asked bluntly, "Why?"

"I'm the girls' governess, and have been for the last three years."

Charlotte was fascinated by the incredulous look he bestowed on Miss Tremere. "Impossible!" he scoffed. "My aunt said you were to marry that intolerable bore, Bayhurst."

"Your aunt was mistaken, Lord Steyne."

His aunt, he decided grimly, had been purposely mistaken. Purposely, cruelly mistaken. "But you left Chipstable when he did."

"To come here, Lord Steyne. Mrs. Holmer was kind enough to recommend me to Lady Eastwick." Theodosia glanced significantly at the wide-eyed Charlotte. "I don't believe Charlotte's uncle had mentioned whom he was bringing. Will you be going on to visit your aunt?"

"No." Obedient to her hint, he turned to Charlotte to express his admiration for the house and grounds. "Do you know when the house was built?"

"Precisely," Charlotte laughed, "though I wouldn't have a few weeks ago. In 1492 it was completed, originally, but several later owners have made improvements."

Steyne held the door for them as they entered the Long Gallery where the family customarily gathered for dinner when they had houseguests. It was paneled in oak, embellished by carved walnut medallions and portraits of dozens of Heythrop ancestors. They were the first to arrive, but Lady Eastwick shortly joined them.

"Oh, Mama, the most famous thing! Miss Tremere and Lord Steyne are known to one another."

"How nice," her mother replied, pleased. "Did you meet in London?"

"No," Lord Steyne answered, "in Somerset. My aunt lives near Chipstable where Miss Tremere's father had the living."

James had entered in time to gather the essence of the exchange and he quickly tried to remember whether he had actually intimated to Steyne on their drive earlier in the day that he had succeeded in seducing the governess. Deciding that his statement had been open to interpretation, he dismissed the matter from his mind. Even parsons' daughters were seducible, after all, if not perhaps this one.

Dinner conversation was lively, and rather heady stuff for Charlotte, who did not often sit down at table with two gallants just come from London. She was disappointed to learn that neither of them had met her friend Christina Winchmore, but it was a minor disappointment. London was a large city, with several different entertainments to go to each evening, so one could quite easily miss one single lady, no matter how charming. And besides, both her uncle and Lord Steyne were considerably older than Christina, who doubtless had a circle of friends closer to her age. Though her uncle directed most of his gossipy conversation toward Lady Eastwick, Lord Steyne divided his attention equally among the members of the small party. What pleasing manners he has, Charlotte decided. Though he was not nearly so handsome as Mr. Winstanley she found him quite one of the nicest gentlemen she'd met.

During the course of the meal Theodosia found Steyne's eyes on her, puzzled, even perhaps a little angry. After the initial shock of seeing him, she had rapidly regained her composure, and whenever she met his gaze, she smiled her normally calm, warm smile. Nonetheless, it was disturbing to see him again and it cost her an effort to maintain her placid demeanor. When the gentlemen joined them in the Gold Parlor after dinner he crossed to where she sat with Charlotte on the Sheraton sofa. As he lowered himself into a ridiculously low tub chair, he commented, "I was sorry to hear of your father's death, Miss Tremere."

"Thank you. He had been ill for some time."

"Not for three years, I think." This time there was no question of the spark of anger in his eyes.

"No." She did not meet his gaze.

"And you left Chipstable after his death?"

"Yes."

There were obviously other questions he wished to ask, but Charlotte's presence prevented him. She was aware of the tense undercurrent between them and thought to join her mother, leaving them to speak in peace, but Lord Steyne turned with a smile to include her in the conversation. "Chipstable hasn't quite the same drama of setting as Channock, Lady Charlotte. Have you ever been there?"

"I don't believe so. I'm not sure where it is."

Theodosia laughed. "Our geography lessons don't include such unimportant spots, Lord Steyne. We've been studying the New World recently because of Lord Eastwick's sojourn there."

How easily a conversation could be diverted from its origins, Theodosia thought with gratitude. Charlotte was pleased to talk of her father's travels, and Steyne listened with apparent absorption, his gaze wandering now and again to Theodosia, his countenance unreadable. The younger children were brought in to see their uncle and his guest, and soon a game table was set out for them to have some sport at lottery tickets while the others sat down to whist. Theodosia and Charlotte joined the children, Steyne partnered Lady Eastwick against James and his nephew. Edward was not much interested in cards, and the stakes were so low as to prove an irritation to James, so there was a relieved acceptance of Lady Eastwick's suggestion that they stroll in the gardens before dark. Immersed in their game, the children decided to remain where they were.

Steyne had been seated where he could watch the

younger party. The governess's back was to him, but he could tell from the familiar low chuckle that she was completely involved with the game and her charges. Not once did she turn to glance at him. There was no sign that her concentration was disturbed. How the devil could she accept meeting him after all these years with so little perturbation? Had it been so easy for her to forget? Steyne rose along with the others, wanting to invite her to join them in the gardens, but realizing that her position made it impossible for him to do so. Even as they headed for the French doors she did not look up.

On their return they found the room deserted. Supper was a leisurely meal, and not attended by Miss Tremere or Charlotte. Steyne supposed that Theodosia ate with the children, and he tried to picture her in the schoolroom pouring out tea for them and toasting muffins over the fire on a long fork. It was not difficult to envision. He could clearly remember her doing the same at the vicarage in Chipstable for her father and himself. And the cranky old man complaining that his muffin was burnt and that the butter was not sweet enough, that the tea was bitter and cold. He had admired her patience, her ability to laugh off the complaints and cajole the old man into a better frame of mind.

Lady Eastwick excused herself after the meal, and Edward was not long in following her example, nudged perhaps by his uncle's obvious boredom with his company. Steyne and James sat sipping at glasses of excellent brandy.

"We'll ride over to Fairlight in the morning," James assured him.

"Borrowing horses from the Charton Court stables, no doubt."

"Why shouldn't we? Eastwick keeps dozens of breasts; prime blood, too. They'll not mind our taking a couple for the day."

Steyne said nothing.

"I'm not down often enough to make it worthwhile

having anything but a nag or two at Fairlight," James said carelessly. "If we decide to live in the country, of course I'll see to the restocking of my stables here. I know your sister likes to ride."

And you know she has half a dozen high-bred horses in the country which you would expect to grace your stables. "Did you intend to leave early?"

James gave him a comical look of despair. "Not so early as we rose this morning, if you please. One should be more relaxed in the country. By eleven, certainly."

"Very well." Steyne sipped the last of his brandy, set down the glass and rose. "I'll see you in the morning."

If he was put out at Steyne's defection, James did not show it. "Ring for anything you need. My sister-in-law runs an efficient household."

"Thank you." Steyne's tone was ironic, both because James took so much license with his brother's home, and because the one thing he wanted to know—where Theodosia's room was—he could not very well ring to ask.

Chapter Five

When Steyne came to his own room, he paused but did not enter. The house was in silence now; very likely everyone but James and he were already in their beds. There was little use in searching for her room. The house was enormous and he had only the indication from meeting her in the hall that she had come from the West Wing. She could as easily have been there to fetch Lady Charlotte. He had already opened the door before he recalled telling her where he'd been headed, and he closed it again soundlessly, turning on his heel to stride purposefully toward his previous goal.

The door out onto the entrance porch roof was closed, the rooftop bathed in a pale glimmer of moonlight. He could see no one there but he stepped out into the warmth of the summer evening thinking to wait there awhile. She might have come and gone, or she might have stayed with one of the girls to answer some query or comfort some fear. Possibly it wouldn't occur to her to come; it very nearly hadn't to him. Possibly she wouldn't have the courage to face the questions which even Lady Charlotte, he felt sure, had known he was burning to ask.

A flutter of movement startled him as Theodosia detached herself from the shadows beside the building.

She was dressed as he had last seen her in the Gold Parlor save for the addition of a light shawl about her shoulders. Her face looked colorless in the pale light, and there was no smile to greet him.

"I'm glad you came," she said at once. "There is little opportunity for private conversation in this household, and your public questioning of me is only likely to embarrass the Heythrops, or frustrate you. Do feel free to ask me anything you wish while we have the opportunity."

"I want to know why you're here."

His voice was coolly unemotional and she responded similarly. "If you mean, do I have to earn my living?—the answer is a little difficult. I could manage on what I have with a certain amount of frugality."

"Nonsense! Your father was reasonably well-off, and your mother had left you something as well. I distinctly remember my aunt saying that your father's living was only a part of his income. He had some property from his family as well."

Theodosia hugged the shawl closer about her shoulders and looked off toward the hills rising black against the night sky. "My father sold his property and left the money to the parish church so they could add a needed aisle."

There was a sharp intake of breath from her companion. "With a plaque dedicating it to him for his generosity, no doubt."

"Something of that sort."

"And your mother's money?"

"It wasn't entirely intact. My father had used it over the years for my maintenance. His solicitor had told him that was perfectly legitimate."

"Exactly how much income do you have, Doe?"

"A hundred pounds a year, not counting my salary here."

A curse escaped him, and he made no effort to apologize. "And that was the man you thought it your duty to stay with and care for."

"I see no need to argue about that now, Lord Steyne.

It's all in the past. I could, as I said, manage on the one hundred pounds. Father's curates had less. But it would have been a rather dull life and I chose instead to come to Lady Eastwick. I like it here."

"You can't seriously expect me to believe you are happy being a governess. What kind of life is that for a young lady?"

Theodosia laughed. "Ideal, my dear sir. They're a delightful family and I have something useful to do. I'm not treated as a glorified nursemaid, you know. The family has accepted me almost as one of them."

"Almost," he muttered, his hands clenched at his sides. "For God's sake, Doe, don't you realize how undesirable such a post can be? You might as easily have found yourself in a household where you were treated as a servant."

"No, you are forgetting that I *am* independent. If I had chanced on an unlucky or unfortunate position, I should simply have left. Fortunately I have that option, and fortunately Charton Court has proved to be marvellous. I couldn't ask for more."

His eyes were angry again. "Really? And what of James and your hat pins?"

Instead of the embarrassment he expected, she chuckled. "Now I wonder who could have told you about that? I hope he didn't suggest that he had his way with me, but he probably did, knowing Mr. Heythrop. Why are you here with him?"

"I don't think I wish to explain that," he said stiffly.

"No, of course not. I am the one being questioned. Had you anything further you wished to know, sir?"

He ran a hand through his hair. "It's not that I wouldn't tell you.... Actually, it's a rather delicate matter and I don't think I should."

"As you wish."

"You haven't explained about Bayhurst."

"There's nothing to explain. If your aunt wrote that I intended to marry him, she was wrong. That's all."

"But you left Chipstable when he did. He must have offered for you."

"There was never any question of my accepting him, and I have no idea when he left the village. If he left when I did, I was not aware of it. I certainly didn't leave *with* him, if that's what you're suggesting."

"I wasn't suggesting anything."

"Your aunt said she would let you know of my father's death. Obviously she took the opportunity to pass on a little gossip. I think she knew perfectly well where I was going. She was a friend of Mrs. Holmer's, after all, and it was Mrs. Holmer who recommended me to Lady Eastwick."

"My Aunt Margaret sees what she wishes to see. I have never understood why she so objected to you and your father."

Theodosia's lips twitched with amusement. "My father once asked her to marry him."

"Oh, Lord. Was there no end to his folly?"

"None, apparently," she retorted as she turned toward the door. She felt his hand grab her wrist, urgent but not painful.

"I'm sorry. Don't go yet. There are still several things I would like to know."

The interview had been more difficult than Theodosia had expected and she strove valiantly for that composure which had become so natural but which in this instance seemed to have entirely deserted her. She had forgotten how overwhelming he could seem with his intent dark eyes and broad shoulders, forgotten how that rugged face could become devoid of expression while still exuding an aura of command. She turned slowly from the door and stood patiently waiting.

"Thank you. When my aunt wrote, it was to tell me that your father had died and that you had left Chipstable with Mr. Bayhurst. No, you don't have to explain that again. What I wish to know is whether you left immediately after your father died."

"How could I? You must know there are any number of things to be done when a relative dies. I was there a month, perhaps six weeks, afterward."

"Did you know ahead of time how you were situated, how little money there would be?"

"I suspected. Father started to talk about the church and how the addition would be a memorial to him. He assured me that I would be well taken care of."

"Did he expect you to marry Mr. Bayhurst?"

"No. Toward the end he took no interest in anything outside himself and his soul. We never spoke of Mr. Bayhurst; there was nothing to say that had not been said a dozen times over the years. Harold was not, to my father's mind, my equal, so he never pushed for a match. My father had a rather...vaunted idea of his own social consequence, or he would never have offered for your aunt."

Her first admission of her father's fallacy, a small admission but a real one, did not give him any apparent pleasure. "So he literally believed that a hundred pounds a year would be sufficient for you to live on?"

"He probably thought it was more. His records were never kept up-to-date and hadn't been balanced for years. He drew on Mother's money to maintain the household and me."

And himself, Steyne thought bitterly. The old fool—a sanctimonious, selfish, narrow-minded hypocrite without the least affection or care for his own daughter. Leaving her barely provided for while he gave what should have been her inheritance to buy his way into heaven. Steyne's eyes flashed with anger.

"If that's all you wish to know, I should be returning to my room," Theodosia said evenly.

"I'll walk you there."

"That's not necessary."

"You forget James is in the house. I would suggest you keep your door locked."

"I shall."

They walked in silence down the corridor to her suite. A lamp burned on the table beside her bed and he stood in the doorway after she entered, saying, "Have a look around. I wouldn't trust James further than I could see him."

Obediently she walked into her study and cast a hasty glance around. All was perfectly in order. She returned to find him surveying her bedroom with interest.

"They've given you a remarkably fine and spacious set of rooms."

Theodosia smiled. "I told you they treat me as almost one of the family."

His eyes met hers for a brief moment. "Yes, you did. Good night, Doe."

"Good night,...Lord Steyne."

"And do you know what he called her?" Charlotte asked her sister dreamily. "He called her 'Doe.' Isn't that perfect? Her eyes are just like a doe's, all warm and brown and trusting."

Eleanor snorted. "It comes from Theodosia, silly."

"Oh, I know, but it's perfect anyhow. He must have known her very well to call her by a nickname, don't you think? I mean, even if his aunt was especially close to her, you'd think at most he would call her Theodosia, don't you? Mama calls her Miss Tremere like we do."

"That's because she's our governess. Oh, she's Mama's friend, too, but she couldn't very well call Mama Joanna, could she? So Mama calls her Miss Tremere."

"Eleanor," Charlotte said disgustedly, "have you no poetry in your soul? I'm not discussing what Mama and Miss Tremere call each other, but what Lord Steyne called her. You should have seen his face when we came around the corner. He was absolutely astonished!" She frowned slightly. "But he seemed a little angry, too. He said, 'What the devil are you doing here?'"

Eleanor giggled. "You shouldn't repeat something like that, Charlotte. What if Edward should overhear you? He'd tell Mama to lock you in your room on bread and water."

"Oh, no, he wouldn't. At least, Mama wouldn't do it. Anyhow, I was only telling you what I heard. Isn't that strange? Of course, I'm sure it was a surprise for him to meet someone he knew here but he was upset about it; I feel certain. Later on you could see he wanted to ask her all sorts of things, but he didn't because I was there. And, oh, Eleanor, he said someone—I can't remember the name—had asked Miss Tremere to marry him. But she hadn't, of course. Lord Steyne said the fellow was a bore."

"Then I'm glad she didn't marry him," Eleanor returned prosaically. "I cannot imagine anything worse than being married to a bore."

"Sometimes I worry about you, Eleanor. Can't you see what I'm driving at? Haven't you the least interest in romance? *I* think Miss Tremere and Lord Steyne were once *interested* in one another, but Miss Tremere was to marry this Mr. Bore. Then Lord Steyne went away and Miss Tremere realized that she couldn't marry the Bore because her heart was given to his lordship. How very sad!"

"*I* think you've been nipping at the wine," was Eleanor's pungent reply, though they were only on their way to breakfast. "Miss Tremere doesn't go sighing about the house with tragic eyes the way you do when you haven't seen Mr. Winstanley for a few days. She is undoubtedly the most cheerful lady I've ever met. How can you weave such a fairy tale? They were probably childhood friends."

"I'm sure they weren't. It was obvious that he met her while visiting his aunt at Chipstable."

"Where he has probably visited off and on for the last—oh, I don't know how many years. He's rather old, isn't he? Over thirty, I'd say. You know we both call Alexander Stapleton Alex simply because we've known him since he was in leading strings."

"She called him Lord Steyne."

"Well, of course she did. You wouldn't expect her to be the least bit familiar with him in our house, would you? And I'll bet you won't find him calling her 'Doe' any longer, either, now that he's found out she's our governess," Eleanor said knowingly. "Thomas told me Lord Steyne is top of the trees as a sporting gentleman."

Charlotte allowed a wistful sigh to escape. "Perhaps

you're right. Miss Tremere doesn't act as though she's had an unhappy moment in her life, does she? Hmm, do you suppose we could sort of promote a romance between them? I would hate to see her leave, but he's a charming man."

"Much as we love her, you must remember she's a *governess,* goose. He won't give her a second glance. And besides, I don't think Uncle James plans to stay very long."

"That, at least, is a blessing." Charlotte shared a grin with her sister as they entered the Breakfast Parlor.

While Lord Steyne and their brothers rose, Lady Eastwick beamed a greeting. What a handsome family she had! It was always a pleasure to present them to a stranger, though rarely did a guest make such an effort as Lord Steyne to draw each of them out, from Charlotte down to John. Amy, who was usually first, had not as yet arrived, but even as she wondered why, her youngest burst through the door, tugging Miss Tremere after her.

"Their eyes are open! I've taken Miss Tremere to see them! Oh, may I keep one in my room now?"

"Make your curtsy to Lord Steyne, dear," her mother prompted with an apologetic smile for his lordship. "Kittens, you know. Amy is devoted to them."

"Are you?" he asked as he seated her next to him, perfectly aware that Edward was urging Theodosia to a seat beside himself. "At Kingswood we have an orange and white striped cat that sleeps under the range all day long and glares at the cook whenever he thumps the pans about. Our cook is a rather volatile Frenchman who professes to despise cats, but the housekeeper tells me she's seen him more than once offer the creature a dollop of the very best cream. What do you make of that?"

Other than her family, it was a new experience for Amy to claim anyone's attention, let alone that of a gentleman of fashion. There was nothing the least reserved about her, however, and she grinned at him.

"I think your cook is embarrassed to admit he likes the cat. Some people are like that, you know. Edward sometimes pretends he doesn't like us, but I've seen him smiling at the boys' antics when he didn't know anyone was watching."

Her eldest brother flushed to the roots of his hair and appeared to choke on the bite of egg he had just forked into his mouth. Lady Eastwick regarded him sympathetically, but a smile twitched at the corners of her mouth. Theodosia calmly poured tea in his cup.

"I think," Steyne replied judiciously, "that it would be difficult to be the eldest son in your family. Lord Heythrop must feel a deep sense of responsibility for all of you, especially since your father is in America. My sister is older than I, and a grown woman, but she's a widow now and I probably treat her just as your brother does you."

"You mean you tell her what to do and what not to do?" Amy asked, wide-eyed.

"Well, I *advise* her about things occasionally. Since her husband died she has no one to turn to when she has an important decision to make."

"Why couldn't she decide for herself? Miss Tremere would."

Steyne met Theodosia's dancing eyes across the table. "Yes, well, Ruth usually makes her own decisions, too, but sometimes it helps to have another person's opinion." He bestowed a look of mock dismay on Amy. "My dear child, it was a great deal simpler discussing cats with you."

Impetuously she laid a small hand on the sleeve of his riding jacket. "I never meant to distress you, sir. Miss Tremere says you must always have a care of other people's feelings, no matter how curious you are. So when I asked Edward where the kittens came from, and he looked like he was going to have an attack of some sort, I immediately said 'Never mind.' After all, Miss Tremere knows, and she didn't mind telling me."

Poor Edward looked as though he was again going

to have an attack of some sort. "Really, Mother, you're not going to let her go on that way, are you?"

Because Lady Eastwick had a napkin pressed to her lips, Theodosia said kindly, "Amy dear, you mustn't monopolize the conversation at table. You should give Eleanor a chance to speak with his lordship."

Looking slightly deflated, Amy murmured, "Oh, yes, of course."

But before she could remove her hand from Steyne's sleeve, he pressed it, saying, "Perhaps you'll show me the kittens after breakfast."

In her most polite voice, but with a triumphant glance at Edward, she replied, "I should be honored to do so, Lord Steyne."

Edward excused himself and the meal resumed light-heartedly. Eleanor thought she had nothing to say to Steyne, but he soon had her talking about her water-colors and the landscapes she most enjoyed painting. He even found himself promising to exhibit his skill as a whip to Thomas and John, if Edward would allow them the use of his curricle. Having no children of his own, and no nieces or nephews, he had never had much interest in young people. He excused his change of heart by assuring himself that the Heythrop children were unique in their enthusiasm and openness.

"You mustn't let them impose on you, Lord Steyne," Lady Eastwick protested when Thomas had extracted his promise. "I'm sure you have other things to do than entertain a houseful of schoolchildren."

"I'll be going with James to Fairlight later in the morning, but I doubt he's even abroad yet." He turned to address Theodosia. "I wouldn't want to keep them from the schoolroom, though, Miss Tremere."

Eleanor gave Charlotte an "I told you so" glance. John hastened to assure him, "Thomas and I are on long vacation now. Only the girls have to study during the summer."

With a mournful shake of her head Theodosia said, "As though studying were a penance. And here I thought you were all enjoying our summer activities."

"We are!" her alarmed charges assured her eagerly, far from ready to give up their search for the treasure. Thomas added carefully, "Studying family history isn't really like working."

Steyne was amused, if perplexed, by the conspiratorial glances which passed between them. Their conspiracy apparently included Theodosia, for they made no effort to avoid her eyes as they did his. What's she up to with the little devils, he wondered. Apparently something that had Lady Eastwick's approval, for his hostess beamed on the lot of them. Steyne took the opportunity of questioning Amy on several matters as he accompanied her to the stables.

"Do you like Miss Tremere?" he asked.

"Oh, yes, she's wonderful. The boys were only teasing about the studying. Half the time they join us when they're home. And I think she's very pretty, don't you?"

"Ah...yes, lovely. I understand she came to you three years ago."

Amy had much the same habit as her mother of screwing her face up when she concentrated, and looked no less charming for all her seven years. "Let's see. I would only have been four then. Well, of course she did, because she came just after Katey was born." Amy's lips quivered slightly. "Katey died in the spring."

"Yes, I heard. I'm sorry. You must miss her."

"I do." She extended her little hand and he enclosed it in his large one. "We all miss her, and we were very sad, but Mama says that she would want us to be happy again now. Do you think so?"

"I'm sure she would."

"Yes, Miss Tremere thought so, too. So we all laugh again, and we're very busy hunting for the treasure."

"The treasure?" Steyne asked as casually as possible.

"It's a family treasure. We don't tell other people about it." Amy looked up, far up, to where his face seemed outlined against the sky. "You won't mind if I don't tell you about it, will you?"

"Certainly not. But is Miss Tremere not 'other people'?"

"Not really. She's one of us, and of course she's seen the inscription on the mantel now for years. I don't think Papa would mind her knowing, though Edward might. He's a little stuffy, you see."

"I hadn't noticed," Steyne lied without a qualm.

"Most people do," she said matter-of-factly. "Perhaps it's because you're one of Edward's heroes. He saw you at Jackson's boxing parlor last year when Papa took him to town and I heard him tell my other brothers that you had a 'handy bunch of fives.' And he saw you take a corner on one wheel in your curricle."

"It must have been an off day," he laughed.

Something had been troubling Amy and with the freedom of youth she asked, "Are you a very good friend of my Uncle James?"

"No, we are merely acquaintances."

"Then why did you come here with him?"

Steyne pursed his lips and considered her for a moment. "If I tell you, it's not to go any further. Can you keep a secret?"

"Not so very well," she admitted. "Perhaps you'd best not."

He squeezed her hand as they entered the dark interior of the stable. "Sensible girl."

Chapter Six

There were times, Edward decided, disgruntled, when he wished he had no siblings. Imagine Amy putting him to the blush that way! And just when he had considered himself sufficiently master of his emotions to seat Miss Tremere next to him again, to say nothing of having such an out-and-outer as Steyne sitting there drinking it all in. The viscount hadn't so much as blinked an eye at the child's blatherings but that was only natural. Steyne was the consummate gentleman: cool, imperturbable, unfailingly polite. He had heard every word, though, and what could he think but that Amy was a fool, or that Edward was?

Edward had more than once considered the possibility that he was a fool. Look at the hash he was making of standing in for his father. And his unfortunate attraction to the governess. He *had* been too hard on the children. From the window of the study he watched Amy and Steyne walking toward the stables and saw her put out her hand to the viscount. To Edward's astonishment Steyne clasped and held it as they continued on their way. This was rather a revelation to Edward, to see a man of Steyne's renown befriending an unruly child. It should have been me, Edward thought. She should have turned to me for comfort. But he knew that she couldn't, and he tried to convince himself that one could not be mentor and friend at the same time. A stupid argument, when all one had to do was observe his own mother, and Miss Tremere. How he wished his father hadn't had to be away at this time!

Upstairs his rascally uncle was probably still in bed, and Edward had yet to see the family document he was supposed to have brought back with him. It would be just like James to arrive under the pretense of returning it, and to have left it in London. And there wasn't a member of the family who didn't wonder how it came about that Lord Steyne had accompanied him. Probably Amy would ask him, Edward realized with a mental groan. The child had no sense of propriety. Well, Steyne was undoubtedly a master at dealing with impertinence; he'd have no trouble handling her.

Reluctantly Edward rose and made his way to his uncle's room in the South Wing. Better to get it over with, provided the older man was awake. Even Edward wouldn't dare rouse him. A soft tap at the door brought a gruff summons to enter.

"Good morning, Uncle James. I trust you slept well."

A tray with chocolate and toast was balanced precariously on James' knees, his nightcap jauntily stuck over his right eye. "Tolerably. The brats playing in the courtyard woke me."

"Unfortunate." Edward showed not a shred of sympathy. "Lord Steyne indicated that you would be going to Fairlight this morning and I wish to get that document from you before you leave."

"I'll be returning."

Despite James' sneer, Edward stood his ground. "I should like it now, please."

His uncle continued to sip at his chocolate, but when Edward made no move to absent himself, he said, "Bring me my valise, then."

Being treated as a lackey by James was nothing new to Edward. With no change of his impassive countenance he walked to where the valise rested on a stool and carried it over to the bed. James waved for him to remove the tray, managing to jiggle it so that chocolate slopped on Edward's coat. Edward ignored it, setting down the tray on a table and swinging the valise up beside his uncle, though he was sorely tempted to ram it down his throat.

James enacted a mock ceremony for removing the document and placing it in Edward's waiting hands. As the younger man had feared, it was not in particularly good condition and he said coldly, "You should have taken better care of it."

"Be grateful you have it back," James snapped. "Now get out so I can dress."

Without another word, Edward left, the paper held gingerly in his hand. In the hall he brushed angrily at the chocolate-soaked coat with his handkerchief, his teeth clenched and his eyes scowling. How it galled him to have to be reasonably polite to his scapegrace uncle! And how unfathomable it was that his gracious, warm-hearted sire could have such a scoundrel for a brother. Edward experienced a sense of shock as he realized it was entirely conceivable that his own brothers and sisters might have wondered how *he* came to be related to *them*.

After changing his coat, Edward sat in his room for some time going over the first earl's poem. The parchment was discolored and frayed, but still largely legible. He hoped Miss Tremere would make an exact copy of it so that future generations would have the key available to them without the necessity of using the original until it crumbled into dust. Edward had largely forgotten the contents, though not the first earl's gallant but untrained hand at poetry.

Proudly passeth from father to sonne
Ye glorious name, ye illustrious treasure,
We who carry ye trust of ye past
Must constantly stryve to be worthie.

Honour hath comme again
As in those days longge passed.

To celebrate this dignity
Lette it be scribed at laste.

Legend hath risen to tarnish,
Fables disguise ye truth
A dozenne engagements in triumph
But bravest of all facing deathe.

Buried alike are ye brave men
Ye leader of battle and this
Ye treasure so honoured, so costlie
Reward for ye bloode so well spente.

Such spoiles as these after battle
No familie yet doth lay claime
Be worthie ye trust so exacting
And defend ye reward with ye name.

Kepe it hidden with those who are gonne
'Nethe ye scenes of valour and stryfe
Arise from the land drenched with
  life's blood
Regen'rated glorie and lite.

Heed well ye location most worthie
A place bothe safe and secure
Be guided by Faith and our grant landes
Forget not ye valu of lore.

Buried. Yes, Edward could remember the tales of digging in graveyards, especially the family plot, despite the sacrilege. It was far more the habit in days past to bury riches, but apparently every inch of the family plots in both Bicknoller and Channock had been searched at one time or another. There was no other burial ground, though sufficient lore of battlefields. The area was strewn with tumuli, settlement rings, the odd quarry, fort, enclosure and barrow. Reading the poem Edward felt a stirring of interest and rather wished that he were part of Miss Tremere's search. He could clearly remember his own fascination when his father had first allowed him to read the documents relating to the treasure. Sure that he would be the one to succeed, he had spent hours puzzling over the clues, only to find himself as hopelessly confused in the end as all the previous searchers had been.

At least the paper would give him an opportunity to speak with Miss Tremere. Surely she would want his opinion of the poem's meaning. But when he arrived at the schoolroom he found her involved in a lesson with the girls and at her suggestion simply left the paper on her desk.

"Would you like to read the other papers, Lord Heythrop?" she asked, indicating them where they lay on a table close by. "The first earl's letter has no doubt stirred your remembrance. Thank you for bringing the poem."

Edward wished she wouldn't smile at him that way; he found it most disturbing. Hastily he gathered up the papers she indicated and returned to his (father's) office, where he sat down to stare for some time at the inkwell before picking up the ninth earl's letter. It was dated 1667 and read:

I take this opportunity to write down the history of the Heythrop "mystery," as even now we are two generations from the last ancestor who was in possession of any real knowledge on the subject. My grandfather, whom I never met, died without conveying the secret to his son, my father, for the simple reason that he was out of sympathy with him at the time he rode forth with the Marquis of Hertford and the royalist forces to meet Sir William Waller. The seventh Earl of Eastwick died from a wound sustained at the battle on Lansdowne Hill in 1643 before his son could be summoned to him.

Although the clue to the mystery was not conveyed to the eighth earl, my father, he was aware that traditionally the eldest son was made privy to this information on his coming of age. My father had arrived at two and twenty years, but had been in dispute with his revered parent for two years over my father's wish to marry my mother, which was opposed by his father, she being not of a station equal to his own, and a purported dissenter. (My mother conducted her life by Church of England standards to the day of her death five years ago.)

No hint as to the nature of the mystery was ever given my father, except of course, the inscriptions on the fireplaces: Proudly Passeth From Father to Son, the Glorious Name, the Illustrious Treasure, along with the Heythrop coat of arms. These mantels were installed during the rebuilding of the house completed in 1492. They have not, to my knowledge, been altered in any way.

That there is actually some *item* of value held by the family does not seem to be in doubt, but what it is or why it is hidden is entirely unknown. Both my father and I have made thorough searches of the house and outbuildings, including the windmill. No trace of anything unusual was ever found except the bones of a small animal which apparently was walled in when one of the changes to the house was made.

It occurred to my father that some written clue to the mystery must be contained in the family archives in case of a sudden death before the eldest son came of age, and he made a search of his father's, and indeed of all his ancestors', papers which were contained at Charton Court. As he felt sure the mystery was an honorable one, he discarded any cryptic references to anything to do with scandal in the family, but not being so scrupulous, I have searched through again and gathered what evidence I could from which to work. Fortunately, I was able to discard after careful consideration any disreputable enigmas, including the coded diary of a lecherous old gentleman— I blush to call him an ancestor—who apparently lived during the reign of King Henry VIII.

Only three possibilities remained after eliminating obviously irrelevant material. Not only the wording, but the locations, of these references is significant, I believe. The first is a letter in poetic form with the broken seal of the first earl which had no direction on it. This was found not with the other documents relating to the first earl, but with my grandfather's papers. The occasion of this juxtaposition in time is unexplained, with the probability that it has been handed down from generation to generation as an (obviously obscure) clue to the location and meaning of the mystery. It must be borne in mind that the first earl did not live at Charton Court but at Seagrave Manor near Bicknoller, which has since burned down. The first earl's letter is attached.

The second item is part of a letter written by the seventh earl when a young man to his father. After discussing various estate matters and the condition of his equally youthful bride (who was apparently increasing), he asked: "Have you determined to remove the treasure from its resting place? I would caution you in doing so, as it has been safe these many years and any change is likely to arouse curiosity. Your fears that someone has guessed the secret are, I feel sure, simply the anxieties of your advancing age. Be content that I share this responsibility and shall do so to the minute of my death. Pray leave the treasure where it is, or if you must move it, summon me to undertake the task. If you should—God forbid!—be struck down before I have a chance to learn of its new location (which cannot, of course, be transmitted other than by your own voice in my ear) there would be a chance of its being lost forever. Your devoted son, etc."

It was this same man, it will be noted, who managed to lose our treasure, possibly forever!

The third article is entirely different from these communications, but seems to have a great deal in common with the first. This is the bronze plaque, undated but of unquestionable antiquity, which has apparently been through a fire at some point (making it probable that it was brought to Charton Court from Seagrave Hall). The plaque is not entirely legible, but the Latin inscription appears to be Keepers of the Trust. The figure of an animal (possibly a dog, a boor, a bear, a lion?) has been largely eradicated by the heat of the fire. This plaque is located on the tower wall of the chapel at such an unusual height—only a foot from the ground—that my father was certain it was highly significant. He had the wall there removed and the stone floor beneath, but found nothing.

One particular must be kept in mind when searching for the treasure, which is that the Heythrop family has moved from Seagrave Manor to Charton Court. It is entirely possible that the item for which we search is still located in the vicinity of Bicknoller rather than Channock. The sixth earl may have considered moving it to Charton Court, or he may simply have considered changing its location here. There is absolutely no evidence to show that he did anything at all, though it is a fact that he died several years after his son's letter, giving him sufficient time to take any action he wished. On the other hand, the seventh earl might well have returned the treasure to its original location (if it was moved) when he came into the title and lands.

My own search for the treasure has been devoid of any tangible success and yet I have confidence that one day it will be restored to the family, through the efforts of a future generation. I cannot and I will not believe that through the petty quarreling of my father and grandfather a special trust has been lost forever. So I wish the coming generations well and hope that the evidence here contained will somehow shed enough light to lead to the restoration of our family inheritance.

Edward set down the last sheet and stared out the window for some time. Really, it was a hopeless tangle and there was no chance at all that Miss Tremere and the children would find the treasure; no one else had. He should not have made such a fuss when his mother allowed the governess to take the papers. Still, he had every intention of keeping an eye on the situation. Come to that, Miss Tremere might yet need his help.

Chapter Seven

As Steyne had expected, it was past eleven before he and James left Charton Court for Fairlight, on horses borrowed with Lady Eastwick's permission. Amy had long since left him to join her sisters and Miss Tremere in the schoolroom, and the viscount had taken the opportunity to observe the inscriptions on the mantels. So the Heythrops had lost an "illustrious treasure," and Doe intended to help them find it again. How enterprising of her, he decided ruefully, and just the sort of thing she would do to distract the children from their grief. Not a trace of her discomposure of the previous evening had been apparent at breakfast. He thought it would be very interesting to hear her explanation of where kittens came from.

When he arrived at the stables James was wearing his own version of country clothes: not the leather breeches Steyne wore, but an expensive and well-cut doeskin, and a brass-buttoned coat rather than the loose one his companion sported. His narrow-brimmed, straight-crowned hat contrasted also with the soft, low-crowned felt hat considered most appropriate by Steyne for such an excursion, and an exaggerated version of the town Hessian boot replaced the more usual mahogany-colored top boot. James made no concessions to country living so far as his dress was concerned; he had no intention of being taken for a country bumpkin by anyone he chanced to meet, and it bothered him not one jot to appropriate Edward's valet for an hour at a time, despite his disparaging remarks on that lad's abilities.

The countryside through which they passed held no fascination for him and it was only with an effort that Steyne urged him to point out the local landmarks. He had, after all, been raised at Charton Court, but his continual residence in London seemed to have blanked out his memory for the local scenery. His standard reply was, "Oh, there's a beacon there, all right, but I don't remember what it's called." The subtleties of combe and moor eluded him, and he exhibited no acquaintance with anyone they passed on the road, though several of the local people raised their hats to him.

Fairlight was approached through an avenue of unkempt oaks and the house itself showed signs of neglect. One of the chimneys was crumbling and the door frame paint was peeling, while the lawns straggled into what had been flower borders and the hedges were so overgrown that one could no longer see above them to the outbuildings. The house itself, though well designed, was depressingly dusty inside with most of the furniture in holland covers and the draperies drawn and faded from the sunlight.

If Steyne was appalled by the condition of Fairlight, he showed no sign of it. James merely said offhandedly, "I rarely come here so it's a waste of time and money to keep the place manicured and polished. I'd rent it out if I could find someone to take it as it is, but no one will pay the price I ask."

Although a due deference was shown James by his tenant-farmers as they rode around his holding, Steyne was not impressed by the condition of any of the farms, either. Five minutes' conversation with James' estate manager was all he needed to take that man's measure, and he sat down over the estate books with a feeling of mingled anger and loathing. Steyne spent a good deal of time on his own estate and knew precisely how much one could expect to reap from good husbandry. James had managed to almost double that figure, and, though it obviously served as a source of pride to Fairlight's owner, Steyne was disgusted. But no sign of his antipathy was allowed to surface. He contented himself with a rigorous questioning of the estate manager, keeping his opinions of that fellow's greedy practices to himself.

James was well content with the visit. "Well, what do you think, Steyne? It's a handsome income for a property its size, isn't it?"

"I'm surprised you haven't invested in more modern equipment, and your rotation isn't regular enough to replenish the land. You're working the soil to uselessness."

"Nonsense! Harding is very clever in choosing the crops that will bring the most profit in any year. If we let a field lay fallow there's no income from it at all." James cast a superior glance at his companion. "I dare say you haven't nearly the profit per acre at Kingswood."

"Very true. On the other hand my home and lands are in much better repair than yours."

Knowing the viscount's pique to be mere jealousy of his own clever management, James was conciliating. "If Ruth wishes to live here, I will certainly see that the place is put in prime condition. But I don't think she'll wish to, you know. She's been stuck out in the country long enough and is enjoying the civilization of London. I don't blame her! There's not a decent entertainment down here from one year's end to the next, even when my sister-in-law decides to do the pretty. All you get is a lot of rustics discussing the price of corn and country misses who don't even know the latest dance steps. Not that you could find the musicians to play for them! I promise you, this is the middle of nowhere. You're fortunate Kingswood is within such easy reach of London. Which reminds me—you won't mind staying a few days, will you? There are some matters to attend now I'm here."

It was the first thing James had said in the three days they spent together with which Steyne could feel in charity. Why he should suddenly wish to remain an uninvited guest at Charton Court he did not wish to consider, but he knew that he was not ready to return to London. The journey to Somerset had not been particularly tiring and he had often enough traveled for days on end with perfect equanimity. But the Heythrops were a congenial family and one he would like to know better. A few days' observance would ascertain whether they offered the suitably genteel position for a governess which they appeared to. Steyne turned to James to say, "No, I won't mind staying, so long as Lady Eastwick can tolerate my presence. I'd like to have a look at the area."

"She won't mind. It's not often they have company with Eastwick in America. I'm afraid you'll have to amuse yourself, though, since I shall mostly be out and about. I'm sure you can appreciate the demands on my time made by a property such as Fairlight."

Now what the devil was he up to, Steyne wondered. He did not for a moment believe that James had the least intention of attending to matters at Fairlight, and it would be foolish beyond permission for him to conduct any sort of liaison with Steyne in the neighborhood, considering the ostensible purpose of their journey. "Feel free to see to your business," he said dryly. "I'm sure I can find sufficient entertainment."

While Lord Steyne and James Heythrop made their tour of Fairlight, Theodosia and the children decided to explore the church at Bicknoller, on the theory that when the Heythrops were burned out of Seagrave Manor and before Charton Court was built, they must have needed a safe place to hide the treasure. The drive took them along the edges of Fairlight land. A hot sun beat down on the ragged lawns and fields beyond where there could be seen broken tubs and troughs, duck baskets and trussels. They caught no glimpse of James or Steyne, but watched men lopping branches from a felled tree and a traveler with a loaded donkey.

The small village of Bicknoller they entered had a lone dog wandering the dusty street but there was no one about. On a hot summer's afternoon the small cottages provided a cool place to spin and rest. In the churchyard stood the shaft of an ancient cross and the building itself dated from Norman times. After the glare and heat outside, the interior felt dark and almost chill. Before Theodosia's eyes accustomed themselves to the dimness, she was startled by a voice, seemingly disembodied, which declared, "Welcome to God's house!"

Eleanor gave a little shriek and Charlotte tittered nervously; Thomas and John stepped forward to protect their female entourage. From the gloom emerged a gentleman dressed in clerical garb, smiling.

"Forgive me! I had no intention of frightening you. Having been in here for some time, I am perfectly accustomed to the light and forgot that you wouldn't be. May I introduce myself? Robert Oldbury, your most obedient servant."

Since he addressed himself to Theodosia, but included her charges in a wide-ranging glance, she made him known to each of the children. "And I am the girls' governess, Miss Tremere. We had in mind to inspect the church, if you've no objection."

"None whatsoever. May I offer myself as guide?"

Theodosia caught the dismayed looks of the children and made a small, restraining gesture to them. "If you would be so kind. You won't mind if the children sketch items of interest and wander about on their own, will you? And I do think we might purchase a few candles to light their exploration."

She allowed herself to be led through the interior while the young people went about their tasks with single-minded purpose. Theodosia had no difficulty inducing Mr. Oldbury to comment on the fine old screen (from 1500) with its beautiful fan tracery, nor on the capitals in the North arcade with their bands of Dev onshire foliage. The cleric was further encouraged by the interest she took in the momument to John Sweeting of Thornecombe (died 1688) and the squint in the chancel pier, as well as the piscina and some of the good seat-ends. By the conclusion of their tour the children had finished their own work and escaped into the churchyard.

Not until they emerged into the sunlight was Theodosia able to obtain a reasonable view of her guide, and she found then that he was rather older than she had expected, perhaps thirty, with wavy blond hair and frank blue eyes. He stood only slightly taller than she and had a square-jawed, open face.

"Thank you for the tour," Theodosia said, extending her hand. "I never meant to take so much of your time."

"It was my pleasure, Miss Tremere. Have you lost your students?"

"No, they'll be rooting amongst the tombstones, looking for anything of interest."

"Are they Lord Eastwick's children?" Mr. Oldbury asked, not eager for her to leave.

"Yes, we're just over near Channock at Charton Court. We plan to make an excursion to see Fairlight, their uncle's home."

Mr. Oldbury frowned momentarily. "I hadn't heard that Mr. Heythrop was in residence."

"He's not, actually. He's staying at Charton Court."

"I haven't seen Mr. Heythrop but twice in the two years I've been here."

Theodosia laughed. "I understand he's not fond of country living. Did you know him before you came?"

"No, the parish living is in the hands of my college at Oxford. It's a peaceful spot and I enjoy hiking in the Quontocks, so I couldn't ask for better. Perhaps you would consider attending a service here some Sunday. Dr. Trainer is a fine speaker, of course, and I could not hope to compete with him, but the young folks might enjoy a change once in awhile."

Dr. Trainer, the vicar at Channock, was a prosy old man who frequently fell asleep while the choir sang.

He tended to address his congregation as though he were preaching at St. Paul's, with a finely dramatic and piercingly loud voice. Theodosia's lips twitched. "I shall suggest it to Lady Eastwick, Mr. Oldbury."

He read the amusement in her eyes and smiled. "Channock is rather a small congregation for the use of his powers, I fear. He really should have been made a Prebend at Salisbury Cathedral. Too many men with country livings are overlooked when a more prestigious position opens. I am not speaking of myself! I haven't Dr. Trainer's years of experience nor the tenth part of his knowledge. And one's political persuasion often carries weight as well. I'm sure you know he's a staunch old Whig and though there were hopes that the Prince Regent would bring that party to power.... Listen to me rattle on! I'm sorry! I'm keeping you from the children."

"Not at all. They'll keep quite busy until the barouche returns. In fact, I'll probably have to drag them away. But perhaps I should keep them in sight."

Mr. Oldbury walked with her into the churchyard where they could see Charlotte and Eleanor tracing letters on a marble stone while Thomas transcribed the words. Not far away John was doing a somersault in the grass while Amy delightedly clapped her hands.

Theodosia sighed. "I hope you won't think them sacrilegious, Mr. Oldbury. They're only children."

"They act exactly as I would expect on an outing. The younger ones, at least. The others are rather industrious for a pleasure jaunt."

"Oh, they enjoy finding the oldest tombstone."

"But writing down the information on it?" he asked quizzingly.

In order to divert his attention from this odd behavior, Theodosia said, "My father was the vicar at Chipstable. I don't think he'd have allowed children to cavort among the tombstones."

"Is your father no longer there?"

"No, he died several years ago."

"I'm sorry to hear it."

"Thank you. It was a great loss." Theodosia did not add, "to me," as she might have three years ago. She had had sufficient time since to obtain the distance necessary to see her father in a less prejudicial light than she had then. Not that she hadn't been aware that he was a selfish, sanctimonious man, but one had to stand by one's parents, one's family, or so she had always been taught. If one lives in a family such as the Heythrops it would not be so hard. Except, perhaps, for the Honorable James, she recalled. It was difficult, when one was young, to know where one's duty lay. Theodosia realized that Mr. Oldbury was speaking to her. "I beg your pardon. My mind was wandering."

"I was just saying that Dr. Trainer is planning a trip to Scotland soon and has asked me if I would serve his church for him. My own service is at half after ten and his not until one, and I was considering the possibility. There's really no one else close enough to do it."

"We would have the opportunity for a change without even a longer coach ride that way, Mr. Oldbury. I do hope you will."

Her smile was so sincerely appreciative that he decided on the moment. "I shall, then. I'll send a note round to him tomorrow."

The carriage could be heard approaching and Theodosia called to the children to finish their exploration. "Just one more minute," Eleanor begged. "We haven't quite finished copying this."

By the time Phillips had climbed down to assist them into the barouche, all but John were gathered about the governess. There was no sight of the boy in the grassy churchyard. For a moment Theodosia thought he must be hiding behind one of the larger tombstones in an undeclared game of hide and seek. He was full of mischief, never malicious but in perpetual high spirits. Mr. Oldbury offered to find the lad and quickly made a pass through the stones, with no success. With a slightly furrowed brow, he disappeared around the corner of the church to an area which had formerly been open pasturage but was recently given over to the church for additonal burial ground.

The gravediggers had spent the morning preparing a spot for the ninety-one-year-old Mrs. Borrow's coffin. In his exuberance John had managed to somersault straight into it, which had vastly startled and slightly shaken, but most of all had intrigued him, for in falling into the relatively shallow cavity his foot had dislodged a clump of earth to lay bare a section of metal. Regardless of his condition, which must be admitted to have already suffered from his tumbling in the grass, he began eagerly to scratch away at the earth to clear a larger section of the discovery. His fingernails were no match for the hard-packed ground and when he at last thought to call for assistance, he looked up to see the worried face of Mr. Oldbury gazing down on him with a sort of horrified fascination.

"Are you hurt?"

"Oh, no, sir, but I've discovered something! Do you have a shovel?"

"I don't usually carry one with me," Mr. Oldbury confessed, "but the gravediggers will have left theirs in the church."

John hastily scrambled out of the hole, brushing ineffectually at the muddy streaks on his fawn-colored breeches. "There's a metal box or something there. It could be a coffin but there's no marker. I'll get a shovel and finish uncovering it."

"Miss Tremere and your brother and sisters are waiting for you, young man. Have you forgotten them?"

John's face was a study in dismay. "We can't leave now! Not when I've just found something! Where are they?"

"The coach is at the church entrance."

Ever polite, John called, "Thank you," as he galloped around the corner of the church and out of sight. He arrived at the waiting group out of breath and almost inarticulate with excitement. "I've found something! I don't know it it's the treasure; in fact I have no idea what it is. I fell in a grave and there it was! Imagine!

Mr. Oldbury said I could use the gravedigger's shovel in the church to unearth it. Thomas can help me. It's metal, you see, and I couldn't get the dirt away with my hands."

They all gazed at Theodosia expectantly. Phillips coughed discreetly and said, "I could perhaps be of help, ma'am. The boy can keep the horses in the shade for a bit."

Theodosia gave a helpless shrug and laughed. "I suppose it's what we're here for. But if we are gone too long, Lady Eastwick will worry, so get the shovel quickly and lead on, John."

The whole party trooped to the site of the would-be grave and John enthusiastically pointed out his find. "First we should determine how big it is, I think," he suggested. "If it's very large, we'll need more help."

Trying not to think about the reaction Lord Heythrop would have to seeing his two brothers, to say nothing of the coachman, arrive home covered with dirt, Theodosia gave permission for them to climb into the hole and work at unearthing the metal object. John's eagerness outpaced his strength, and even Thomas soon tired of scraping at the hard-packed earth, but Phillips set to with a will and a metal box of modest proportions was soon outlined on the side of the grave. Its length was short of two feet and its height not above four inches, Theodosia guessed, as they worked alternately to remove the box from its resting place. Surprisingly, it was buried rather deeply, at least three feet under the surface, with nothing on the ground above to indicate its location.

The boys gave a triumphant cry announcing the release of the metal box from its burial ground. There was a lock on the box and Theodosia turned to Mr. Oldbury.

"I think you should be the one to take the next step, sir. The box is, after all, on church property, and until it can be identified as belonging to anyone else, I suppose it is your responsibility." Her eyes danced with laughter. "Of course, the children would be horridly disappointed not to see what's in it."

He offered his boyish grin. "So would I! May I have a look at it?"

Thomas reluctantly handed him the box, at the same time casting Theodosia a look that clearly betrayed his opinion that she was being hopelessly scrupulous. However, Mr. Oldbury did not tuck the box under his arm and march off to the privacy of the rectory. He examined the rusted lock, asked for the shovel and neatly smashed the lock off in one vigorous stroke. There was a breathless silence while he dusted the box with his sparkling white handkerchief and quickly prised open the lid.

"Papers!" Thomas exclaimed disgustedly. "Just a lot of old papers!"

Mr. Oldbury shook his head sorrowfully. "And here I thought we'd have found mounds of guineas and perhaps a few pairs of solid gold candlesticks at the very least." He carefully sorted through the stack of handwritten sheets, pausing here and there to note signatures and subject matter. "They appear to be old church registers and related documents. I can't imagine why anyone would bury them."

"That will give you a mystery to solve," Theodosia suggested, "and possibly a fascinating one. I wonder, if you find anything relating to the Heythrops, would you let us know? The children have been...ah... researching their family history, so to speak."

"With pleasure." Mr. Oldbury rose and dusted off his hands. "I'll go through them minutely and let you know if there is anything you would be interested in."

"Thank you. Come, children, we're already much later than we'd planned." As the disappointed group moved off toward the carriage, Theodosia offered her hand to Mr. Oldbury with a grateful smile. "You've been most helpful, sir, and very indulgent of my charges."

"It was my pleasure, Miss Tremere." He hesitated to offer his dirty hand but Theodosia kept hers out, and at length he shook it warmly. "I hope we meet again soon."

"I'm sure we will."

They had reached the carriage and Mr. Oldbury handed Theodosia in. If she had intended to say more to him, there was no opportunity, for the children all started speaking at once about what they had found and what a disappointment the box had been and what they would do next. Theodosia smiled ruefully at Mr. Oldbury and waved as the carriage clattered off down the dusty village street.

This time as they passed Fairlight they did catch a glimpse of James and Steyne riding across country back toward Charton Court. Thomas watched admiringly and exclaimed, "Did you see him take that hedge! And he's on Clover, by God! Who would have thought it? Uncle James held Trumpet in too long, don't you think, John?"

Theodosia followed Steyne's retreating back until it disappeared beyond the trees. He had always looked perfectly at ease in the saddle. She could remember how, when he had ridden out with her the first time, he had attempted to hide his astonishment at the broken-winded nag on which she was mounted. There were two fine horses in Mr. Tremere's stables, a fact of which all were aware. But Theodosia's father considered them for his use alone, and she was reduced to seeing her sidesaddle grace the shaggy flanks of a mare which should have been put to pasture years before. On subsequent expeditions he had brought one of his own horses which where stabled at his aunt's and he had grinned at her delight in a superb piece of horseflesh. "No one would ever know from the way you ride that you were accustomed to toddling about on a hobby-horse," he had teased.

And it was on one of those rides, her persistent memory reminded, that he had first kissed her. They had ridden toward Heydon Hill and dismounted to have a closer look at a birdhouse made in the shape of a windmill, totally incongruous in the rough countryside. No dwelling could be seen and the trail was rough and partially overgrown.

As she had watched the little windmill spin in a gust of humid air, he had gathered an armful of yellow-wort and corn flowers and presented it to her as though the flowers were from one of his hothouses at Kingswood. He had told her father, who had an interest in horticulture, that in his hothouses there grew an astonishing variety of fruits, vegetables and flowers, but Mr. Tremere had scoffed at the tales, declaring that God designated in what seasons a plant should grow and that man should not tamper with the arrangement.

Theodosia had looked up from the yellow and blue petals, her eyes aglow, and Lord Steyne had touched her lips softly with his. The kiss startled her; she had never been kissed before. In confusion she had sunk her face into the flowers and even now she could remember his voice, ever so gentle, saying, "Don't be alarmed, my dear. The flowers are a homage to your beauty, and the kiss a homage to your spirit. I would never harm you, believe me."

No, he had never intended to harm her, had in fact treated her like some treasured discovery, perpetually astonished at his good fortune. But that was long ago. Theodosia sighed as she turned her attention back to the children.

If James had rejected his obligation to entertain Lord Steyne, several of the Heythrop youngsters were determined to assume the burden. To their minds nothing could be more entertaining than having him instruct them in how to handle the ribbons on Edward's curricle, or showing him how the kittens were beginning to cavort, or having his opinion, shyly requested, on a favorite drawing. And even after the younger ones went off to bed, there was Edward ready to proudly display the archive room and expound on family history. Though Edward had recently read the ninth earl's letter, he had already forgotten its strictures on the contents of an old journal in cipher which lay temptingly on a shelf. When Steyne happened to flip it open and ask if he might take it with him, Edward gulped down his natural inclination to bar any document from leaving the room, and politely (James would have said fawningly) agreed.

Lady Eastwick and Theodosia had already retired for the night and Steyne took the journal with him to his room. Before he so much as untied his cravat, however, he set the book on a table and left the room again, headed for the entrance porch roof. Very few words had passed between himself and Theodosia that evening, owing to the efforts of the family to keep him occupied, but he had attempted to indicate that he wished to speak with her again.

There had been no sign that she understood him, and he found the rooftop vacant. Since he had been delayed by Edward's tour of the archive room, he was not surprised. She might have come and left again; more likely she had not come at all. The temptation to knock at her door was strong, now that he knew where her room was, but he refused to make that move. He did, however, stand outside it to ascertain whether there was movement within.

Damned if he couldn't hear her humming. Humming, for God's sake! As though she had not a care in the world. As though her mind were entirely at peace. Was it possible she didn't know how badly she had cut up *his* peace all those years ago? Did she imagine he had forgotten her as easily as she had apparently forgotten him? Well, she was right, after all, wasn't she? When he had received her letter in response to his on her coming of age, he had entirely put her from his mind, lived his life as he had done previously, determined in his anger to see that she held no place in his mind.

For a while he had seriously considered marrying the Wilberfoss girl, but he hadn't been able to bring himself to do it. That inability had nothing to do with Miss Theodosia Tremere! Clara Wilberfoss had turned out to be as empty-headed as she was flirtatious; not exactly the sort of wife he had in mind.

Let Doe enjoy her life as a governess! Apparently it suited her perfectly, all those people depending on her for good humor and advice. If what she wanted was to be needed, she had chosen the ideal situation. Certainly *he* didn't need her! For six years he had proved that to his own satisfaction, and evidently to hers. There was nothing less appetizing to a man of his inclination than a martyr, and only a martyr would have stayed with that cantankerous old man when she might have married Steyne and lived a life of luxury and position. He would have seen that her father had someone to care for him if his income didn't run to it. There were always neighborhood women looking for a position of that nature.

Steyne wondered if she had remembered to lock the door against James, but he didn't dare try it to find out. Instead he walked as silently as possible away from her door, hoping she wouldn't know that anyone had been there. She needn't think he took the least interest in her welfare after she had so carelessly rejected him, he decided as he yanked off the square of starched muslin which served as his cravat. And if falling asleep that night took longer than usual, he had the journal to entertain him, its code almost childishly simple to decipher. Steyne found the Elizabethan gentleman's amorous adventures diverting.

Chapter Eight

Theodosia sat late that night sorting through the information she and the children were accumulating on the history of the Heythrop family. Their excursion to Bicknoller had provided little new intelligence, but it was part of a well-organized effort to extract every piece of evidence they could as to where the treasure was *not* hidden. In addition to several excursions in the neighborhood of Channock to determine the possibility of hiding places, Theodosia had the children working their way through various family documents looking for clues.

"It is all very well," she told them, "to rely on the ninth earl for his synopsis of available information, but we will do better to cover every piece of the ground ourselves." And, surprisingly, the children had not complained. The weather might have had something to do with that, she thought ruefully as her candle burned lower. For a while it had turned foggy and cold, with occasional showers to induce the cautious to stay indoors when possible. The children were not by nature particularly cautious, but with a fire burning in the schoolroom grate, and constant infusions of tea and cakes, they worked their way through the papers Lord

Heythrop had grudgingly allowed them to remove from the archive room.

Working on the chart was a good way to keep her mind from wandering to Viscount Steyne, for it required her concentration and she even found herself enjoying it, humming as she worked. The chart was not precisely a history of the Heythrops, but more a conglomeration of ancestry, residence and years of birth, death and marriage. Most of the facts were available after Sir Arthur Heythrop was created the first Earl of Eastwick in 1485 by Henry VII after the Battle of Market Bosworth. The first earl had died shortly thereafter, passing on the poem and the title to his son and a long line of succeeding Heythrops.

Having sat for some time bent over the chart Theodosia rose and stretched. The night was clear, with only a few clouds scudding across the moon. Outside the oriel window she could distinguish the Quantock Hills with their stands of trees and dark peaks, a familiar sight now in daylight or dark. Theodosia, lulled by the serenity, allowed herself to consider how she would conduct herself with Lord Steyne. Really, it was a difficult business. How did you behave as though he were a mere acquaintance when there was a time when you had loved him? Especially unnerving when you caught a glimpse of laughter in his eyes or heard the note of concern in his voice and all the old feeling rushed back. She must, of course, show him how content she was at Charton Court, how comfortable her life was with these kind people—her new family. Perhaps he didn't care if she was happy, but she could not help believing that he did. It must be rather painful to see a woman you had once offered your name and your heart reduced to presiding in a schoolroom. Certainly he was glad she did not preside at his table, but that would not reconcile him to what he must consider a most unfortunate fate. Wearily she stifled a yawn and returned to her seat at the desk.

The knock at her door surprised her and she glanced

at the mantel clock to find that it was only a few minutes short of midnight. "Who is it?"

"Edward."

Alarmed that someone might be ill, she picked up the candle and hurriedly unlocked the door to him. "Is there some problem?"

"No, no. I saw your light when I was passing and thought you might not be well."

It was a very simple excuse, and not a very good one, since there was no reason for him to be in her wing at all. He didn't appear as awkward as on his last call, however, and Theodosia was reluctant to turn him away. She was aware that despite his being surrounded by a large family, he felt lonely and often segregated from them by the nature of his position.

"No, I'm fine. I've been working on a chart of your family. Would you like to see it?"

His hesitation was minimal. She was still dressed and he felt left out of the children's perpetual chatter about their researches and exploration. "Yes, I'd like to see it if you wouldn't mind. Perhaps I can be of some help." He followed her to the desk, leaving the door slightly ajar for propriety's sake.

"As you can see," she explained, "I have concentrated largely on when each of your ancestors lived. After all, the first earl already had the treasure, but there is little documented before him. His great grandfather was made a baronet, and he himself has left sketchy details of those who came before him, but nothing we can find which in any way reveals the secret of the mysterious inheritance. He died in 1485 and his son became the second earl. In 1487 Seagrave Manor burned to the ground, though the archive room is witness to the fact that there was time to remove at least the most valuable of the Heythrop articles from the house. Charton Court was built between 1487 and 1492 around an old manor house that stood here. I'm sure you know all that, Lord Heythrop, but I mention it because we have been unable to discover where the

Heythrops lived during the five-year building period. It may be significant."

"It is unlikely that the treasure was left there," he protested.

"I'm sure you're right, but if a secure spot was found, it is just possible that it was. Unlikely, I agree. Every indication is that the family lived in the immediate neighborhood, probably somewhere around Bicknoller or Channock."

Edward considered her chart and the map which lay beside it. "The Heythrops have owned or inherited several properties in the neighborhood. Even when Seagrave Manor stood, they had the manor house here. Aren't there records which show?"

"No, which leads me to believe they may not have owned the place in which they stayed for those five years. I dare say it's not important, but it's a piece of the puzzle I'd like to fill in." Theodosia moved her finger down the list of earls until she came to the seventh. "Here is where the chain of passing on the secret broke. He was born in 1600 and died after the Battle of Lansdowne Hill in 1643. His son began the search, and his grandson wrote the letter we have with its few clues."

Her nearness was doing alarming things to Edward's emotions. Although he would not even acknowledge it to himself, he had glanced to see whether from the open door they could be seen by the desk, and found they could not. And he doubted very much that there was another soul at Charton Court abroad at this late hour. Not that he contemplated doing anything outrageous. He simply wished to touch the gleaming brown hair, to hold one of those soft, shapely hands. But when she glanced up from the chart, her full lips smiling and her eyes friendly, he had an almost uncontrollable urge to kiss her.

With the unerring instinct of a woman of her beauty and precarious position, Theodosia did not need the slightest movement on his part to tell her how matters stood. Before he could even decide what to do—pull her into his arms, or set the candle down, or grab her hand with an impassioned speech of his regard for her—she stepped hastily to the door and asked, "Did you hear Lady Eastwick call? I thought I heard something."

Poor Edward felt as though he'd suffered a severe blow to the stomach. He didn't believe for a moment that his mother was awake or calling for anyone but he knew the turn such a suggestion gave him. In a choked voice he murmured, "I didn't hear anything. I'm sure Mother is asleep, but I'll check if you wish."

"If you would, Lord Heythrop; it would ease my mind. No doubt it was simply one of those creaks or groans for which old buildings are famous, but I would rest better knowing you had checked." She pointedly noted the time. "Oh, dear, it's gone midnight. I'll have to finish this in the morning. Thank you for your help."

In no time at all Edward found himself in the dark hall, her door closed behind him. Shame was uppermost in his mind. How could he have even considered approaching Miss Tremere in such a situation? Was he not responsible for the welfare of every resident at Charton Court? The governess was an employee of his family and he had almost made a most improper advance to her. Of course he would not have been so lost to all honor as to have seduced her, but neither was he in a position to offer marriage. She was not as wellborn as he, and he had a very strict sense of what was required of a Heythrop when it came to allying himself to a young lady in marriage.

There had been moments over the last few days when he had thought of arguments against his being so severely handicapped. Miss Tremere was, after all, quite obviously of gentle birth. His mother liked her extremely well. The children had shaken off their grief and plunged into the search with renewed vitality simply because of the governess's contagious enthusiasm. What a picture she had made as they arrived home late from Bicknoller, her cheeks glowing and her eyes laughing when she had related to Lady Eastwick the suspense of the wait to see what the old box contained.

Miss Tremere—Theodosia—could make the most amusing story out of the dullest expedition imaginable!

Edward admired her, and the calm efficiency with which she dealt with the family and the servants alike. She seemed to find no ambiguity in her position: above the servants and below the family. Always good-humored and sure of herself, others could not help but be drawn to her. And Edward had allowed himself to think of her in quite another way altogether! It never occurred to him that the object of his infatuation would have rejected him. He was, after all, heir to the Earl of Eastwick, one of the most illustrious titles in the land! When one enjoyed a truly remarkable situation, neither age nor inclination was likely to stand in the way... and Edward was very aware that Miss Tremere was several years older than he.

If he had thought the suggestion would have received even the least attention from his mother, he would have broached the possibility of replacing Miss Tremere. It would be a good thing to remove temptation from his sight. Of course, he would have helped to find her a new position, preferably in Yorkshire or somewhere in that vicinity. Anywhere that he had no chance of falling under her spell again. But he knew his mother and he knew precisely what her reaction would be: "You can't be serious! Replace Miss Tremere? Have your wits gone begging, Edward? Even in my fondest dreams I have never imagined a more perfect governess for the girls. And have you forgotten that she has earned the respect of your brothers as well? I think you must be suffering from the onset of a fever, my dear. I'll have Dr. Horner come around."

No, there was no chance that she would leave. He would have to keep a very strict guard on himself in future. Wrapped in his thoughts, he entirely forgot to pause at his mother's door, but stomped disconsolately to his own chamber, setting the candle on his bedside table and calling for his valet. And with Amy only seven, it might be another ten years before the Heythrops pensioned her off!

* * *

At the breakfast table Theodosia found Edward polite but distant. He refused to join in any discussion of the children's activities, making a point of studying a newspaper, though it couldn't have been current, for none had arrived for two days. Lady Eastwick offered to show Steyne her gardens and Theodosia proposed a jaunt into the Quantocks to the children for an overview of the area. The Honorable James Heythrop had not, of course, arisen as yet.

The Quantocks are not a lengthy range, running only ten or twelve miles from the area of Taunton to the northwest. On the eastern side are woodland dells and heathy moorlands, while on the west side, from which the Charton Court party ascended, there are steeper, barer slopes covered with bracken, heather, scrub oak and whortleberries, which ripen just in time for the released schoolchildren to go "whorting." The range is narrow with only a few noticeable peaks, but the red deer roam them and Theodosia was not averse to allowing her charges to explore.

They wandered as far as Will's Neck, the tallest summit, to survey the various combes which stretched down from the hills and into the flatter land beyond, identifying villages and locating the estates which housed their neighbors. Theodosia pointed out the sites which were marked on the old map of the treasure-seekers but their locations brought no fresh ideas and the party sat down to their picnic lunch. After discussing Bicknoller Hill, Trendle Ring, Quantock Moor, Thorncombe Hill, Black Hill and the various ancient barrows and tumuli, Theodosia turned to Charlotte.

"Have you heard from Christina Winchmore, Charlotte? Are they back from London?"

"We expect them any day now. I can hardly wait to hear what she has to say of the season." Charlotte knew a moment's hesitation at showing so much interest in the frivolities of a London season, when she remembered that they were still mourning poor Katey, but Miss Tremere smiled encouragingly. "I'm sure she'll send a note as soon as they reach Basing Close. We can go to visit her, can't we? It's been months since I saw her."

"As Basing Close is one of the estates we wish to visit, I should certainly think so. Remember what we saw from the hill, the four estates clustered about Charton Court: Old Lodge, Lovelands, The Beeches and Basing Close. On the old map they are each marked, and I can see no reason why, so I think we had best investigate, as we did at The Beeches. Are there any ties with the Heythrop family? Are there any mysterious carvings on the mantels? That sort of thing."

"But we've all been to each of them dozens of times," Thomas protested.

"Ah, but we weren't looking for the treasure then. That is a significant difference." Theodosia made an airy gesture with her hand. "We must see everything with new eyes. The ninth earl said they had searched the windmill, but I for one intend to do so again. Unless we cover every bit of the ground again, we may miss some clue, if not the treasure itself."

Her confidence in their eventual success, or at least in the possibility that they would be successful, never failed to inspire them. Homeward bound once more, they did not consider the day's journey wasted, but the beginning of a new direction. Theodosia herself had different cause to rejoice, and it had nothing to do with their treasure hunt. Christina Winchmore was the answer to her most recent dilemma, she felt sure, if the girl had not attached someone in London. When Christina had left with her family in the spring, Theodosia was aware that the girl had a decided *tendre* for Edward, and she would make a perfectly suitable match, if that stuffy young man's eyes could be opened to her attractions. Despite his obvious resolve, displayed at the breakfast table, to ignore her in future, Theodosia knew she would be a great deal more comfortable in her role as governess at Charton Court if Edward's attention were directed elsewhere.

Charlotte was handed the awaited note the moment

they entered the house, and she gave a delighted cry. "At last! Oh, she doesn't say anything at all but that she is happy to be back. And that she wishes me to visit her as soon as may be. May I go this afternoon, Miss Tremere?"

"They'll just be settling in, my dear. You must ask your mother and see what she thinks."

As Lady Eastwick was frequently to be found in the Gold Parlor at this time of day, Charlotte skipped excitedly to the room, threw open the door and sang, "Mama, Christina is home! May I go to see her today?"

Only at the end of her impulsive speech did she become aware of a visitor in the parlor. For just a fraction of a second she thought (or perhaps hoped) it was Mr. Winstanley, but the gentleman rose and turned to face her while the others poured into the room.

"I beg your pardon, Mr. Oldbury. I had no idea Mama had a guest," she apologized, and then, realizing the significance of his visit, "Have you found something among those old papers?"

Lady Eastwick forebore with patience the excited inquiries of her offspring before saying firmly, "You forget your manners, children. Mr. Oldbury cannot answer all of you at once. Eleanor, if you will ring for the tea tray, the rest of you may be seated."

There was an expectant hush as Mr. Oldbury cleared his throat and addressed his opening remarks to Miss Tremere. "I never meant to create such excitement. Would that my parishoners hung on my words with such interest," he said ruefully. "Knowing that you were all eager to learn anything about the Heythrop family, I have brought what references there were. I confess I do not find them very significant myself, but perhaps they will lend some small new fact to your inquiries."

Beside his chair he had placed a satchel from which he withdrew a stack of the old papers. Though he offered them to Lady Eastwick, she indicated that Theodosia was to have them, saying, "Take them to the escritoire, my dear. Nothing is worse than sitting on a chair and being expected to juggle a lot of dusty, crumbling papers."

Theodosia smiled appreciatively and found herself surrounded by all the children as she spread the old records out before her. Mr. Oldbury pointed out the first reference, which was the confirmation of a child, William Heythrop, in the year 1482. The second was no more auspicious, the churching of a Madeleine Heythrop in 1491.

"What years do the parish records cover?" Theodosia asked curiously.

"Apparently 1480 until 1520, though many of the registers for those years were with the church documents we already had."

"Was there any indication why these records were hidden?"

"I can't be positive. At first sight, none, but on closer examination each of the pages had at least one reference to the Gregory family, and for the years in question there was not a solitary entry concerning them in the church books we had. I'm not from this part of the country, myself, and am not familiar with the family. No one by that name resides in the parish now."

Theodosia looked questioningly at Lady Eastwick. "Are you familiar with the family, ma'am?"

Her employer's face wore its charming puzzled expression. Though she cast her mind in a multitude of directions, she could not capture even the glimmer of a memory. "I don't believe so. Certainly not here in Somerset. It's not an uncommon name in some parts of the country, I suppose. Eastwick would probably be of more help."

"Perhaps the Winchmores would know," Charlotte suggested hopefully.

"Now, dear, you must give them a chance to rest after their journey," Lady Eastwick insisted. "Send Christina a welcoming note, and I will add a line to her mother. Tomorrow morning is the very earliest we should go, I think."

"Yes, Mama."

Theodosia turned her attention again to the papers in front of her. "Now here is something that could be of interest. The Madeleine Heythrop who was churched in 1491 is stated to be 'of Whortle Hall.' If she is a member of the second earl's family, that may prove to be where they lived during the building of Charton." A frown puckered her brow. "Whortle Hall? I'm afraid that serves no memory with me."

"It would have had to be in the Bicknoller parish," Mr. Oldbury mused, "but there is no such place now. It could have been abandoned, or destroyed by fire, of course."

"Or its name could have been changed," Thomas suggested.

Theodosia regarded him admiringly. "Very good! That's quite possible, you know. Perhaps we should have a look at the rest of Mr. Oldbury's parish records, if there's no help here." A minute examination of the papers, however, gave no hint, and after 1492, when the Heythrop family presumably moved to Charton Court, there were few mentions of the name. One Jane Heythrop was married to Charles Datchet there in 1502, and George Heythrop Datchet was baptized there in 1505. Thedosia made careful notes of each of the Heythrop entries and checked to see that Whortle Hall was not mentioned again before she handed the papers back to Mr. Oldbury. "We're grateful for your assistance, sir. You were kind to be so thorough in your search."

"I'm grateful to Master John for finding the records, and only wish they might have proved more useful to you."

Her eyes danced. "But you have given us a new mystery to untangle! We can only be thankful, I promise you."

"Would you allow me to see what I can find about Whortle Hall—from the rest of the parish records, and from my parishioners? I'd enjoy doing it."

Theodosia took a silent survey of her charges, who nodded agreement. "We accept your generous offer. Of course, in our own area we'll make inquiries as well; one can never be sure where the most useful information is to be found."

"Very true. I've agreed to stand in for Dr. Trainer while he's in Scotland. He was so pleased he's decided to leave earlier than planned." His eyes plainly showed his amusement at this turn of events. "I'll be taking the service this Sunday."

Charlotte was watching with fascination the exchange between them, the spoken as well as unspoken messages. Well, on his part, in any case. Miss Tremere was her usual calm, cheerful self, but Mr. Oldbury most decidedly had an *interest* in Miss Tremere, Charlotte decided, and heaved a satisfied sigh. She was so pleased to discover this that she had one of her rare inspirations, and hastened to whisper in her mother's ear while Mr. Oldbury took leave of the children.

Surprised, but willing, Lady Eastwick extended her hand as he approached and said, "As you are to be in Channock for the service, I do hope you will join us for dinner, Mr. Oldbury."

His acceptance, Charlotte noted ecstatically, was with quite evident delight. She threw Eleanor a conspiratorial wink, though her dear sister hadn't the least idea why.

Chapter Nine

teyne, perhaps in an effort to prove to James his
tention of exploring the area, had spent most of the
ay riding about on Clover, stopping at an inn in West
agborough for a midday meal. On returning to Char-
n Court he passed a gentleman in clerical garb leav-
g and lifted his hat in salute, though just prior to
eeting him he had been meditating once again on Mr.
remere's many grievous faults. The fellow looked
armless enough, however; was in fact a rather fine-
oking figure of a man with a suitably warm smile as
e said, "Good afternoon, sir!" Probably the local vicar,
eyne decided, and a frequent visitor at the Court. He
smissed him immediately from his mind.

Strangely enough, as Steyne left the stables his eye
appened to fall on the windmill on the hill and he,
o, was reminded, as Theodosia had been earlier in
e day, of the first time he had kissed her. That silly
tle windmill-shaped birdhouse had been spinning fe-
rishly as he presented her with the flowers and
aned down to embrace her. He had wanted to do that
actically since he met her but he had been terrified
frightening her away. She hadn't darted off like a
artled doe, but her eyes had widened before she
opped them to avoid his gaze. From that moment he

had always thought of her as Doe, though it was som
time before he actually called her by the pet name. Th
compulsory visit to his aunt, which he had intended t
last no longer than two weeks, had stretched into a
many months.

Thomas and John came racing out a side entran
of the house and, spying him, begged for another lesso
in driving Edward's curricle. "Obtain your brother
permission and I will be happy to oblige," he assure
them, firmly thrusting his thoughts of Miss Tremer
from him.

But the thoughts refused to keep a distance for lon
Steyne found himself dressing once again for dinner i
the only respectable outfit he had brought, and he wor
dered if his predicament amused Miss Tremere. Ha
he not dressed with particular care that summer, a
tually going to the length of sending for more clothin
from London when he determined to outstay his ori
inally intended two weeks? Not that she had seeme
to notice particularly. Her own wardrobe was limite
no doubt because her father thought it unnecessary fo
a woman in her position to possess a lot of worldl
finery. And nothing she wore was the least bit fasl
ionable, by London standards. But the neutral co
tumes could not detract from her natural radiance an
served only to make him want to see her rigged out i
style.

Steyne had induced his aunt to invite the vicar an
his daughter to dine with them. He had not realized a
the time why she made such a storm about the matte
but he had assured her that if she did not, he woul
have them as his guests at the nearest inn. Not wishin
to become the object of local gossip and conjecture, sh
had reluctantly acquiesced. How could Mr. Tremer
have had the nerve to ask Margaret Sommers to marr
him? The very idea was ludicrous. Even the idea of he
first husband having married her was ludicrous. N
one should ever have married such a dried-up prun
at all. Steyne could not think of even one redeemir
quality in her makeup: she was rude, cold, ugly an

piteful. Thank heaven she had never produced any offspring!

The dinner-party Lord Steyne remembered as not a notable success. Mr. Tremere had smirked, thinking that Margaret Sommers had reconsidered her decision, and she had let him know in no uncertain terms that she thought him the closest thing she could imagine to a worm. Theodosia had been uncomfortable, wishing that they had not accepted the invitation, and confused by Steyne's frequent attentions to her. He made sure that she had the finest selection of curried lobster and the roast saddle of lamb, the lemon blancmange and the baked gooseberry pudding. He had turned her music when she played the piano-forte after dinner. He had admired her gown and her grasp of the economics of the countryside. But Theodosia had been intimidated by her father's and his aunt's presence, and had not really appeared to advantage.

Where she had always been at her best was in an animated discussion between just the two of them. As Steyne absently checked the folds of his cravat in the mirror he more clearly saw the two of them wandering down some dusty lane near the vicarage, Theodosia swinging her bonnet by the ribbons as she tried in all earnestness to explain her efforts to see that the neighboring landlords did not come to an arrangement with the local publican whereby the laborers' wages were paid on the latter's premises, so that the proceeds were drunk up before ever they reached home. Her indignation had amused him—no, that was condescending. It had touched him, her simple faith that such matters could be rectified by her concern and her exertions. For the life of him, he could never remember afterward why he had agreed to speak to the landlords, urging the wisdom of discontinuing the practice. Not that he didn't agree with her, but simply that he had allowed her to involve him in that community which was so foreign to his own interests.

Steyne had thought it only fair, when his promise had been extracted, to insist on a forfeit for his good services. He would never forget the astonishment which had widened her eyes, nor the hurt which had caused her lips to tremble. "Surely you cannot be serious, my lord," she had whispered. "I don't sell my kisses." Her face had flushed and her eyes moistened with sternly repressed tears. "If that is how you view the matter, I would prefer you forgot the whole thing."

Even her chin, held high as it was, trembled by then and he silently cursed himself for his lack of sensitivity. She was not accustomed to the sophisticated bantering of society. Actually, he had intended to kiss her again when the opportunity arose and they were well shielded from prying eyes by leafy trees on either side of the path, but this was obviously the wrong time to press her. She had made him feel, for perhaps the first time in his life, as awkward as a schoolboy. It had been a week before he made the attempt again, and that was long after he had fulfilled (and not mentioned) his promise.

Lost in his reverie, Steyne had not noticed the passage of time and was surprised to hear the dinner gong resound. Dear God, he was becoming as careless as James. He hastened to join the assembled Heythrops, minus James, and to take Lady Eastwick in to dinner, apologizing for his tardiness.

"No, no, don't say a word," she protested. "I know the boys cozened you into instructing them in driving again and barely gave you time to dress. I do hope you won't let them become a nuisance."

"How can they be a nuisance when they so apparently admire my skill with the ribbons?" he laughed. "Nothing could be more flattering."

Lady Eastwick had invited the Hedgerleys for an evening of cards, assuming that James would be there (since she had reminded him in the morning), but he did not appear until late in the evening, making it impossible for two tables to be formed. He offered no excuse for his absence, nor did he willingly make a forth for a second table. Barely civil to the Hedgerleys, James was bored and allowed it to show. His eyes wandered speculatively to Theodosia who ignored his suggestive gaze, but he decided that the risk of trying anything there with Steyne in the house was too high. Soon enough he would return to London and marry the succulent widow with the gold-filled pockets. And with luck he would have something else to show for his journey to Somerset. James was quite sure that his reading of the first earl's poem must be accurate. How fortunate that Eastwick should be abroad at just this time!

No one was the least sorry that James declined to join them the next day when they set out for the Winchmores. Edward came because Steyne did, and not because his brothers and sisters deputed him their spokesman in asking Sir George if he knew of a Gregory family from the Bicknoller area.

Sir George dug a hand into the pocket of his coat as though searching for the answer there, his brows drawing down in vigorous thought. "None to my knowledge. Used to be, of course. Oh, eons ago. Some scandal attached to the name. Can't rightly remember what it was, but it's of no importance nowadays. A long time back one of the Winchmore girls married into the family, and I remember a great to-do in some of the letters of that day which passed back and forth. Should she do it? Had the scandal been forgotten? Was there still a blot on the name? And, good Lord, this was two hundred years after...whatever happened, happened. Hadn't lived in the county for a century by then."

If Edward was satisfied with this hazy recollection, the younger children were not. Christina was the Winchmore's only child, and the Heythrop youngsters rapidly became restless in the drawing room. Theodosia suggested that she walk with them down to the pond to see the ducks since there were no mysterious sayings carved on the mantels. To her surprise, Christina and Charlotte expressed a desire to join them, and then Edward and Steyne did likewise. The whole party, minus Sir George and Lady Winchmore, Lady Eastwick and Eleanor, wandered through the neatly trimmed gardens down to the artificial pond. Charlotte avidly drank in tales of Christina's London season while Theodosia listened with half an ear and attempted to keep the boys from frightening the ducks.

"Bet I can make a stone skip more times than you can," John challenged his brother.

"Ho," Thomas snorted, "you've hardly gotten the knack of it yet." He stooped down and searched for the flattest one he could find, sending it skimming over the placid water. "Six times. You can't better that!"

"It was only five," John protested, reaching for one of his own.

Steyne was standing apart from the others, surveying the gazebo at the furthest end of the pond, but at their words he turned and met Theodosia's eyes across the expanse of gravel path. Suddenly they were alone again, as they had been that summer day at Oakleigh his aunt's home. Mrs. Sommers had taken the carriage to go shopping in Wiveliscombe, not bothering to invite him to join her. Steyne had been delighted at the chance to bring Theodosia for a walk by the artificial lake where they would be undisturbed by anything more annoying than a honking goose. The charming setting of the lake had been no testament to his aunt's taste but to that of a former owner. Mrs. Sommers had threatened to serve every last one of the graceful geese on her table.

A dryness developed in Theodosia's throat as she found herself unable to look away from Steyne's intent gaze. He must be remembering, as she was, that day at Oakleigh when he had taught her to skip stones on his aunt's lake. She had been clumsy at first, unable to duplicate the motion of wrist and arm that he exhibited for her. Carefully he had chosen the flattest stone he could find. Then he had come around behind her, pressing the stone in her hand and putting his arm alongside hers to guide its motion as she flung it across the water. Theodosia swallowed hard as she remembered what had happened next.

His closeness had set her heart to pounding and his

id not withdraw when the stone had disappeared in idening circles on the lake. Instead he had turned her face him. There had been a question in his eyes; not demand or even the lightness of humor, but a gentle uery: Are you ready now? Theodosia had been ready r days, expecting him to kiss her each time they were lone. When he didn't she had begun to wonder if he ad taken her previous upset so much to heart that he ever intended to kiss her again, and she felt bereft.

Her own gaze must have given him the answer he ished, for he drew her toward him and kissed her ather differently than he had that first time. His lips ere tender on hers but it was not a simple passing uch. She had no desire to draw away from him but he had not previously experienced the chaos which ripped her, and she was shaken. When he at length esisted, she found that her hands were on his shoulers and had no idea how they had gotten there. Beused, embarrassed, she let them drop to her sides, eling as though she had done something terribly improper. He had smiled at her, the most charming, deghted smile she had ever witnessed, and her heart ad felt as though it turned over in her body.

Steyne was not smiling at her now. There was no iscernible expression on his face at all, in fact, while eir eyes were locked. Theodosia knew, though, that e was remembering that kiss, and the dozens that had llowed in the succeeding weeks. Remembering how he had once, in despair, come running to fling her rms about him for the last time, the tears streaming own her cheeks. Theodosia could feel them pricking t her eyes now and she turned aside abruptly to ask homas and John, "Shall I have a try? I haven't done is in years."

Six years, to be exact. Six long, but not always painl, years. Years when she had learned to live with the isappointment, when she had done her duty, when she ad found new friends and occupation. Years when she ad learned to lock the love away and to smile at the emories, to cherish them instead of mourning them.

She must learn to live with them even now that he w
present again. There would be no new memories
store. Forcing herself to smile, she said, "Lord Stey
taught me to skip stones, you know. I once saw one
his skip a dozen times." The stone she had just toss
sank ignominiously the moment it hit the water.

There was a movement behind her and she felt
stone pressed into her hand and his arm alongside he
again, directing its arc toward the water. "You haver
practiced, Miss Tremere. You don't wish to disgrace r
lessons, do you?"

Theodosia felt a tremor run through her body a
immediately stooped to find a stone, saying in a chok
voice, "I'm sure I'll catch the hang of it again in time

"Yes, I'm sure you will," Steyne said softly.

Joining them, Edward assumed the responsibility
reinstructing the governess. He hadn't the temerity
actually grasp Miss Tremere's hand as Lord Stey
had, but he demonstrated with a rather stiff grace. I
stone skipped no more than thrice and his brothe
hooted at him, causing Edward to move along to whe
Charlotte and Christina sat chatting on a wood
bench in the shade of a willow tree.

Amy, who had been watching the ducks and id
listening to their conversation further down the bar
of the pond, now came to stand beside Steyne, gazi
up at him with puzzled eyes. "Is it important to kn
how to skip stones? Why did you teach Miss Tremer
Will you teach me?"

"Of course I will teach you, young lady. And it
excessively important to know how to skip stones. Wh
would you do on a lazy afternoon by the water if y
did not know how to skip stones?" He smiled. "I'm su
prised Miss Tremere has not included it in her lesson

"Is that why you taught her? So that she could tea
us?"

Steyne frowned at the back of Theodosia's head. "N
I taught her because it was a lazy day and we were
the water, and because it's a pleasure to teach oth

people new things. I think Miss Tremere learned several new things that day."

There was no question that she heard him. He could tell by the very stillness of her stance and the way she gripped the small, flat stone she was about to toss into the water. But it was Amy who said cheerfully, "Miss Tremere likes to learn new things. She's told me so. But usually she teaches. Did she ever teach you anything in exchange?"

For a moment he didn't answer. When he spoke his bantering tone was gone and his voice, to Theodosia, sounded almost brusque. "Yes, she taught me several things. I haven't forgotten them."

"Well," Amy hastened to assure him, "I am sure she hasn't forgotten, either. Sometimes it just takes awhile to familiarize yourself again—like doing multiplication tables after a vacation. After all, you don't have an opportunity to skip stones every day."

"Very true." He chose a flat stone for her and demonstrated the swing of the arm without letting go of it. "Here, you have a try."

By the time a footman came to inform them that Lady Eastwick was ready to leave, Theodosia found that she had regained some of her ability at skipping stones, a fact which Amy jubilantly pointed out to Lord Steyne. He nodded and met Theodosia's eyes once more. "Apparently it was solely a lack of practice," he admitted, moving over to walk beside her.

With Amy on one side and Steyne on the other, Theodosia felt sure she would not be able to avoid further disconcerting revelations unless she took charge of the conversation herself. "In the winter, if the roads are in decent condition, the children and I sometimes drive to Quantock's Head to see the long-tailed ducks that migrate there. Sir George says their call-notes sound like a pack of baying hounds. We see scaup-ducks and pintails inland, too, sometimes."

"How interesting," Steyne murmured, his eyes dancing.

"Oh, yes," Amy contributed politely, "we have made

quite a fascinating study of birds. Miss Tremere can identify hawfinches, skylarks, whitethroats, green plovers, wagtails—oh, any number of them."

"Wagtails, Miss Tremere?" Steyne asked mischievously.

"Yes, wagtails," she replied, her attempt at firmness belied by a slight quiver of her lips. "We've seen both the pied wagtail and the yellow wagtail this summer, haven't we, Amy?"

"Indeed we have. The pied likes the farmyard, but the yellow prefers the open fields. Would you recognize a wagtail, Lord Steyne?"

"I'm sure I would. In fact, I have pointed one out to Miss Tremere in the past."

The man was incorrigible, Theodosia thought ruefully. She had always *tried* to walk in a perfectly ladylike manner, but he had, more than once, in those long past days, remarked teasingly that her walk, especially from behind, was what had first attracted his attention to her. Since her father, a notable critic of anything improper or unladylike in her, had never mentioned the matter, she was sure it was only a joke—well, almost sure. Good heavens, they had spoken with uncommon familiarity in those days, hadn't they? When she glanced up at him his set expression of the last few days was gone and he was smiling. Theodosia felt her heart quicken.

Unfortunately, they had reached the house, where Lady Eastwick already had the carriage waiting. "Eleanor is not feeling quite the thing, I fear," she explained. "Nothing serious, I'm sure, but she should be at home resting."

Theodosia instantly took charge, sitting beside Eleanor in the carriage and shepherding her to her room as soon as they reached Charton Court. Though she joined the family for dinner while Eleanor slept, she returned to the girl's room in the evening to read to her before retiring early for the night. She sat for some time at her dressing table brushing her hair, not really paying the least attention to her reflection in the pier glass.

His smile meant nothing, really; just the sort of shared memory one had with old acquaintances—ludicrous, perhaps, in the circumstances, but undeniable. At most it meant he was beginning to remember the amusing as well as the disturbing aspects of their past and she should be grateful. Theodosia had not dared hope all these years that he would regard the episode with anything but bitterness. His letter....

Well, that was something she had forced herself to soften in her own mind, understanding his exasperation, his frustration after his self-imposed wait of several years. She had not asked him to wait, though she had dreamed that he might. How unfortunate that her father should have been so ill when she at last came of age and found that Marc had indeed waited. A lump rose in her throat and she set the hairbrush down gently on the dressing table and extinguished the candles. They were really too alike in their stubbornness to have gotten on well in the end, she reminded herself as she had so many times before. And he would still believe that he knew what was best for her, as he had then. Hadn't she found a wonderfully comfortable niche for herself without his help? She was loved and needed here. Even he could not deny that. Theodosia sighed as she climbed into bed.

Chapter Ten

Sunday was a day on which the Heythrops broke their usual routine. In addition to church attendance, the girls were not expected to do any studies. The day was not given over to a surfeit of religious observation by any means. The children, in fact, viewed it entirely as a day of freedom and looked forward to it despite the lengthy and usually unintelligible (to them) sermons delivered by Dr. Trainer. He had a habit of choosing obscure texts which led to even more obscure sermons, and his choice of music was almost intolerably lugubrious. But Lady Eastwick had vetoed Edward's suggestion that he read some edifying verses from the Bible at home after church to instill a proper regard for religion into his younger brothers and sisters.

"Nothing is less likely to inspire virtue than being made to sit still and listen to someone prose on at you about goodness," she had responded with a certain asperity. "You forget that you yourself were once happy enough to return home from church and run round the orchards in your best clothes, Edward. And don't be suggesting that we shouldn't have music or play cards, either. I can't fathom where the idea came from that one must be miserable in order to show a proper reverence."

So Sunday was perhaps the favorite day of the week for the younger children, and they weren't at all surprised to see their uncle shab off before they all walked into Channock for the service, though they had assured him that Dr. Trainer was on holiday and would have a much livelier replacement. Eleanor's indisposition had passed, and Lord Steyne accompanied them, walking with Lady Eastwick and sitting beside her in the family pew. Miss Tremere strolled along with the children despite Edward's attempts to draw her into a theological discussion of the Trinity. And they found their hopes for Mr. Oldbury not unjustified. His sermon was understandable, with no trace of condescension, but a rather positive approach to handling life as it came.

Edward, however, was incensed at the attention Mr. Oldbury paid Miss Tremere after the service, and chose to distinguish Christina Winchmore with his conversation to show the governess he couldn't care less. Charlotte, according to her plan to match Miss Tremere and Mr. Oldbury, made every effort to keep her younger brothers and sisters at her side so the governess and the clergyman would have a chance to speak with one another uninterruptedly on their walk back to Charton Court.

Theodosia brushed back a loose strand of hair and viewed Mr. Oldbury with laughing eyes. "We enjoyed the service, Mr. Oldbury. Amy told me next week she intends to leave her finger-knitting at home, as she won't need it."

"Praise indeed! Dr. Trainer will be gone a month, at the very least. A trip to Scotland at his age is not a matter to be taken lightly, or hurried. I'll try to bring my best sermons to keep the young ones from being restless. They must be quite a handful."

"Oh, they're most enjoyable. I only have the girls under my charge, really, as Thomas and John are largely away at school. After growing up an only child, I find all of them refreshing."

"Is Mr. James Heythrop still at the Court?" Mr. Oldbury certainly hadn't seen him at his earlier service in Bicknoller.

"Yes, but he was unable to make it to church. He brought Lord Steyne down with him, and I'm afraid the children are rather monopolizing his lordship's time. The boys want him to teach them to drive a curricle to an inch and the girls are forever showing him the kittens or their drawings or embroidery."

Mr. Oldbury turned his gaze to where the viscount had his head bent listening to Lady Eastwick as they walked. "I don't suppose he minds. Is he related to the family?"

"No. At least, not that I know of. His aunt lived in the village where my father was vicar."

"So you knew him before he came here?"

"I met him some years ago." Theodosia gestured toward a lush growth of whortleberries. "Were you able to find out anything about Whortle Hall?"

"I nearly forgot!" He regarded her with a crooked grin which, oddly, seemed not at variance with his clerical garb. "Several people I talked to said it's Wildcroft Grange, though the name was changed ages ago. And there is the supporting evidence that the whortleberry grows there in hearty profusion. Do you know the place?"

"The Winstanleys are friends of Lady Eastwick's. I've been there a number of times. How fortunate that this will give us an excuse to visit."

He regarded her questioningly, but she shook her head with a mischievous smile. Lord Steyne happened to glance around at just that moment, and jumped to a most imaginative conclusion. Theodosia, intent on her companion, failed to notice the arrested look in his eyes.

Mr. Oldbury was familiar with the Winstanley family, since they were his parishioners, and he met her smile with one of his own. "Their son is home just now. A very dashing naval fellow."

"The children love to hear of his exploits."

Unerringly, Mr. Oldbury's gaze sought out Charlotte. "I'm not surprised. He's an engaging young man."

"Fancies often change when you're seventeen. I believe Mr. Winstanley will be returning to duty shortly."

As Mr. Oldbury agreed, Edward moved up to join them, unable to keep to his resolution of ignoring the governess when she so clearly didn't even notice. His reason told him that the clergyman should be given this opportunity to converse with her alone, but his rebellious emotions could not allow it. After all, she would probably be placed at table near him and that would give them sufficient time to talk. What in heaven did they find to talk about, anyway, when they hardly knew one another? Edward found it immensely difficult to find subjects when he had the rare chance to be alone with her.

Lord Steyne was finding it difficult to concentrate on Lady Eastwick's discussion of the boys' school curriculum. When he glanced around again and found that Edward had joined Theodosia and Mr. Oldbury, he felt distinctly relieved, but a moment's reflection showed him that such a reaction was beneath him, or at the very least alien to him. Why should he wish to keep her from an intimate discussion with the clergyman? She no longer meant anything to him. Steyne surprised Lady Eastwick by politely interrupting her to suggest that Edward might have some thoughts on schooling and peremptorily gestured to the young man to join them. Reluctant to leave Miss Tremere's side, but even more hesitant to give offense to his lordship, Edward went.

Sunday dinner was the one meal to which the younger children were customarily invited to join the adults, but on this occasion, with two visitors, (and possibly James, who was nowhere to be found) Lady Eastwick considered revising their routine. Both Steyne and Mr. Oldbury appeared at ease with the young folk; still, sitting down to dine with them was another matter. Lady Eastwick clearly remembered the previous morning's breakfast wtih Amy's artless comments and she was not sure she wished for a repetition at the dinner table.

Theodosia recognized the puzzled frown and suggested quietly, "Why don't I eat with the younger children in the Small Dining Parlor, ma'am?"

Although she had said this very softly, a chorus of protests rang out. Edward's "No!" was the most adamant of them, but Mr. Oldbury was heard to murmur a negative as well, and Steyne with his usual polish remarked, "I beg you won't banish the children on my account, Lady Eastwick."

Lady Eastwick blinked at them all in surprise and then turned to Theodosia with a beaming face. "How delightful to have company who tolerate children! I'm not sure Eastwick would approve, mind you, but they shall join us as usual. And I would certainly not have denied our guests your company, Miss Tremere; the housekeeper could have sat with them."

Learning this did not seem to appreciably lessen the approval of her decision, though Edward did mumble, staring directly at Amy, "I trust they will behave presentably." He received only an angelic smile in response.

Dinnertime arrived and James did not, so the rest of the party was seated. For all the good it did Edward having Theodosia there, she might have eaten with the children. She was seated beside Mr. Oldbury, as he had known she would be, and quite at the other end of the table from himself. In fact, most of the children were between him and the governess, and due to their chatter he could not hear one word of the discussion there. His mother regarded him sympathetically, with Eleanor and Amy at his sides, but there was no other possible arrangement than to put their two male guests on either side of her. Theodosia, too, smiled at him, that warm, companionable smile that set his pulses racing.

If Steyne had previously been unaware that Edward nurtured a *tendre* for Theodosia, and he had been, his eyes were opened during the walk home from church and the time they had spent in the Long Gallery. The boy's eyes seemed drawn to her almost against his will, and he got the most idiotic look on his face when she smiled at him. Steyne regarded her closely during the meal but could not see that she encouraged Edward. True, she smiled at him from time to time, but it was not the sort of smile to capture a man's heart, not that dazed, enchanted smile she had....Enough of that, he apostrophized himself sternly. That was long ago, and she was little more than a girl, eighteen and intoxicated with her first love.

Maturity had changed her. Steyne could not see that she regarded Mr. Oldbury with more than her usual warmth and frankness, her ready laugh and intelligent conversation. That was one thing for which one could not condemn her father: He had educated her himself in every field of study in which he was proficient and had not objected to her pursuing other branches of knowledge if she chose. And her interests, Steyne well remembered, had been wide and varied, and often not the least feminine. He wondered if she encouraged the Heythrop girls to expand their horizons beyond the usual ladylike achievements.

The conversation had strayed from Caxton's first efforts on his printing press in Westminster to Gibbon's *Decline and Fall of the Roman Empire* with scarcely a pause. Lady Eastwick was not a scholar but she delighted in the educated flow of discourse which so clearly brought to mind her husband's presence. Steyne purposely directed the topics in an effort to assess Mr. Oldbury's intellect and grudgingly had to admit there was nothing amiss with the fellow on that score. Nor was he overly pious, certainly not sanctimonious. And of course Theodosia would be familiar with life in a country rectory since she had acted her father's hostess and helpmate from the time she was old enough to walk. The old scoundrel had used her services as housekeeper, errand girl and maid without the least hesitation. Many were the times when they had planned to meet that she had arrived late, breathless; those glorious brown eyes wide with concern, begging his pardon and explaining that Mr. Tremere had sent her off on yet another of the endless tasks he should have taken care of himself. Not that she had put it that way. Steyne had, at first verbally but later, when he saw it upset her, he had merely thought it.

Apparently Lady Eastwick was unconsciously moved by the undercurrents in the small group about her, for she aided Steyne's efforts by unearthing, in the most genteel way possible, Mr. Oldbury's social position.

"Are you related to the Hertfordshire Oldburys, sir?"

"Very distantly, ma'am. My family resides in Surrey but I spent one long holiday with them near Stevenage when I was a boy, and they've visited Weybridge from time to time. Mrs. Francis Oldbury is a great friend of my mother's, which accounts for it more than the connection." He turned to Theodosia with an engaging grin. "And perhaps that my older brother and their daughter are likely to make a match."

"You're Roger Oldbury's younger brother?" Steyne asked, astonished.

"Why, yes, do you know him?"

"Very well. I run into him frequently when I'm in London. I'm surprised I've never met you."

"I spend very little time in town. Aside from my parish duties I'm at work on a history of Somerset. I fear I am of a more scholarly than social temperament," he explained apologetically.

Theodosia's eyes lit with interest. "A history of Somerset? But that's wonderful! I presume it is more than an ecclesiastical history."

"I should hope so," he laughed, meeting her eyes with mock reproach. "A great deal of interest occurred here before the first church was built. No, I trace the beginnings from the Britons or Celts, and the Saxon tribe that gave Somerset its name was preceded by the Romans. Surrey, too, derives its name from the Saxons though not a tribe. Suthrea—south river, which is occasioned by its being on the south side of the Thames."

Steyne wore a thoughtful frown. "Then it was you who wrote the history of Surrey I read a few years ago?"

"My first attempt, and rather a feeble effort, I fear,"

Mr. Oldbury admitted. "I've since revised it, however, and hope the next edition will prove more worthy."

"I thought it eminently readable—both informative and lively. A remarkable combination for a history."

"You are kind, Lord Steyne. I've never found history dull, myself, but only the historians who frequently write it, concerned overmuch with facts and dates and forgetting that it is the people in whom we are interested. How did they live, why did they do that they did? And most of all, I find the legends intriguing, the folktales that are passed from generation to generation, growing, changing, but almost always with some kernel of truth to them." He stopped abruptly and addressed himself to Lady Eastwick. "Forgive me! I never meant to ramble on so."

"Not at all," she assured him. "Eastwick is a history buff. Perhaps I could find your book for him."

"I would be honored if you would allow me to present you with a copy. I always keep several on the off-chance I can convince someone to accept one." He turned to Theodosia. "And I would like you to have one, too, Miss Tremere. I only regret the history of Somerset is not completed, as it might have been of some small help in the children's researches of the Heythrop family history. But I've gathered extensive materials, and my brother sends me anything he finds in London, so I hope you'll call on me even at this stage. Covering the whole county means I cannot concentrate on any one area, but being in Bicknoller I've acquired a fair share of local history as well."

"You've already helped by identifying Wildcroft Grange for us. Perhaps you would allow the older ones to look through any local materials. I would, of course, supervise them."

"Certainly." Mr. Oldbury looked as though nothing would give him greater pleasure. "Bring them to the rectory one day, and I'll show you what I have."

Some perverse devil in Steyne would not allow this to pass. "I wonder if I might join the party? It would

be fascinating for me to see how one goes about su
a project."

Theodosia bit her lip to suppress the gurgle of laug
ter she felt bubbling in her, but Mr. Oldbury readi
assented. Steyne scowled at Theodosia's twitching li
and pointedly turned his attention to Charlotte, wl
further disconcerted him by suggesting that she ha
thought he and her uncle would only be at Charte
Court for a few days.

"Your uncle has some business to attend that ma
take longer than expected. Of course, we would n
delay our departure for a whim of mine."

Charlotte was not at all sure why he glared at Mi
Tremere at this point, but she set herself, as she ha
been taught, to distract his attention and relieve hi
of the irritation into which he had unaccountab
fallen. The romance between Miss Tremere and M
Oldbury, she decided with satisfaction, was progressir
very nicely, and she determined to further it by su
gesting that she and Miss Tremere would show him tl
topiary after dinner. Lord Steyne would stay with h
mother, and Edward, if he came with them, wou
surely not pass up a chance to answer Charlotte's que
tions on the day's Bible lesson. Charlotte would tolera
even that to promote Miss Tremere's happiness.

This scenario, with major variations (such as eve
one of the Heythrop children accompanying them), du
came to fruition. Theodosia cheerfully organized
game of Prisoner's Bar for them and sat with Mr. Ol
bury on a white iron bench watching as their voic
rose in excitement and they dashed about among tl
fantastic shapes of the carefully tended trees an
bushes.

"I remember playing...." turned into a swift repar
tee between the governess and the clergyman. The
was cricket, of course, but also battledore, peg top, pi
in the ring, hoops, trap ball, steal baggage, puss in th
corner, cut gallows, Tom Tiddler's Ground and a doze
others. And the awe one had felt at his first "magi
lantern" show, or the surprise she felt at seeing learne

pigs and mermaids and horses with five feet at the country fairs. Dwarfs and giants and puppet shows were linked irrevocably in one's mind with luscious gilded gingerbread and syllabubs. Theodosia didn't mention that her father, on these festive occasions, had always been a trifle bosky, as though he could not enjoy himself unless he had downed more than his ordinary quantity of brandy, and her memory of conjurers, contortionists and men who drank fire and ate knives was accompanied by the fumes of strong drink.

As though the whole family were conspiring to throw Theodosia with Mr. Oldbury, she found herself partnering him at whist against Lady Eastwick and Lord Steyne. His lordship was intent on winning her few pennies, or so she assumed from his concentration on his cards. But Theodosia had played against Lady Eastwick enough to know precisely how her mind operated, and with Mr. Oldbury willing to enter into her whimsical method of attack, the two of them came out the winners of three and six apiece by the end of the evening.

Chapter Eleven

It was after Mr. Oldbury had left, and Lady Eastwick was helping Charlotte gather her shawl and workbox, that Steyne cornered Theodosia and murmured,
"I want to talk to you."

"About my winnings?" She dug in the tiny reticule
and produced the three and six. "I could tell it upset
you to lose this evening, my lord. Are you hard-pressed?
Here, have them. They won't go far, but I could make
you a loan if you wish."

"Don't be absurd, Doe." He was tempted to shake
her, goaded by the teasing light in her eyes. "On the
porch, in ten mintues."

"I don't think...."

"Be there...please."

"Very well, but twenty minutes. I should see Charlotte to her room and she will likely wish to talk for a
moment."

Steyne nodded and moved away from her to allay
any suspicions Edward might have. The boy had glared
at Mr. Oldbury throughout the card game, though he
had himself offered to sit out. In his opinion there was
less opportunity to make a fool of himself on the side-
lines than playing whist; he was a wretched card
player. When Steyne asked if there was any decent

fishing in the neighborhood, his gloom abated considerably, and he offered to take the viscount with him in the morning to a spot he knew where the trout were biting. His offer was accepted.

After bidding his hostess good night, Steyne went directly to the balcony over the entrance porch where he waited for close to half an hour before Theodosia joined him. She smiled composedly but did not apologize for her tardiness.

Without prelude he asked, "Are you going to marry him?"

"Marry whom?"

"That...that fellow, Mr. Oldbury."

"You are as bad as Charlotte, Lord Steyne. For heaven's sake, I've only met him. There is no question of marriage. From a girl of Charlotte's age I might have expected such a flight of fancy, but not from you. And really," she said, the gentleness in her voice softening the reproof, "it is no concern of yours."

He stared at her for a moment before speaking. "There is no one to take an interest in your welfare. I think our...acquaintance from the past might allow me to give you some well-intentioned advice. True, I cannot see anything amiss with Mr. Oldbury but that is no excuse for rushing headlong into an irrevocable contract."

"Were you listening to me, Lord Steyne?" she asked quietly. "Less than a week ago the children and I explored the church at Bicknoller, where we first met Mr. Oldbury. Several days later he brought some papers over for us to look at with regard to our search. Today we heard him preach in Channock and he returned with us to Charton Court. Those are the only occasions on which I have seen him; previous to them I did not even know of his existence. I presume this excessive concern with finding me a husband has to do with my advanced age and the possibility of poor Mr. Oldbury being my last chance to snare an eligible catch. He is an engaging gentleman, and I hope we will have the opportunity to meet again in future, but there is nothing more. Can I not make a friend without all this fuss?"

"You are being purposely obtuse. Mr. Oldbury is not thinking of you as a friend, any more than Edward is."

Theodosia ran her hand along the top of the stone wall. "Lord Heythrop is young and confused. I hope you are not suggesting that I have in any way encouraged him. He has far too great a sense of his consequence to consider marrying me, and too great a sense of responsibility to try to seduce me. Poor dear, it leaves him in the very worst bind."

Steyne surveyed her rueful face. "I don't see how you can jest about it, Doe. The boy is like a moonstruck calf, following you with his eyes everywhere you go. Just what do you intend to do about it?"

"Well, I have no wish to leave, if that's what you expect me in my generous-heartedness to do. He'll get over it. I've been trying to push him toward Christina Winchmore. She would be a perfectly suitable match for him, and if I am not mistaken she has had the same idea for some time now."

"So you have taken to orchestrating their lives, have you?"

The coolness of his tone only made her smile. "My dear sir, I think you have lost your sense of humor. There was a time you would have found the situation vastly diverting. Do you not recall...."

But a movement in the grounds had caught his eyes, and he motioned her to silence. As the figure approached the house, Steyne drew Theodosia back into the shadows, his arm about her shoulders as though for protection. There was something ungainly about the intruder, but not until he came close to the entrance porch were they able to distinguish the reason. The ragged clouds obscuring the moon parted briefly to disclose James—carrying a shovel! Without so much as a glance around him, he disposed of it by pushing it behind some shrubberies growing along the entrance porch wall. Afterward he dusted off his hands, stomped his boots against the wall and casually strolled toward the front door.

Theodosia's brows were drawn down in a worried frown. "I don't like that."

Steyne immediately removed his arm from her shoulders and said stiffly, "I beg your pardon."

"I wasn't referring to your arm, my lord, but to Mr. Heythrop. I very much fear.... But you are a friend of his and doubtless you would consider my fears groundless."

"You think he's been hunting for the treasure on the sly?"

Theodosia regarded him with incredulity. "How in heaven's name do you know about the treasure?"

"I don't know much. Amy said she couldn't tell me about it, but I've read the incriptions on the mantels. You may be jumping to a hasty conclusion about James."

"I thought you would defend him. You don't think it's significant that he has just returned the poem and now we see him with a shovel skulking about?"

"He was hardly skulking, Doe. I can't imagine James skulking," he said thoughtfully, "but I grant you he was acting surreptitiously. What poem?"

Theodosia shivered. "I'm cold. If you will excuse me, Lord Steyne, I should like to go to my room."

"I'll come with you."

She thought he meant that he would accompany her, but when she opened her door and turned to say "Good night," he impatiently entered with her. "You really can't come in," she protested.

"Don't be missish, Doe. I *am* in. Now close the door and explain to me about the poem."

Theodosia stood uncertain, rubbing her forehead and trying to decide what to do. Steyne closed the door and locked it, his dark eyes never leaving her face.

"I...I really can't tell you Heythrop family secrets. You will have to ask James; perhaps he would be forthcoming, as you are his friend."

"That's the second time you've said that. I'm not his

friend, never have been, and certainly never intend to be."

"Lord Steyne, it makes me nervous having the door locked," she said unhappily, ignoring his reply.

"Oh, for God's sake, Doe, I haven't the least intention of harming you." Angrily he unlocked the door but left it closed. "Is that better?"

"Somewhat, but I would prefer if you left."

"I'm not going to leave until you explain to me."

"I can't do that."

Steyne disposed himself comfortably in one of a matching pair of comfortable Windsor chairs and said nothing.

If he was going to be stubborn, Theodosia could easily match him. "I am going to bed. You may as well leave."

Steyne draped one elegantly clad leg over the other.

"Steyne, if it were my secret, I would be happy to explain to you, but it isn't. Ask James, or even Edward. I will have to speak to Lady Eastwick about what we saw tonight. I won't tell her you were with me."

"You may tell her if you wish."

"Well, I *don't* wish. Now be a good fellow and run along...please."

Steyne toyed with his watch fob and made no attempt to rise.

Exasperated, Theodosia went over to her bed where a nightdress was laid carefully across the folded-back coverlet. It was one of her prettier ones, with a green ribbon woven through the eyelets, and she picked it up and took it with her into the study, closing the door rather vigorously after herself. There was no light in the second room and she quickly shed her dress and put the gown on over her chemise. In her agitation she had forgotten to bring a dressing gown as well, but there was nothing she could do about it now. Returning to her bedroom, she did not so much as glance at his lordship but went directly to her dressing table where she removed the pins from her hair and brushed it determinedly before tying it back with a ribbon. She washed her face and hands in the lukewarm water of the basin and dried herself thoroughly with a large, fluffy towel. For a minute she contemplated not brushing her teeth but decided that she must. Surely nothing could possibly be more inelegant than watching someone else brush her teeth.

Finished with her preparations, she calmly stepped to the lamp and extinguished it, making her way in the dark to her bed, where she climbed between the cold sheets and wished she had taken the time to heat them with the warming pan. Steyne had made no sound or movement during the whole, even when she extinguished the lamp, but she knew he was still there, not only because she had caught a glimpse of him in her mirror, but because she could feel his presence as clearly as though he were touching her. Though she wished to lie very still in the bed to simulate sleep, she found her position exceedingly uncomfortable. What if he had fallen asleep and didn't awaken until the maid brought her chocolate in the morning? *That* would lose her her job without a shadow of a doubt.

Ten, twenty, thirty minutes passed and nothing happened. Theodosia was accustomed to falling asleep almost directly she climbed into bed, but under the circumstances she was not surprised to be wide-awake, listening to her own heart pound. Could he hear it? No, of course not: She couldn't hear his. Again she shifted restlessly in the usually comfortable bed. Why didn't he leave?

Steyne was asking himself the same thing. She had totally outmaneuvered him and the only gentlemanly thing to do was give in gracefully, but he felt strangely reluctant to go. The brazenness of her tactics had at first astonished and then amused him. So that was what she would look like preparing for bed each night, with her bare feet padding along the carpet and her long brown hair falling almost to her waist. She had lovely ankles. He almost laughed when she turned away from him while she brushed her teeth. How ridiculous she was! Did she think seeing her do that would offend him? And did she care?

Being alone in a dark room with a desirable woman was working its mystique on him. Was she still desirable? His body very clearly told him she was. But so were dozens of other women. He hadn't realized she was so stubborn. Imagine parading in front of him in her nightdress! It was beside the point that she looked beautiful in it; no one but a brazen hussy would behave so. It was—was it not?—a clear invitation. Yes, he told himself mournfully, a clear invitation for him to make himself disappear in the only manner she could think of to rid herself of his annoying presence. She had asked him to go; she had assured him that she could not share secrets which were not hers. Ordinarily he could respect that, but not from Doe. She should not have a will of her own, opposed to his. Had she not totally disrupted his life once already by exerting her will? And for what? To stay with that sanctimonious old man who neither treasured her nor enjoyed her company. Wrong-headed women made the worst possible mates. They were worse than spendthrift or vain or stupid or frivolous women. They made one's life miserable, uncomfortable, exhausting.

When Steyne had completed this litany of evils, he became aware that there was a subtle change in the room. Was she crying? He would thrust aside his pride and comfort her. It had not been his object to distress her. But no. The sounds were not of stifled weeping or shuddering breath. Rather her breathing had become deeper, more regular. By God, the little minx had fallen asleep. How dare she? Steyne was tempted to shake her shoulder to waken her and tell her what he thought of her.

Instead he rose and, taking care there was no one to observe him as he came from her room, left her to her righteous sleep, remembering to lock the door after himself and push the key under the door.

The sun was streaming through the window, glinting off the mirror and catching specks of dust in midair. The whole room seemed aglow with the light and warmth, and Theodosia thought sleepily that she was glad it wouldn't be an overcast day, as she had feared when seeing the clouds the previous evening. A horrid thought struck her and she peeked cautiously over the coverlet toward the Windsor chair. He was gone. How could she possibly have fallen asleep when he sat there, silent, disapproving? She sat up in bed, looking down at the nightdress and shaking her head at her own temerity in appearing in it in front of him. Of couse, it had been a great deal darker last night, with only the lamp burning. Not at all as revealing as this morning's sunlight.

Theodosia climbed out of bed and padded over to the door. He had locked it, thoughtful man, and she found the key at her feet. Since the maid would soon be coming with her chocolate, she unlocked it and left the key in the lock as usual, but, being up, she also retrieved her clothes from the study and dressed herself in a primrose jaconet round dress whose color was more flattering than the duller ones she ordinarily wore. But she made no further concessions in her toilette, dressing her hair as always and affixing a pelerine to disguise the low neckline of the dress.

There was time while she sipped her chocolate to make a list of the salient points the children had noted when each of them read the poem. Today especially, after seeing James with the shovel, she intended to push their hunt forward with all possible speed. Having some conception of his character, Theodosia felt sure he had no intention of turning the treasure over to the family if he found it. And what would his reaction be if Lady Eastwick or Edward spoke to him of his nighttime activities? A denial? A concocted story? Perhaps, Theodosia mused, it would be better not to confront him with the story at all.

Knowing what he was up to, and not letting *him* know that they knew, had distinct possibilities. If he found the treasure, they would have the opportunity to retrieve it from him with the least possible aggravation. If he didn't find it, there would be considerable embarrassment saved. Theodosia was turning the alternatives over in her mind as she headed for the Breakfast Parlor and was so intent on her thoughts that she did not notice Steyne standing in the hall until she was almost upon him.

"I've been waiting for you," he informed her. His exaggerated air of indolence made it perfectly obvious that he had been waiting for a considerable time.

"I hope you don't intend to badger me again about the treasure."

"No." Steyne had no intention either of apologizing for his behavior the previous evening. Having weighed the matter for some time on his own particular scales of justice, he was convinced that he had suffered sufficiently after returning to his room to serve as reparation for any misguided action on his part, without the necessity of knuckling under to his former (and obviously heartless) love. If she could so easily dismiss their previous affection, he thought she could as easily forgive his boorishness, possibly even expected it of him. She was probably surprised not to find him still in the chair when she woke in the morning! He pictured what she would look like as she woke from a peaceful sleep with the sun shining on her and her long brown hair cascading about her shoulders, the big brown eyes perhaps further softened by the haze of dreams. Had she dreamed of him? He stared at her as though the answer might be written on her face.

Theodosia cocked her head inquiringly. "Was there something in particular you wished to say, Lord Steyne?"

Recalled to his initial purpose, he cleared his throat and rasped, "Of course there was, or I would hardly have waited for you, would I?"

Instead of answering him in kind, which she could easily have done, Theodosia smiled. "Tell me."

Why was she being so damned patient with him, he asked himself irrationally. If he was going to act like a boor, she should treat him like one. "I don't think you should tell Lady Eastwick about James," he replied in

138

a lowered voice, remembering the possibility that his companion across the hall might be awake, though he thought it unlikely. He took Theodosia's arm and guided her further down the hall.

"She will have to know, Lord Steyne. It would be unfair to ignore the episode. I am sorry if it reflects ill on your friend, but there are matters of more moment at stake...."

"I've told you he isn't my friend."

"But you haven't told me why you are here with him, so I can only assume there is some connection between you which you feel might be jeopardized by his being called to account for his actions." She regarded him speculatively for a moment, a scrutiny which made his dark eyes flash. Hesitantly she went on. "I will have to trust you, Lord Steyne. I'm sure you would not approve of James doing anything dishonest. It has occurred to me that it might be best if neither Lady Eastwick nor Edward mentioned anything to him, though I will of course tell them what I saw."

"Have to" trust me, he roared inwardly. The fact that he had stood waiting for her in the hall for nearly an hour to suggest precisely what she was proposing had nothing to do with the matter. Since when did she "have to" trust him? That was the crux of their estrangement in the first place. She had never trusted him to know what was right for her, had never accepted that his age, his experience, his position, his, yes, his being a *man* were the only credentials he needed to proclaim the obvious truth—that she should leave her demanding, unloving father and make her life with him. Steyne found himself virtually speechless.

Theodosia was concerned by the way his face had suffused with color, rather as though he were choking. A muscle in his jaw jumped sporadically and the veins in his neck stood out rather prominently. "Do you think perhaps you should loosen your cravat, my lord?"

"No, I don't, Miss Tremere! Don't touch it" (as she reached to assist him) "It took the boy fifteen minutes to even make it presentable."

"Don't you do it yourself?"

"Not when I only have half a dozen of them wit[h] me." Distracted from his useless rage, he resorted onl[y] to sarcasm. "So you have decided to trust me, have you[?] How very discriminating of you. And you're not afrai[d] I shall go directly to James and tell him the whole?"

"If you did, we would merely have to keep a sharpe[r] eye on him," she returned with her usual practicality[.] "You do understand why I must tell Lady Eastwick[,] don't you?"

"I believe I may truthfully say I have not understoo[d] anything you've ever done, ma'am." The sardonic not[e] remained in his voice and he regarded her with a blight[-] ing stare which had crushed innumerable impertinen[t] pups over the years.

Its effect on Theodosia was to make her grin. "I won'[t] contradict you. Shall we go down to breakfast?"

"Together?"

Apparently she gave this incredulous query seriou[s] consideration, for she gazed furtively up and down the[e] corridor before whispering, "You think someone wil[l] suspect? What is your usual arrangement, Lord Steyne[?] Does the lady go first and the man follow a few minute[s] later? I am open to suggestion."

Her impish eyes made him strongly desire to giv[e] everyone in the household something to suspect, bu[t] he refused to let her cozen him out of the sullens s[o] easily. "We will go down together," he said stiffly.

"Ah, well, I don't suppose anyone would have sus[-] pected, anyway," she repined. "There is a very hig[h] moral tone in this house. When James Heythrop come[s] down with a woman, Lady Eastwick assures me tha[t] he stays at Fairlight, though how he could I am at [a] loss to know. The place is entirely in holland covers[.] I doubt he comes down very often.

His lordship deigned only to murmur in reply, noth[-] ing intelligible, but Theodosia proceeded, "Yes, you ar[e] quite right. He *is* rather a court-card, isn't he? Lady

Eastwick is astonished that you should come here with him, I can tell."

Steyne gave her another blighting look intended to depress her impertinence.

"Oh, I see. You should have told me sooner. If I had known it was all the fashion to travel about with your worst enemy, I would have passed the information on to Lord Heythrop. He's immensely interested in the goings-on of the *ton,* though you wouldn't necessarily know it to observe him. Here in the country we still tend to cling to our friends and avoid our enemies. I can't think why."

"It's not your concern why I am here with James," he told her coldly. "I feel no necessity to explain my actions to *anyone.*"

"Yes, I remember you feel that way, and yet you expect others to explain theirs to you."

Impossible to tell if she was speaking of their night-time talks or the distant past. They had reached the foot of the stairs and he pulled a letter which he had franked from his pocket and set it on the salver. Fyfield daily collected any items deposited there and had them taken into the village by his most reliable footman for posting. It was not on Theodosia's account that Steyne turned it upside down, but because he preferred that James not note it, since it was to Ruth. In the letter he had explained (there, he sometimes did) that he had been delayed and that there would be sufficient grounds at Fairlight to deny the match if his man in London was unable to come up with further proof of James' profligacy and debts. He paused to consider whether it would be worthwhile to include any mention of James' nocturnal activities. It would mean breaking the seal, the letter having been written the previous morning and not set out since it was Sunday. His hesitation cost him only a few moments but he found that Theodosia was halfway to the Breakfast Parlor before he decided not to bother.

"I thought we had agreed to enter together." His long

strides quickly brought him abreast of her, and he frowned. "Did you think I had changed my mind?"

"No," she laughed, "but I'm famished." And she waited as he held the door for her to enter.

Chapter Twelve

After breakfast Lord Steyne left with Edward to go fishing and Theodosia followed Lady Eastwick to the Summer Parlor for a moment's private conversation. Sunlight sparkled on the crystal chandelier and the gilt chairs and sofa with their flowery beauvais tapestry coverings. The painted roundels on the ceiling were by Angelica Kauffmann, and were echoed in the geometric design of the carpet. Lady Eastwick urged the governess to a seat by the windows.

"Possibly I should have told Lord Heythrop," Theodosia began, "but I thought it wisest to approach you first. You are aware, I presume, that James Heythrop has returned the first earl's poem?"

"Yes. I won't comment on how he came to take it," Lady Eastwick said dryly.

"The poem purports to give a clue as to where the treasure is hidden. Obscure, of course, but the only clue which seems to be available to your family."

"The children must be excited to have a chance to study it."

"They are." Theodosia sighed. "It is difficult for me to.... Well, let me just say that last night before going to bed I saw Mr. Heythrop returning to the house with a shovel, which he hid in the flower border before entering."

Startled eyes met Theodosia's. "You think he'd been out looking for the treasure?"

"It does seem possible."

"More than possible," Lady Eastwick murmured, frowning. "And not beyond him to abscond with it if he finds it. Lord, how I wish Eastwick were here! Edward will only make a hash of it: He doesn't like James in the least. Did anyone else see him return?"

"Lord Steyne." Though she realized this must sound suspicious, Theodosia did not allow her gaze to drop.

For a moment Lady Eastwick studied her, and then nodded, saying half to herself, "Steyne is a gentleman. I needn't fear for your virtue with him, but I do hope you are keeping your door locked with James in the house."

Theodosia grinned. "I am, but he hasn't paid me the least attention. Not that I'm complaining!" She was immediately serious. "I was wondering if perhaps it would be better not to confront Mr. Heythrop with his midnight excursion. If he found something, he might intend to present it to you. And if he didn't...."

"...Fyfield could search his room before he left," Lady Eastwick finished for her. "How very tactful of you, my dear. Yes, I like the idea very well, and I'm sure I can convince Edward. He will have to be told."

"Of course." Now Theodosia did look away from her employer. "Lord Steyne seems to know a bit about the treasure—perhaps from the children's chatter. Seeing Mr. Heythrop with the shovel he immediately knew I assumed he might be looking for it. I didn't feel I was in any position to discuss your family secrets, but I am afraid his curiosity is aroused."

"Doubtless he'll have the whole from Edward if he's persistent. Though Edward has made a great fuss about keeping all knowledge of it within the family, my son is hardly likely to resist Steyne's charm. *I* wouldn't hesitate to tell him, simply because I would feel more comfortable knowing that he was keeping an eye out for us."

"Even when he came here with Mr. Heythrop?"

Lady Eastwick pursed her lips in thought. "I admit there is a mystery in that, but I think I could trust his integrity as I would Eastwick's. You must remember that I knew him slightly years ago, and his sister was one of my dearest friends. Poor love, to have her husband taken from her so young!"

As though the idea were in the air, the two women were apparently struck by it simultaneously. Lady Eastwick's face registered horror. "Dear God, not Ruth and James! Steyne could not possibly condone such a match!"

"But he couldn't really prevent it," Theodosia pointed out. "His sister is a mature woman."

"I cannot believe Ruth would ever consider a man of James' ilk. Why, Morrison was a paragon! She adored him! And James is.... Well, never mind, but it simply would not do."

Theodosia felt a constriction in her chest but forced herself to say calmly enough, "Perhaps Lord Steyne is pressing for the match. If his sister is devoted to him...."

"I will not believe it," Lady Eastwick declared emphatically. "There must be some other explanation. You may be sure Steyne knows precisely what James is, and he would have no reason to desire such a match."

The two ladies sat contemplating the situation for several minutes, but there seemed no salutary solution to the mystery, only discouraging possibilities. Eventually Lady Eastwick shrugged and stated, "It is not something we should concern ourselves with, I dare say. If Lord Steyne wished us to know, he would tell us. And James has said nothing, either. You may be sure he would be crowing if he were to marry Ruth. I understand she was very well provided for, and there were no children. How empty her life must seem without husband or children. And I bemoan Eastwick's temporary absence. What a silly woman I am!"

"No one has ever heard you so much as breathe a syllable of discontent," Theodosia laughed as she rose. "I should go to the children. They are intent on doing some treasure hunting of their own today."

"There is one thing.... Why do you suppose James suddenly conceived the notion he would be able to find the treasure *now*? Surely he had looked for it with the rest of them when he was a boy."

"I wondered about that, too. The poem says it is kept beneath scenes of valor and strife in a worthy location; that the place is both safe and secure, and that one should be guided by faith and the land grants, not forgetting the value of lore."

"How helpful," the countess murmured.

"Yes, isn't it? But you must remember that the poem was written when the first earl lived at Seagrave. Undoubtedly the treasure was moved to Charton Court, and I would think it would have been near impossible for the third earl to have duplicated a site such as had been used at Seagrave. On the other hand, it is general enough to apply to all sorts of spots: graveyards, old fortress sites, ancient battlegrounds, mythical holy places and so forth. Mr. Heythrop took the poem with him in the spring, didn't he?"

"Yes."

"Something might have spurred his interest at that time."

Lady Eastwick could only picture the lonely little grave of her daughter, and shuddered.

To distract her, Theodosia continued, "It might have had to do with some discovery of an old burial site written up in the local, or even the London, papers. Do you recall anything of the sort?"

"Not offhand. It is not the sort of article I am likely to read."

"If it was of that nature, Mr. Oldbury might be aware of it," Theodosia said thoughtfully. "Surely he would collect anything he found, and his friends might send him items that appeared in London, knowing he would be interested. I shall ask him tomorrow when we go.

In the meantime, I hope you won't mind if I allow the children to do a little digging about the estate. I don't think they can restrain their energies much longer."

"A few muddy articles of clothing are a small price to pay for their renewed spirits, dear Miss Tremere. Have I told you how pleased I am with how they've come out of their gloom? I hope you know how much I appreciate your endeavors."

"I've enjoyed it."

"This evening after they're in bed I'll show you the artifact my sister sent as the 'treasure.' It's a handsome Roman belt buckle found somewhere in Somerset. She thought that would lend it more authenticity. Will it do?"

Theodosia rose as Lady Eastwick did. "Admirably. We can weave a wonderful tale around it, ma'am. Now all I shall have to do is discover an appropriate spot to hide it, and a new set of rules to point to its location. It can be an exercise in deductive reasoning to parallel the real family treasure. I shan't try to fool them that it's a true 'find.' They're far too clever for that, anyhow, I fear. On the other hand, I shan't help them find it, either! And again Mr. Oldbury might be able to assist by instructing me where such an item would logically be found. A lesson in archeology for the children, as it were."

The children were poring over a map, and arguing the most logical place for the treasure to be buried when Theodosia arrived. Each had some idea to offer but there was no concensus.

"I want to start digging." John glared at his brother and sisters. "It doesn't matter much where. Can I, Miss Tremere?"

The governess nodded her understanding. "Yes. For today we'll simply choose the most accessible spot which conforms to the terms of the poem. Would you hand me the map, Thomas? Very well, we shall, for the time being, assume the church as 'faith' and the barrow above the park as the 'burial ground,' if that is agreeable. The estate itself can serve as the boundary,

147

though the first earl was granted a great deal of land in the area. We may find that there is only a small area of the barrow from which the church is visible. It will give us a starting point, at least."

By the time the children had changed into their oldest clothes and several shovels had been rounded up (none of them finding it at all strange that one was missing from the stables), the better part of the morning had escaped. Undaunted, the large party set off on foot, having decided that horses would just be a nuisance, and not wanting to have one of the grooms with them when they made the big discovery. John led the way, awkwardly shouldering one of the shovels, but delighted to finally be at the real crux of their hunt—the dig. They had only climbed the lower slopes when they met Edward and Lord Steyne returning from their morning's fishing.

It took no second sight for Theodosia to tell that Steyne had learned the whole. The very blandness of his countenance, coupled with the amused intentness with which he regarded her, were sure signs. Edward wore the air of a man who had made important decisions in spite of the odds against which he had struggled. They had caught no fish.

Amy tugged at Steyne's sleeve. "Won't you come with us? We're going...digging on the hill."

Ordinarily a governess might have shuddered at the child's presumption, and hastily stepped in to assure his lordship that Amy didn't understand that she was imposing. Theodosia said nothing, returning Steyne's startled look with a serene smile.

When Edward appeared about to protest, Steyne looked down at Amy and said, "You don't think perhaps I would be in the way?"

"Certainly not!" she cried indignantly. "You would be of the greatest assistance! Thomas and John are bound to tire of digging very quickly. I dare say you would be able to keep on for hours!"

Now Edward did protest, and most of his siblings with him, but Theodosia had found it necessary to retrieve a pad of foolscap she had dropped. Steyne could see her shoulders shaking with laughter and, to the surprise of all of them, he gave a hoot of mirth himself as he gently touched the tip of Amy's nose. "Not quite hours, urchin, but for a while at least. What do you say, Edward? Shall we join them?"

The younger man gaped at him, unable to picture the Corinthian hard at work with a shovel, his sleeves rolled up and his shoulder muscles bulging under the effort of shifting earth at little Amy's request. But Steyne wasn't quizzing him; he meant precisely what he said, and eventually Edward croaked, "If you wish, sir. They'll be looking for the treasure."

His brothers and sisters stared at him, and he stiffened. "It's all right. I told him about it for a very sufficient reason. You will have to trust my judgment."

Theodosia intervened to set them on their way again, discussing as they went the various categories into which the search would fall. On the foolscap pad she was jotting down ideas as they occurred to her, separating them on the basis of whether they would have marched with the first earl's poem, a later earl's situation at Charton Court, or neither. A second sheet listed the various meanings which might attach to such terms as "Faith," "grant lands," "lore" and being hidden beneath scenes of valor and strife. She glanced up to find the viscount studying her.

"Did you have a suggestion, Lord Steyne?"

"I would have to see the poem first. Edward has only told me about it." He had shouldered John's shovel, assuring the boy that it was only right that he have some of the burden if he was to share in the fun.

"There is a copy in the schoolroom, but I've replaced the original in the archive room. You might wish to see my notes on the Heythrop ancestry, and the time when they moved to Charton Court. The earldom was created in 1485, and the treasure was misplaced between the seventh and eighth earls in 1643, but it may have been in the family for some time before the first earl."

"With Edward's permission," he assured her, all

righteousness, "I would be fascinated to see anything relating to it. Not that I would be likely to discover anything you had missed, ma'am. I have the greatest respect for your...competence."

"There is always the possibility that a new view on the documents would be beneficial. The Heythrops are so familiar with them that they may be overlooking something very simple that an outsider would notice—a gentleman, that is." Her eyes danced in the noonday sunlight. "Something to which a mere female would attach no significance."

"I never said....!" Steyne seemed to recall abruptly that there were any number of interested onlookers to this conversation and finished lamely, "that it would be easy to find such a long-missing treasure."

"It could be anywhere," Edward grunted, swinging Thomas' shovel from one shoulder to the other. "I don't see why you want to go digging up here."

His younger brothers were pleased to inform him of their purpose, and soon both Steyne and Edward found themselves digging in the one area of the mound of earth from which the village church could be seen. Their greatest find was a piece of a stoneware mug which certainly did not date from the fifteenth century.

Eleanor studied it carefully before giving her judgment that it was possibly fifty years old. "Do you think it was left here on a previous search?"

Her query was directed to Theodosia, who admitted it was likely. As they trudged wearily back to the Court, Steyne chatted amiably with the girls while Edward kept close to the governess' side and made sure that they brought up the rear of the party.

"I only told Lord Steyne about the family secret because of what he...and you...saw last night," he told her, his eyes vaguely accusing. "He did not enlighten me as to how it came that you both saw my uncle so late at night."

Though he waited for some comment from her, Theodosia merely regarded him with interest.

"Anyhow, I decided it was proper for him to know. He won't tell anyone else, and he might even have some suggestions. I can't think why you thought it likely the treasure would be buried in the barrow."

"Not likely," Theodosia explained, "but a start had to be made somewhere. John especially was eager to get down to the digging."

"He didn't do much of it," Edward grumbled, brushing a smear of dirt from his coat. "Did you tell Mother about last night?"

"Oh, yes."

He seemed surprised. "And what did she say?"

"She thought it would be wisest not to confront Mr. Heythrop with the knowledge."

"I wasn't speaking of my uncle," he rasped, "but of your being with Lord Steyne."

Theodosia regarded him with wide brown eyes. "She didn't say anything about it."

"Then you didn't mention you were with him." The statement was made belligerently, but he refused to meet her gaze.

"Of course I did. There was no harm in the situation, Lord Heythrop, any more than when I have seen or spoken with you late at night."

Edward's face suffused with an unbecoming flush. He was tempted to point out that he was (temporary) master at Charton Court and Steyne a guest, but there seemed no purpose. His late calls *had* been harmless, he assured himself, if not in his mind, then certainly in their execution. Had Miss Tremere handled Lord Steyne in the same manner? Was he attempting to seduce the governess? Unlikely he thought, since Steyne had known her some years ago and must be aware of her gentle birth. Edward stomped along beside her in silence for some time and eventually said, "You should keep your door locked."

"I do."

Not knowing what to make of that, Edward fell silent again.

Chapter Thirteen

Lady Winchmore and her daughter Christina wer
at Charton Court when the searchers returned. Wit
Lady Eastwick they were cozily ensconced in the Sun
mer Parlor, cups of tea in hand and plates of tarts an
biscuits at their sides. Theodosia's charges were hardl
dressed for the occasion but their mother allowed ther
to join, fearful that they would starve, having misse
the cold luncheon which only she and James had en
joyed before her brother-in-law had left the house, n
bothering to explain where he was going. Christin
cast a shy glance at Edward as he entered, but it wa
Charlotte who hastened to her side.

"Have you been here long? I'm so sorry we weren
here to greet you, but we've been...walking in th
hills."

Perhaps it was perverseness on Steyne's part, but h
paid a great deal of attention to Christina, asking he
about her London season and regretting that he ha
not had the opportunity to encounter her there. Hi
charm was wasted on the girl, as she kept dartin
glances at Edward, where he sat with his mother an
Lady Winchmore. The younger children disappeare
as soon as they had stuffed themselves with sufficien
nourishment to sustain them until dinner time, an

Theodosia excused herself with them. Lady Eastwick, thinking she looked a little tired, made no effort to stay her.

None of the children went to the schoolroom; Theodosia hadn't expected them to, but it was her destination, nonetheless. From the schoolroom window she watched Thomas race John across the drawbridge, their unbounded energy renewed by a little sustenance. The aroma of newly mown hay drifted up to her, along with that of freshly baked bread from the kitchen wing. Stands of oaks stood gloriously green in the heat of the afternoon and the cry of birds echoed from the wooded park. Later she would take a book into the topiary, when the heat of the day diminished a bit, but now the schoolroom was one of the coolest spots in the house. Theodosia settled herself in an overstuffed chair, drowsily reading the notes she had made on the foolscap, her mind not completely on the task, but finding it simpler than the other questions which rose to tease her.

Her eyelids drooped and she thought she might just let them stay that way for a minute. The heat and the morning's exercise and the lateness of the hour when she had gotten to sleep the previous night combined to enervate her. She was soon dozing peacefully, a faint smile on her lips and the breeze from the open window stirring a few stray strands of the luxuriant brown hair.

When the Winchmores left, Charlotte and Eleanor drifted off to their rooms and Steyne decided to take Theodosia up on her offer of studying her notes about the Heythrop family. There was no answer when he tapped at her door and he climbed the stairs to the second floor, sure that the schoolroom must be there. He had no trouble finding it: The door was open and from the doorway he could see her fast asleep in the chair, the foolscap pages under her folded hands.

As though she could feel his gaze on her, her eyelids fluttered but a haze of dreams clung about her. She was in her father's house in Chipstable, waiting. Waiting to see if he would come. She had been waiting for more than a month and could only stay a few days longer. The new vicar wished to move in with his family; she must make a decision on whether to go to Lord Eastwick's. So many times she had half expected to look up at the doorway and find him there, smiling at her. And at last, just when she had almost given up hope—there he was. In a daze of dreamlike happiness she extended her hands and said, "Marc! You came."

Shaken out of her stupor by her own voice, confused, she still could not fail to comprehend the stunned look on his face. She was not at Chipstable but at Charton Court, and he had not come, not when she needed him. Slowly she rose from the chair and smoothed down her skirts with the uselessly extended hands, saying, "Lord Steyne, I beg you will forgive me. I seem to have been dreaming. Did you come to see the notes on the Heythrop family?" In her embarrassment she busied herself at the desk, sorting out anything that might be of interest to him.

Two long strides brought him to her side. "My aunt didn't write until you had left Chipstable."

She lifted her head from perusing the papers and gazed calmly at him. "I realize that now, and I suspected it then. It's of no importance. I don't dream of the past very often. Now, this is a copy of the first earl's poem, and a list I have made of the...."

"What do you mean 'it's of no importance'?" His countenance was grim, his hands clenched at his sides.

"We leave the past behind us, with all its joys and miseries. What seemed crucial then is only a memory years later. I'm sure you've noticed."

"I haven't." The dark eyes regarded her intently. "You could have written me yourself."

"No, I couldn't. You know I couldn't."

Steyne thumped a fist against her desk and muttered, "Doe, I.... You know I never meant what I wrote you. I was upset! You had come of age and you still wouldn't leave him!"

"He was very ill at the time. I explained that to you in my letter."

"But you had always let him convince you that he was ill! He didn't die for almost another year!"

Theodosia smiled sadly. "You must believe what you wish, Lord Steyne. And you have always believed that I was a fool to do my Christian duty."

"Duty!" he growled. "No one owes a duty to an irrascible old man who thinks of no one but himself. It would have done him no harm to lay out a few pounds for a housekeeper and a boy to replace your domestic services. You will never convince me that he had any other use for you."

"I would never try." Theodosia tapped the papers so their edges aligned and offered them to him.

Steyne stared at them uncomprehendingly, as though his valet had handed him a candlestick instead of his hat. Impatiently he jammed them into his coat pocket. "Did you want me to apologize? Did you expect me to bow down to that aggrandized, pompous...? Have you never realized that I only felt so strongly about him because of what he did to *you?* Treating you like a servant, finding fault with every effort you made, returning no affection for the devotion you poured on him."

"Steyne," she said, her voice sharp with anger, "I don't wish to discuss my father. I don't wish to discuss our past. In fact, I don't wish to discuss anything with you just now. My head is aching abominably. If my notes aren't clear, I will be happy to explain them to you at some other time—or you might consult Lord Heythrop. Please don't say another word," she cautioned as he looked ready to protest. "I am going to rest until I feel better."

Her anger was something new to him and he stood rooted to the spot as she vanished out the door. At nineteen she had cajoled, she had teased, she had apologized, she had begged him to understand her actions, but she had never spoken a cross word to him, let alone ordered him to silence. His confusion was as great as hers had been on waking, compounded of annoyance and remorse, the memory of the surge of hope he had felt and the despair as their exchange turned to bitter recriminations. Had he been to blame? Was he at fault even now? Steyne walked to the window and watched as dark clouds obscured the sun and the first drops of rain splashed against him. Damn! A change in the weather could well presage a change in James' plans. Steyne closed the window and walked from the schoolroom, the foolscap sheets forgotten in his pocket.

Since it would never have occurred to him to visit the schoolroom, Edward had been unable to locate Lord Steyne. He had opted for a short ride when the storm clouds gathered, and found himself halfway to the stables when the first drops of rain fell. Taking refuge on the terrace outside the Summer Parlor he was about to wipe the muddy splashes from his boots when he realized that Charlotte and Eleanor had sought shelter just around the corner under the overhang. As usual, they were not in agreement on the subject which absorbed their attention.

"Well, *I* think he was decidedly smitten by her," Charlotte pronounced. "How am I to get the mud off these white shoes?"

"You won't be able to," her sister informed her smugly. "They're ruined. You should have worn your boots as I suggested."

"You never suggested any such thing. All you said was that you were wearing yours. Anyway, you didn't know it was going to rain."

Eleanor snorted. "Of course I did, goose. It is exactly on days such as this when the weather gets unbearably hot that a shower comes to cool it off. I never take my sketchbook out when it gets muggy hot this way."

"Why don't you think Lord Steyne was interested in Christina? He certainly paid her particular attention, and you have to admit she is charming and pretty."

"He's far too old for her, Charlotte, for one thing."

"Stuff! Lots of girls marry men his age."

"Christina won't," Eleanor declared in her most definite manner, nicely calculated to set up her sister's back.

"You can't possibly know that!"

"For heaven's sake, Charlotte, she's your best friend and you can't see what's right in front of your eyes. I can understand why she wouldn't tell you, but surely you could have guessed."

Edward, who had considered letting them know that he could overhear their conversation, abandoned the idea of doing any such thing when he heard Charlotte, bewildered, ask, "What are you talking about?"

"Christina has a *tendre* for Edward, silly. Haven't you noticed the way she always glances at him when he's in the room with her? She was hardly aware of Lord Steyne."

"You have windmills in your head, Eleanor! Who in her right mind would find anything the least bit romantic about *Edward?*"

If Edward was miffed by this reference to himself, few outsiders would have been able to tell. He stood transfixed on the terrace, unaware that the wind had changed direction and rain was pelting him unmercifully. Nothing is quite so flattering as learning that you are the object of another's adoration, and though Edward had never until that moment so much as given Christina a thought (other than seeing her as a neighbor and a friend of his sister's), suddenly he was stricken with a most gratifying gallantry. He never doubted the truth of Eleanor's assertion, and barely heard her reply to Charlotte: *"Chacun à son goût."*

Christina Winchmore. Edward could picture her readily enough, though he had not paid particular attention to her that afternoon. Several years his junior, she was just the sort of young lady who would appreciate his finer qualities. Miss Tremere, he decided abruptly, had a certain levity in her nature which was not in keeping with his conception of a truly aristocratic lady. Christina, on the other hand, showed a proper reserve and decorum at all times, and if she was a trifle timid, well, Edward was just the one to give her confidence. Knowing that he had the edge over Lord Steyne in this one particular instance was a marvelously heady sensation. Christina Winchmore was attracted to him, Edward, heir to the Earl of Eastwick, bulwark of his family during his father's absence; she had no interest whatsoever in the noted Corinthian, Lord Steyne. Edward was smiling fatuously when his mother opened the door onto the terrace and expostulated, "For God's sake, Edward, what are you doing standing in the rain? You'll catch your death of cold."

Edward looked at her, bemused, and sneezed.

When dinner time arrived and Theodosia had not reappeared, Lady Eastwick, worried, sent Charlotte to inquire. Her eldest daughter returned to report that Miss Tremere was sound asleep and she hadn't the heart to waken her.

"Of course not, love. I thought she looked a bit peaked at tea. After dinner I'll check on her myself."

But Theodosia was still sleeping soundly when Lady Eastwick went to her room, and she did nothing more than place long, cool fingers on the governess's forehead to ascertain whether she had a fever. Her brow was no warmer than it should be, Lady Eastwick decided as she tucked the bedcovers more closely about the sleeping form. The fact that Miss Tremere had not experienced even the slightest indisposition in the three years she had been at Charton Court, and that she should feel ill today rather worried Lady Eastwick, especially when she had found Edward standing like a love-struck schoolboy on the terrace in the rain.

There might not be any connection between the two events, she mused, but it would be wise to keep an eye on the situation. Then there was the added anxiety from James being in the house. He could very well have upset the young lady with his unwanted attentions. And Lord Steyne....Lady Eastwick had an intuitive feeling about the state of his emotions, if not the reason for his being in Somerset. Her theory on matters of the heart, however, was to allow them to sort themselves out in their own time, whenever possible. She closed the door quietly behind herself.

Questioning eyes turned toward her when she returned to the drawing room—Charlotte's, Edward's, Steyne's. "I don't think she has a fever. She's still sleeping, though, so she must be exhausted. Having the boys home doubles the demands on her time but she has always insisted that she enjoys working with them. Perhaps I should have seen that they weren't so much underfoot."

"I wouldn't alarm yourself, ma'am," Steyne interjected. "Most likely Miss Tremere is simply suffering from the headache brought on by the muggy weather before the shower. My sister is prone to suffer a similar inconvenience."

Charlotte frowned. "It's never happened before, and it's not uncommon for us to have weather like this."

They really did treat her as one of the family, Steyne decided, disgruntled. Their concern was as real as it would have been for any one of them. He listened silently as Charlotte suggested she might go to sit with Theodosia, but Lady Eastwick fortunately thought such a measure unnecessary. Somehow Theodosia's absence seemed to leave them disspirited. Lady Eastwick halfheartedly suggested a hand of whist, but Steyne countered with a request that Charlotte play for them. The girl was midway through her second piece when James entered after being gone since early afternoon.

Three of those present studied him circumspectly for any sign that he had been successful. If he had been out digging in the rain, there was no way of telling, for he wore a fresh cravat and a spotless brown coat. His boots, too, were polished to a high gloss, indicating that they had not even been worn outside the house. Obviously, James had seen fit to change before joining his relations.

Not waiting for the conclusion of the piano-forte performance, James turned to his sister-in-law and announced, "I have finished my business here and intend to head back for London tomorrow."

His words caused a bit of a sensation in the small group. Lady Eastwick replaced the fragile teacup she had been holding on its saucer, her brow puckered. "So soon, James? When you have come such a distance, I thought you would remain for at least a week."

Edward, finally alarmed out of his intriguing daydreams, stuttered, "B-But you hadn't s-said anything!"

His uncle regarded him with a sardonic twist of his lips. "Did you expect a written itinerary, Edward? I felt sure it would not be necessary with my closest family. A few days was all I ever intended to stay. Lord Steyne will wish to be returning to town."

All eyes swung to Steyne, even Charlotte's. She was not immune to the sudden tension in the room. His lordship sat at his leisure, long legs casually crossed, one hand idly toying with his watch fob. Had James found the treasure, then? Or was he merely put off by the rain and lack of success? Steyne couldn't imagine him spending long on any one endeavor; he would cut his losses at the first frustration.

"Tomorrow?" he asked, his voice thoughtful. "After this afternoon's cloudburst the roads are bound to be muddy." Steyne was stalling for time and he disliked the speculative look that came to James' eyes. "However, I dare say if we leave at an hour you would consider reasonable, they will have had an opportunity to dry somewhat."

"True," James retorted with lazy satisfaction. "I have never understood this passion to be off at the break of day."

And the discussion ended, if not the racing thoughts of several of the parties present. Over a hand of whist, Lady Eastwick mutely indicated to her son that his countenance was an obvious testament to his suspicions, and Edward attempted to modify his grim stare into a disinterested gaze. Neither of them could help but look to Steyne for support, but the viscount gave no indication that he was aware of anything the least bit out of the ordinary. Charlotte had excused herself for the night and James, bored by Edward's worse-than-usual performance with the cards, asked, "Where's the governess?"

His condescending tone set up Lady Eastwick's back. He could have called her by name; no one referred to Miss Tremere as "the governess." Calmly taking the trick with an ace of spades, she explained, "Miss Tremere wasn't feeling well and has retired to her room."

"You shouldn't put up with sickly servants," James taunted, knowing full well he was alienating at least two-thirds of his audience and noting with interest the hard line of Steyne's lips. "I give them notice at the first sign of indisposition. That way you haven't any doctor bills to pay. You would be astonished at how healthy my dependents stay."

A cold silence greeted this remark and James laughed. "You become too familiar with the lower orders in the countryside, Joanna. I'm sure you learn all about their aged mothers and arthritic fathers, their sick cows and poor turnip harvests. In London the problem doesn't arise. If they aren't satisfactory, you dismiss them. There are hundreds more where they came from, champing at the bit for a chance to make enough to maintain themselves. Being softhearted with dependents—any dependents," he stressed, his eyes on Steyne, "is a waste of time. They don't admire your weakness."

Lady Eastwick did not deign to reply to his callousness; Edward glared at him. The comments were really meant for Steyne, however, and the viscount realized with something of a shock that James was declaring his philosophy as a direct challenge. For the simple reason that he wished no unpleasantness at Charton Court, Steyne had purposely not commented on the marriage, but James could not resist pushing his luck. Convinced that he had the upper hand in the negotiation, that he was to marry Ruth, he intended to make it clear that he would exercise the upper hand in his marriage as well. He was not merely discussing domestic servants: He was discussing Ruth as well.

For the first time Steyne was forced to reconsider his own attitude. He could feel the anger coursing through his veins at the very thought of James dictating to Ruth, ordering her life, bullying her into obedience. His sister was a courageous, intelligent and strong-willed woman. These attributes had not detracted from her first marriage. Morrison had accepted her as she was without feeling the necessity to dominate. James was announcing his resolution to wield his power over another "dependent." Steyne found his mind wandering to Theodosia and forced it back to the issue at hand.

"You are confusing strength with power, James," Steyne remarked with no show of the turmoil that had seized him. "If Lady Eastwick shows an interest in her servants' personal problems, it is a sign of her ability to accept that the management of a household depends on dealing with human beings, not animals. If Edward treats the tenants with courtesy, it is a sign of his responsibility toward his inheritance and his position. Both necessitate strength rather than weakness, and both will generate loyalty rather than slovenliness. It is the weak man who must use his petty power to cow his dependents, who must use ceremony for want of sense. Privilege entails responsibility and wealth bestows obligations." Steyne trumped the trick James was sure he had won and continued calmly, "A man—or woman—must earn the right to be admired. You are content, I dare say, with servility, but it has a nasty way of turning sour on you. Take, for instance, a man who has made not the least effort to earn his servants' respect. When someone approaches them for information, possibly damaging information, they are not averse to being bribed."

James had been regarding Steyne with a superior smirk during most of this lecture but now his hand paused in midair, holding a card of no value. "What do you mean?" he asked sharply.

As Lady Eastwick took the trick, Steyne met the hostile eyes. "Just what I said. Where there is no loyalty, there is no security. A man has few secrets from his servants, especially a man who considers them beneath his notice. Do you think his parlormaid doesn't notice the stack of duns when she dusts? Or his porter recognize the bailiffs when they come to his door?"

"What his servants know," James growled, "is that they will be dismissed for gossiping about such matters."

"Why should they care?" Steyne countered. "Their employer isn't providing an amiable setting in which to labor. Perhaps they are offered a chance to change employment."

"You wouldn't dare!"

Steyne, unperturbed, observed the furious countenance and said gently, "There is very little I wouldn't dare, James, with the proper incentive, but why should you read anything personal into my comments? We were discussing strengths and weaknesses in the abstract, were we not?"

By now Edward was openly gaping at them but James had forgotten the card game, as well as the other occupants of the fashionable drawing room. His laughter grated in the tense silence. "You would be ill-advised to interfere, I think, my lord."

"Possibly." Steyne turned to Lady Eastwick, smiling. "Rubber to us, ma'am. Shall we play another?"

"I think not, if you don't mind. I'd like to check on Miss Tremere before I retire."

"Of course."

Edward showed an inclination to linger with the two men, but his mother insisted that he accompany her. When the door had closed behind them James was immediately on his feet, pacing about the room. After a moment he stopped behind Steyne's chair, his eyes dark with anger.

"So you've been playing cat and mouse, have you, Steyne? Well, it won't do you any good. No matter what you find out about me behind my back, your sister will marry me. She doesn't need your approval but she does need *me*. Her shame would be on your head if you prevented a marriage she has already consummated." His eyes now glowed with mocking triumph.

Steyne sat perfectly still except for the thumb which rubbed slowly across his watch fob. "No one but a scoundrel would make such a statement, which I know to be a lie. I would be remiss in my duty if I allowed my sister to marry you, James. If you wish to be frank, let us. You are bleeding your estate; you have innumerable debts in London; your life is incompatible with marriage."

"Nonetheless," James retorted coldly, "your sister wishes to marry me, and you really can't stop her."

"You are mistaken, James. My sister does not wish to marry you. I've spoken with her."

If this came as a surprise to James, not by the twitch of a muscle did he show it, but his eyes became colder, more calculating. "I fear your sister has not been wholly frank with you, Steyne. Her behavior has been such as to make a marriage between us highly desirable."

"*Nothing* could make a marriage between the two of you highly desirable, James." Steyne met the cool eyes with a steely gaze of his own. "You needn't spell out for me how you could make life disagreeable for my sister by discussing your connection with her. No gentleman would do so, of course, but you have yet to prove that you fall within that category. I will not be intimidated or blackmailed or coerced, James. You shall not marry Ruth, and if any whisper, any innuendo reaches me, I will kill you. It's as simple as that. You're a spiteful devil and I give you this warning because I know you'll be tempted. You would only be tempting fate. After the effort I have made to come here with you, any reasonable man will assume that I scotched the connection because of your financial standing, and that your tales are mere bravado and malice. Ruth may have removed from London by this time, but I will be happy to see that she writes to tell you the exact state of her feelings on the matter, if you doubt me."

One of the candles guttered, causing a soft hissing in the room. Otherwise there was no sound as the two men fought a battle of wills with their eyes. James turned away first. Another gamble in his long career had failed, his veracity and his honor had been called in question, and he knew he should challenge Steyne for the insult. But he was not, when all was said and done, a particularly brave man, and he had seen Steyne at Mantons any number of times, unerringly accurate with a pistol. James had decided that afternoon to abandon his hunt for the family treasure but now, in an effort to salvage something from the trip, he changed his mind again. He would take one more stab at it.

"I have decided to stay another day or so...if that will be convenient with your lordship," he said, his voice laden with sarcasm.

"As you wish." Steyne was relieved that he would not have to contrive some damage to his carriage to delay their departure. There was one more thing he felt it necessary to say, though it nearly choked him. "Ruth never meant to mislead you, James. Since her husband's death, she has been emotionally over-wrought. I'm sure she would wish me to apologize for any misunderstanding."

It was a handsome concession but James only threw him a look of violent dislike and strode from the room, slamming the door after himself. Steyne rose wearily from his seat at the cardtable and proceeded to Theodosia's room where his light tap went unanswered. Trying the knob he found the door unlocked and slid quickly inside. From the bed came the gentle sounds of breathing and he whispered, "Sleep well, my dear," before taking the key and locking the door from without, and slipping it underneath.

Chapter Fourteen

Theodosia was asleep when Steyne entered, but even the slight sound he made on leaving roused her somewhat, and when she fully woke she was surprised to find it completely black outside. Too exhausted when she went to bed to bother disrobing, she was still fully dressed, with the exception of her shoes, and she climbed out of bed to check the clock on the mantel. Almost eleven! What must they think of her for missing dinner without sending a message?

Very likely they had all retired by now, but Theodosia slipped into her shoes and brushed her hair into place in the dark room. Only a glimmer of moonlight stole through the window, making it difficult for her to see whether indeed she had managed to control all the whispy ends. She would take a candle from the sconce outside her door, where one was left burning each night so the girls could find her if they were frightened or worried. Strange, Theodosia thought, as she tried the door and found it locked. I don't remember doing that. But the key was not in the hole and she knew instantly that Steyne had come to lock her door. As before, she found the key at her feet and let herself out into the hall.

Shielding the flame with her hand, she walked down

several corridors until she reached the main staircase. There was no indication that any of the family was still up—no spare lights or the sound of voices. Fyfield was closing the house for the night and smiled up at her.

"Miss Tremere. I hope you're feeling better. My lady retired some time ago."

Theodosia nodded. "I thought as much, but I wished to check. They weren't worried about me, were they? I feel perfectly fine right now—except that I'm famished."

Her rueful expression met with an answering grin. "Of course you are. Let me bring you something from the kitchen. I've banked the fire in the drawing room, but it won't take a minute to have it blazing."

Despite her protests that she could come to the kitchen herself, Theodosia found herself led firmly to the drawing room where Fyfield lit several candles and promised to bring a tray immediately. Left alone she found her mind had a tendency to revert to the scene in the schoolroom that afternoon. How could she have said such a stupid thing? Amazing that he had realized exactly where her mind had been. Had he, too, pictured her in her father's home, waiting to see if he would come now that she was truly free? Did he regret that his aunt had withheld the information of her father's death until it was too late? Or was he relieved that the responsibility had been taken out of his hands?

He had looked so handsome standing there. Not exactly as she remembered him: His face was thinner, more rugged, and there were lines which hadn't etched themselves across his brow six years ago. His stance was no different, though, just as proud and self-confident as ever, the broad shoulders seeming to block out the entire doorway. She had often thought you could tell a lot about a man by his hands, and Steyne had such wonderful ones—long, strong, well-used, gentle hands. Not like James Heythrop's, which were short and pampered, as though he had never so much as handled a pair of reins with them. When Theodosia had cried out to Steyne, half in a dream, she had extended her hands to him, knowing exactly how it would feel to have them encased in his. And how it would feel to have him hold her in his arms—he had done so six years ago....

Oh, Lord, why was she allowing herself such flights of fancy? He might, out of a misplaced sense of chivalry, consider himself still bound to her, but.... Theodosia's vacant gaze had come to rest on the mantel, where the first earl's lines were legible even in the dim light. Sir Arthur, the gallant knight who fought for his king... Suddenly Theodosia realized where all the Heythrops had gone wrong. Chivalry. The glorious name. Proudly passed from father to son...until the eighth earl, who didn't know which name it was that he was supposed to pass on. Not Heythrop, but Arthur. The first earl had been Sir Arthur Heythrop before he was raised to the peerage. How many Arthurs had there been? Theodosia could not remember exactly. There had been Edwards, but had they been younger sons? She would have to see the list. But she had given the list to Steyne.

Fyfield arrived with a tray loaded with tea, bread and butter and cheese and a variety of cold meats, plus a sampling of cakes which had been served at dinner. Though Theodosia had suddenly almost lost her appetite, she forced herself to do justice to the meal, since the butler had gone to such trouble for her. Her mind raced, linking clues here and there, wondering, trying to remember everything. Did this bring her any closer to the treasure itself? Not necessarily, but perhaps. With impatient fingers she stacked the dishes neatly on the tray and carried it out to Fyfield, who scolded her, affectionately, for her effort.

Taking the candle once more, she thanked him and climbed the stairs, almost wishing she could do it two at a time, as Thomas always did. John's legs weren't quite long enough yet for him to accomplish the same feat. In her headlong rush she had not actually decided what she was going to do when she reached Steyne's room, but she knew there was no possibility of sleep for her that night if she didn't look at her notes. There was one candle burning in the hallway, its light barely reaching beyond the area where Steyne and James Heythrop had their rooms. She knew Steyne's room faced onto the exterior because he had commented at breakfast one morning on the view. Hesitantly she tapped, suddenly astonished at her own courage. There was no response.

The papers were sure to be in his room. Theodosia rationalized that they were *her* papers, after all, and it would do no harm to retrieve them for a few hours. They could be returned to him in the morning, before he even woke. She blew out her candle and slipped silently into his room, closing the door behind her with only the faintest click. If there had been a fire in the room to warm it after the chill of the rain, no embers glowed and the pale moonlight did not reach this side of the house. Unfamiliar with the layout of the furniture in the room, she stood just inside the door for some time allowing her eyes to become accustomed to the dark. When she could distinguish the four-poster bed, with the black lump that was Steyne, she tiptoed over to the bedside table and stretched out her hands to feel along its surface. Her wrists were clasped in a firm grip.

Theodosia gasped, protesting in a whisper, "It is only me—Theodosia. I need the notes I lent you this afternoon."

"What the devil are you doing up at this hour of the night?" he demanded, releasing her.

"It's not at all late. I doubt it's gone midnight. If you were awake, why didn't you respond to my knock?"

"I wasn't awake," he said irritably, swinging his legs over the side of the bed, having momentarily forgotten that he wasn't dressed to receive company. His nightshirt gleamed white in the darkness of the bed-hangings. "Hand me my dressing gown, would you, Doe? It's on the chair."

Fumbling past the nightstand, her toe painfully encountered the claw-footed chair where the silk dressing gown blended so well with the upholstery that only by the feel could she find it. She turned her back as he stood up, shrugged his way into it and tied the cord about his waist.

"Where the hell do they keep the tinder box?" he grumbled as he ran his hands along the nightstand. The only evidence that he found it was a rather noisy clatter as it fell to the floor. "Oh, damn, forget it. Give me your candle and I'll light it in the hall."

"Couldn't you just tell me where the papers are and I'll leave?" she suggested diffidently.

"No, I couldn't. Where did you put your candle?"

"I dropped it when you grabbed my wrists."

Steyne swore again, softly, and banged his head against the nightstand as he stooped to feel around for the errant candle. "If you laugh, I'll strangle you," he muttered.

Theodosia attempted to restrain the gurgle that rose in her throat, and was only partially successful. "Forgive me. Shall I find it for you?"

"Certainly not. Just sit down and be quiet."

Naturally he stubbed his toe against the chair, just as she had, as he stood up and stomped to the hall to light the candle. When he returned he lit the lamp on the bureau and another by his bed. Then he seated himself and regarded her sternly. "If it's not asking too much, I would like to know why you must suddenly have your notes back in the middle of the night."

"I told you it's not the middle of the night." He glowered at her and she continued, "I think I have just uncovered a part of the puzzle, about the missing treasure, I mean. But I need to see the list of earls in order to confirm it, and the poem."

"What have you discovered?" He was interested now, his eyes keen and his lips no longer so grimly pressed together.

Theodosia, surprisingly, dropped her eyes. "Well, I'm afraid it will sound absurd. It seemed so logical in the drawing room....I mean, when I was looking at the mantel and thinking about chivalry...."

Her voice trailed away and he smiled. "Why were you thinking of chivalry, Doe?"

"Heaven knows!" she said crossly. "One sees so little of it these days."

"I didn't mean to upset you this afternoon."

"Didn't you? Strange, I thought you did. Well, that's irrelevant."

"Are you feeling better now?" he asked, belatedly.

"Perfectly fine. I don't know how I came to sleep so long. Did anyone remark on it?"

Steyne grimaced. "Everyone. Lady Charlotte was determined on sitting with you, and her mother checked on you twice. Edward was visibly shaken."

"Such dear people! You have no idea how fortunate I feel to have come to Charton Court of all places. I imagine you know the earl. He and Lady Eastwick made me feel a part of the family right from the start."

"My dear, you are wandering from the issue. I am fully prepared to admit that the Heythrops are an admirable family (with the exception of James), and that their treatment of you is above reproach. Will you tell me what you've discovered?"

"The 'glorious name' refers to Arthur—as in King Arthur."

His eyes narrowed. "How the devil did you come to that conclusion? Surely you must know he wasn't really a king, that those are only legends woven round him."

"Of course I do," she retorted, offended. "But there was a real Arthur. Think of the poem. 'A dozen engagements in triumph, but bravest of all facing death.' Arthur's twelve battles were real enough."

"Presuming they were, what connection could he possibly have with the Heythrops?"

"The first earl had been Sir Arthur Heythrop, and most of the others were Arthurs, too, until the secret was lost. May I see the list? I want to check myself on that."

Steyne made no move to get the notes. "Are you *sure* you're feeling well, Doe? The Arthurian legend is preposterous, and dates from the fifth century. Your Sir Arthur lived in the fifteenth!" -

"I know, I know. Didn't I tell you it would seem absurd? Still, so many things fit. Arthur—the bear on the old bronze plaque. If it is a bear. It might not be, of course."

"I don't think Arthur had any descendents, Doe," he said gently.

"Well, they needn't have been descendents, exactly. Perhaps some ancient Heythrop ancestor was an aide in battle and Arthur bestowed some 'illustrious treasure' on him for his service. Arthur was a *dux bellorum*—a leader of battle. That's in the poem, don't you see?"

No, he didn't see at all. Steyne was shaken by her conviction in a patently ridiculous idea. Her very earnestness was a reproach to him. Somehow he felt responsible for this instability she was exhibiting. Probably she had woken in the dark, disturbed by his plaguing her during the afternoon, and all sorts of fantasies had come to her while she sat in the drawing room, alone, perhaps a few embers flickering in the grate, the ancient words carved in the mantelpiece.

Steyne rose from his chair and came to crouch before her as he took her hands in his. "My sweet, you are a little confused. I'm afraid this treasure hunt has become an obsession with you. Remember, no one else has been able to find it; there is no need that you succeed. I realize that folklore and myth can seem particularly real at times, but in the daylight you will understand the difference. Let me tuck you in bed. I'll stay until you fall asleep."

"Of all the condescending, pompous...." Theodosia withdrew her hands so violently from his clasp that he lost his balance and found himself sitting on the floor. "Haven't you even bothered to read the notes I gave you?"

Stunned, he merely stared at her.

"No, of course not," she answered herself, rising to pace about the chamber. She didn't even notice how

172

gracefully he rose to his feet. "You *cannot* believe that anyone but yourself has any wits about them, can you? I wish you would just give me back my notes and be done with it. If you think I've lost my mind, so be it."

"I meant to read the notes, but I was concerned for you and I stuck them in my pocket. And then having a set-to with James entirely made me forget." Steyne felt defensive. "I looked in on you before I came to bed, and locked your door."

"Yes, I know. Thank you. You have always been willing to protect me, just not to credit me with any will, any purpose of my own. Do you treat your sister that way? Is that why you are here with James?"

She had swung around to face him, brown eyes piercing. Steyne had the sudden realization that if he made a misstep now it would be irrecoverable. And he knew just as surely that he didn't want to make that mistake again. "My sister," he began, and paused to gather his thoughts, rubbing a tired hand across his forehead. "James wants to marry Ruth; she's very wealthy and James is always in debt. He didn't bother to ask her because he thought she had indicated by her actions that she was... amenable to the arrangement. That wasn't at all the case, of course. Ruth doesn't like him but she's been wretchedly unhappy and lonely since her husband died. James mistook her... behavior as an indication that her feelings for him were strong enough that they would outweigh any objections I might have to the marriage, but he wanted to cover all bets and proposed to show me how secure his financial standing was. After speaking with Ruth, I agreed to accompany him here, thinking it wiser to be able to refuse him on that basis than any other."

"So you were protecting your sister."

"What else could I do?" he asked impatiently. "She needed to be protected, Doe. Ordinarily she is *almost* as strong willed as you are, but her husband's death has shattered her. I could have allowed her to extricate herself from the situation, but that would have been heartless of me, and her reputation would likely have been badly damaged. There are times, you know, when women *must* be protected."

"Certainly. And I agree with you that this was one of them. James Heythrop is not a man to be taken lightly." Theodosia sighed as she reached for a candle. "Would you mind if I took the notes with me? I will return them to you in the morning if you wish."

Without a word he went to the wardrobe where his coat was hanging. When he had changed for dinner he had not thought to remove them, and they were still there, stuffed carelessly in the pocket. A quick glance down the sheets told him nothing except that her handwriting was as firm as always and that the notes were apparently well organized. He glanced across the room to where she waited calmly by the door. "Would you...go over them with me? I'd like to understand how you arrived at your conclusion."

Theodosia could see he was struggling not to offend and her eyes began to twinkle. "Actually, my lord, I consider it a working theory. I won't call your intelligence in question if you don't agree with me; on the other hand, I don't like to be dismissed as suffering from delusions. When I was a child, my father took me to Glastonbury on some business of his, and I heard about the supposed exhumation of Arthur and his queen Quinevere there. A child's imagination is easily caught, and I took a special interest in the Arthurian legend." She made a deprecating gesture with her hands. "That would account for my fanciful theory, would it not?"

"Possibly. How thoroughly did you investigate the Arthurian legend?"

She regarded him approvingly. "As thoroughly as I could. My father thought it foolish but it held a fascination for me, even after I learned that all the chivalry was French trapping. A kindly old gentleman in the neighborhood, a historian, took pity on me and procured, from friends, copies of the passages in Nennius relating to Arthur and the turning of the Saxon tide. Then it was that Arthur was wont to fight against them.' Of course, even the *History of the Britons* was compiled long after Arthur's time, so there is no reason that it should be particularly accurate. *Arth* means bear in Celtic, but it could be of Roman derivation. Gildas mentions the battle on Mons Badonicus, too, but doesn't mention the leader, the *dux bellorum*."

"I might have known," Steyne murmured, a crooked smile tugging at his lips. "You really are incredible, Doe. Will you come and go over your notes with me?"

Nodding, she advanced as he set two chairs at the writing table by the windows. Once more she pointed out the cryptic references that could suggest Arthur—the twelve battles, the legends that had risen to tarnish the truth, the fact that the treasure could be the spoils of battle. Going down the list of earls, she was able to ascertain that in every case before the treasure was lost, the first son (whether he had become earl or had died previous to doing so) had been named Arthur. Even the eighth earl, whose father had died without passing on the secret, had been named Arthur. Not knowing the significance of his Christian name, he had named his own son Edward after his grandfather, a second son, and thenceforth the Heythrops had, in all ignorance, named their first sons Edward.

Steyne sat back after perusing the documents with interest. "And what of the plaque you mentioned?"

"The plaque is located on the tower wall of the chapel and says, in Latin of course, Keepers of the Trust. There is a figure of an animal which might be a bear. At one point in a previous search the wall and stone floor were removed but nothing was found. They thought it significant that the plaque was mounted so low on the wall. It had been through a fire and is partially eradicated."

"Moved from Seagrave Manor to Charton Court, then?"

"Presumably." She rested her hands in her lap and looked up at him with anxious eyes. "Well, what do you think?"

The lamplight made the wide brown eyes glow, and

picked out the high cheekbones and delicate lips. He was tempted to tell her that he thought her adorable, but said instead, "I think you may be right, Doe. No, no, I'm not trying to placate you—I really do. Not that the whole theory isn't ridiculous and unprovable, but there is a certain logic to it, despite the eons that have passed since Arthurian times. But does it get us any closer to the treasure?"

"I'm not sure. When we see Mr. Oldbury tomorrow—or is it now today?—I think I will ask him about any Arthurian legends attaching to the neighborhood."

The mention of the clergyman's name brought Steyne abruptly out of the revery into which he had fallen. Though he studied her face closely, there was no indication that she attached any special significance to the coming meeting with Oldbury. She simply looked puzzled by his scrutiny.

"Do you not think that's the thing to do?" she asked.

"You don't want to give him any hint of a relationship between the Heythrops and Arthur," he pointed out. "But then, as we have mentioned, it is unlikely anyone would assume one on the face of things. Asking about Arthurian legends will doubtless seem very reasonable if you're discussing the lore of Somerset in general. By the way, James announced tonight that he plans to leave tomorrow."

"Why didn't you say so sooner? Do you think he's found the treasure?"

"No, and he changed his mind after our discussion." Was she not the least concerned that it would mean the possibility of his own disappearance from her life again? "I think he decided to stay another day or so for precisely that purpose—to hunt for the treasure."

She grinned. "I'm determined to find it first! It's become an obsession of mine, you know, but in the light of day it will probably go away."

Having his own words thrown back at him was a new experience for Steyne but he laughed. "That's all right. I'll still tuck you in bed and stay until you've fallen asleep."

"Thank you, no." Theodosia was very firm, but she could not refuse to allow him to escort her to her room, as late as it was. At her door she turned and smiled at him. "I never meant to disturb your sleep, Lord Steyne. I hope you won't have any difficulty returning to your slumbers—and I hope you don't meet anyone, wandering around the house in the middle of the night in your dressing gown."

Instead of offering her a well-earned set-down, he stooped to plant a kiss on her forehead. "We seem to be making a habit of these bedroom visits, but I promise you I don't mind in the least. Would you like me to come in and make sure your chamber is safe?"

"It's safer when you don't come in," she retorted, slipping through the opening and locking the door after herself.

Chapter Fifteen

Mr. Oldbury's housekeeper was prepared for the group from Charton Court which descended on her the next afternoon. The rectory parlor was dusted and polished, the best jasperware plates were piled high with cakes; the silver tea service gleamed from patient rubbing. As Theodosia had promised to bring only the older children, it was Charlotte and Thomas who accompanied her and Steyne in the barouche. Fair weather made it unnecessary to raise the hood, but, as on the previous day, there was the possibility of a shower later in the afternoon, and Theodosia promised Lady Eastwick that they could all squeeze into the covered portion if necessary. Though Steyne had amused visions of this meaning that Theodosia would sit on his lap, he made no mention of them.

The parlor was comfortably furnished with a scuffed set of shield-back chairs, a drum-top occasional table, an oval writing desk and a satinwood cabinet as well as a settee and a long-case clock. Mr. Oldbury, unaccustomed to playing host for tea, shepherded his guests into the room with some trepidation. Not until this moment had he really noticed that the chairs were a bit the worse for wear, and that the writing desk looked somewhat disreputable with its overflow of papers. The majority of his papers were in his study, of course, but he always seemed to absentmindedly carry some of them in with him, as he had done that morning after the housekeeper was through tidying. He backed toward the desk and tried to at least rearrange the papers as his guests seated themselves.

Ever eager to promote a romance, Charlotte thought it a good idea to illustrate to Mr. Oldbury some of Miss Tremere's outstanding qualities. She mentioned Theodosia's interest in history, her vast knowledge of geography, how readable her copperplate hand was (in case the clergyman was looking for a wife as an amanuensis), her excellent performance on the piano-forte and her kindliness to children and animals. "And her father was a clergyman," Charlotte clinched her argument.

"A truly admirable lady," Steyne murmured as Thomas in anguish nudged his sister with a sharp elbow.

Aware of her charge's intent but unembarrassed by it, Theodosia smiled at the startled Mr. Oldbury. "You see how easy it is to indoctrinate a young mind, sir. Charlotte's modesty applies only to her own abilities, which I assure you are considerable, but I shan't enumerate them." Charlotte flushed and accepted the gentle reproof with lowered eyes. Theodosia gestured to the pile of almost-neatly-stacked papers. "How is your own work progressing?"

"Rather well just at present. I've been working on the small uprising at Chard in 1655 under Colonel Penruddock and Sir Joseph Wagstaff. It was crushed, of course, but showed a remarkable spirit considering the king had already been executed. The Somerset folk have always had strong sentiments."

"Which is only to say we're stubborn," Theodosia laughed. "And do we cling as stubbornly to our legends as to our political views?"

"Even more so," Mr. Oldbury rejoined, smiling. "Every hamlet seems to have its share of lore."

Steyne was aware from Theodosia's glance at him

that he was appointed to take up the questioning. "And are there tales of devils carrying off sleeping boys in church or oddly shaped rocks reputed to be King Arthur's dog?"

"Some of both, actually. A little above Bicknoller there is Trendle Ring, which is the site of an encampment with a history of mysterious doings. You know the sort of thing—witches dance there at the full of the moon. But it's strange you should mention Arthurian legends. I haven't *heard* of any in this area. That is, no one seems to place any attachment nowadays to a particular site as being related to Arthur, but in the parish records for my church there are several references to Arthur's Spring. I don't know of any spring at all, so presumably it has dried up."

Theodosia asked casually, "Was there any way of telling where the spring might have been located?"

"Nothing precise. Possibly it was in the direction of Fairlight because Weacombe Hill was also mentioned in one of the references. Would you like me to look out the instances and write them down for you?" Mr. Oldbury, to Steyne's eyes, looked inordinately eager to please.

"I'm afraid it would give you a great deal of trouble," Theodosia protested.

"Not at all. I couldn't find them just now, but when next I'm working on the records, I shall make a note of them and send it round to you."

"You're very kind."

Steyne received another speaking glance from Theodosia and he cleared his throat portentously. "I imagine there is always exploration going on for interesting archeological sites, and Somerset apparently abounds with them. Did I read something about a discovery in the neighborhood recently? I seem to have a vague recollection...."

Mr. Oldbury was struck by his interest. "What a remarkable memory you have! My brother sent me an article from the *Morning Post* last spring. Not to do with Bicknoller, but in the area of Channock, it was.

I imagine that's the piece to which you were referring; you probably saw it in London. A fascinating tidbit of misplaced knowledge. Sir Lawrence Windoby's archeological diaries were thought to be complete in the collection held by the University, but a short one was recently discovered at Fulbrook Grange. It had been mistakenly tucked away in a trunk with some digging apparatus rather than kept with the others in his library."

"And the missing diary had to do with a find in the Channock area?" Theodosia prompted him when he sat silent, lost in contemplation of the vagueries of fortune.

"Why, yes, right at the boundaries of Charton Court land." Mr. Oldbury rubbed a thoughful finger along his chin, trying to remember precisely what the article had said. "There were three old graves in a row just outside the hedgerows, I gather. Sir Lawrence had noted in his diary that there might be further graves inside the boundaries, but he could discern no mounds, so he made no effort to gain permission to dig there." He surveyed his company with enthusiasm. "You might wish to investigate yourselves! The site was just this side of Rams Combe. I believe Sir Lawrence mentioned that there was no road nearby, simply a footpath."

Thomas entered the discussion for the first time. "I know where he means. The estate is rather untouched in that area—no use for planting or even grazing because it's steep and rocky. Even the boundary hedgerow is a scraggly sort of thing. How does an archeologist tell which mounds are graves and which are just natural lumps?"

While Mr. Oldbury attempted to enlighten him, Steyne studied Theodosia's face. He could not tell from its calm attentiveness that her mind was wandering but he knew it must be. A line of graves pointing directly to the Charton Court boundary—the extent of the "grant lands," was significant indeed. Or at least, James Heythrop was likely to think so. Was the Honorable James digging along the line of the graves even while they sat here? Steyne was impatient to know and he could not understand how Theodosia sat there so much at ease, entering into the conversation, urging Mr. Oldbury to show them the mechanics of his research, delighting in the old sketches he had come across. His impatience turned to something different, however, when Mr. Oldbury took Theodosia over to the desk, leaving Charlotte and Thomas poring over some ancient account books. Steyne feigned interest in a sixteenth-century map of the Minehead area, but his ears were tuned to the low-voiced discussion that went on behind his back.

"It's a pleasure to find someone who shares my interest in history," Mr. Oldbury assured her. "Perhaps, if you had any free time, I could take you for a drive and you could tell me about the Chipstable area. I've not had a chance to visit there as yet, though I would like to go."

"The village is charming but I can't say it abounds in historical merit. I don't have any specific afternoon to call my own, but Lady Eastwick is forever urging me to take more time for myself. I think she worries that if I don't get away more, I'll tire of all of them and leave!" Theodosia chuckled and gazed fondly at Charlotte and Thomas. "But they've become my family and my duties are not so arduous that I need any respite from them."

"Still, you should cater to Lady Eastwick's whim." His serious expression lapsed into an infectious grin. "Let me come for you a week from today at one. My gig is hardly the height of fashion but it's serviceable, and by then hopefully any threat of rain will have disappeared."

"Very well, Mr. Oldbury. I'd enjoy that—and it would ease Lady Eastwick's conscience."

Steyne refused to turn and look at them. He knew perfectly well that Theodosia would be smiling at the young jackanapes, her calm friendly smile. Or would it perhaps be more? Were their eyes meeting in a dawning understanding, a shared secret moment of kinship? Were they silently acknowledging that this was the beginning of a courtship? Steyne could not, would not, believe it possible that Theodosia would ever look at Mr. Oldbury the way she had looked at *him*, Steyne, when they had fallen in love. It wasn't possible! On the other hand, he thought, disgruntled, that she hadn't looked at himself that way recently, either.

After what seemed (to Steyne) a lot of unnecessary further talk among the group, the Charton Court party prepared to leave. Steyne found it difficult to project the proper appreciation for the visit to the young clergyman but he made a valiant effort, born of innumerable years of social expertise. His attempt was of limited success, however, as Mr. Oldbury's attention was quite obviously directed at Miss Tremere.

In the carriage Charlotte beamed with the progress of the call, having listened as carefully as Steyne to the arrangements made between her two protagonists. Nonetheless, she was not so involved in her daydreams as to ignore the approach of Wildcroft Grange. Her wistful gaze went past the intervening fields and lawns to the ancient structure of mellowed stone which was barely visible for the avenue of elms which led to it.

Theodosia followed the direction of her eyes and suggested, "Let's pay a call on the Winstanleys. We haven't visited since we learned that the Heythrops stayed at Wildcroft Grange while Charton Court was built."

Though Charlotte and Thomas were perfectly willing, Steyne stared at her in disbelief. They were seated together opposite the children and he whispered, "What in heaven's name are you doing? Don't you want to see if James is out there digging?"

"Yes, but that can wait. This is more important." When he continued incredulous, she fixed him with a particularly unnerving stare and said, "Trust me,...please."

Somehow he could not help feeling that he was being tested. Momentarily he was irritated, and then a slow, rueful smile lit his darkly handsome face. "I do trust you, Doe." And he leaned back against the squabs as though he hadn't a care in the world.

Theodosia's eyes danced as she murmured, "Thank you!"

Their visit to the Winstanleys was no longer than an ordinary country visit was supposed to be but Steyne immediately realized the purpose of it. Impossible not to, he thought with amusement, when Charlotte and Carlton Winstanley could barely take their eyes from one another, and tended to start when someone else spoke to them. Steyne found that he had developed a proprietary interest in Theodosia's charges which led him to take a few minutes sounding out the young man as he might have one of his sister's suitors. This took a form too subtle to be noticed by anyone but Theodosia who raised a quizzical brow at him across the room. When Carlton saw them to the carriage, Theodosia expressed the hope that he would visit them soon at Charton Court. Thomas, suddenly fired with a desire to join the Royal Navy, added his enthusiastic support to her invitation, and besieged poor Charlotte (who knew very little about the navy) with questions for the remainder of their drive home.

"A nice family," Steyne commented laconically, his eyes intent on the passing landscape, his voice low. "Is there approval among the Heythrops?"

"Things haven't progressed that far. Edward has been a bit stuffy, but Lady Eastwick seems delighted."

"I understand Edward was planning a visit to Basing Close this afternoon."

Theodosia regarded his turned head with astonishment. "How odd! I'm sure I had nothing to do with that. I've made no progress there whatsoever."

"Perhaps he wishes to discuss farming with Sir George." Steyne shifted on the seat so that he sat facing her. "But he did have on one of those high-collared coats that young men seem to think the very height of elegance. I doubt he would go to such an effort for Sir George, especially since he won't be able to turn his head more than an inch if they go to inspect the pig sty."

"I suppose it was the attention you paid to Christina

yesterday," Theodosia mused. "He must have realized her merit when he saw a Corinthian so obviously taken with her."

There was no censure in the statement, which only made Steyne feel it the more. His brows drew down in an uneasy scowl, but he could think of no way to excuse himself, short of admitting that he had been trying to make her jealous, a ploy that had obviously failed. Eventually he said, "Edward did not appear to notice at the time."

"Well, it doesn't really matter how he became interested in her," Theodosia admitted briskly. "I'm just delighted to see that he is, even if nothing comes of it. He needs to be distracted from his worrisome care of his family."

As the carriage swept up in front of the Court, Steyne murmured, "Shall I take Thomas and check the boundary where the graves are? Or would you like to come?"

"I'd like to, but I think I'd best not." She glanced across at the children, still deeply engrossed in talk of Carlton and the navy. "Will you let me know what you discover as soon as you return?"

"Of course. We'll be circumspect; I'll explain to Thomas. If we find James, we won't confront him."

Theodosia nodded and followed Charlotte into the house. Thomas was surprised, but flattered, to have Steyne delay him, and entered with great excitement into the adventure. Apparently the possibility that his uncle was a scoundrel didn't bother him in the least. More likely he already knew.

Charlotte was blushingly telling her mother of the visit to Wildcroft Grange when Edward swaggered into the Summer Parlor. There was no other fitting description for the manner in which he entered: a lordly strut. It was something new in Edward's experience to find himself viewed with unalleviated approbation, and Christina Winchmore had done just that. In his own family Edward was lovingly tolerated with his pompous airs and stuffy pronouncements, but Christina Winchmore, almost overwhelmed by the occasion of a visit from him alone (not that her mother wasn't there, but the rest of *his* family wasn't), had hung on his every word. Heady stuff for one of Edward's temperament, and the euphoria of it had not worn off by the time he joined his family in the Summer Parlor.

"Lady Winchmore and her daughter sent their greetings," he informed the astonished company. "Sir George was out on the estate somewhere and I didn't see him."

"You went to call at Basing Close?" Lady Eastwick asked, her eyes enormous.

"Certainly. I felt I had been a little distracted yesterday when they called and did not wish them to take my preoccupation amiss. Miss Winchmore assured me that she had found me all that was pleasing, however, so I needn't have worried."

Charlotte and Eleanor exchanged a skeptical, even downright incredulous, glance, but Edward didn't intercept it. Lady Eastwick offered a faint smile, saying, "How kind of her!"

"She's a most admirable young lady," Edward intoned, toying with the bottom button on his blue superfine coat. It had occurred to him that Miss Tremere might be alarmed by his defection and he observed her with a shade of apprehension. He had not, after all, ever given her any hint of his passion for her, which now seemed childish and had always seemed reprehensible.

His unblinking gaze prompted Theodosia to enter the conversation. "Yes, indeed. Lady Winchmore confided to us that she could not have been more pleased with her daughter's reception in London. Miss Winchmore needed nothing but a season to complete her education, and she seems to have enjoyed herself thoroughly. A little exposure to society is a great deal more enlightening than a set of schoolroom rules."

Hard as Edward tried to keep the conversation on Christina, it inevitably drifted to other subjects, notably Carlton Winstanley. He frowned when he learned that his sister and brother had called there with Miss

Tremere and Lord Steyne, and he looked to his mother for support.

"I think Charlotte is seeing far too much of Winstanley, Mother. You should put some limits on her." And have Miss Tremere enforce them, was his unspoken addition.

Lady Eastwick fixed him with a doleful eye. "Perhaps you would consider it appropriate for Charlotte to see Carlton with the same frequency you see Christina, Edward."

"I very rarely see Miss Winchmore." He refused to meet her eyes.

"Yesterday, today. Do I take it you don't intend to see her for some time now?"

Since Edward had already arranged to take Christina riding the next day, he mumbled a negative and excused himself. He had not reached the library when Charlotte and Eleanor, too, left the Summer Parlor and he distinctly heard Eleanor say, "He was difficult enough to live with before this; *now* he is going to be insufferable."

And Charlotte's soft reply: "Christina will lose all interest in him once she gets to know what he's really like, Eleanor. She's remembering him as he was when we were younger—full of fun and adventure with none of these exalted airs. When she sees what a prosy bore he's become, you may be sure her eyes will be opened and she won't have a thing to do with him. Why, she told me about the nicest man she met in London...."

But they had reached the first-floor landing and Edward, once again finding himself eavesdropping, could not catch the rest of her words. Disspirited, he stomped into the library, flung himself in one of the leather chairs and contemplated the probability to Charlotte's being right. Edward *knew* he had become a bore. He knew because he had not always been one, and along with his family he could see that he had overreacted to the responsibilities thrust on him by his father's absence.

Probably, if he had not been at home, the estate

manager and his mother together, with the assistance of Miss Tremere, could have done a better job of running things, but he had wanted so badly to prove himself. He had planned to be the balwark of the family, not the petty authoritarian figure he had become. When Katey had died he had thought, "It wouldn't have happened if my father had been here," which was the same thing as saying it was his fault, that he had failed in his duties.

Somehow Miss Tremere had guessed the burden he placed on himself and she had patiently attempted to work him out of the ridiculous belief, but he had stubbornly clung to it, as though he needed it as a proof of his ineptness. Edward had always compared himself with his father, and found himself wanting. His efforts to duplicate his father's elegance were absurd; to duplicate his efficiency a castastrophe. Miss Tremere had said, "You don't have to be like your father to be a good man."

He hadn't believed her. His father was the finest man he knew and he wanted to be exactly like him. Edward was twenty years old and he sat in the library staring at the inkwell, wishing he were John's age so he could put his head down and cry.

A light tap at the door brought his head up and he called gruffly, "Come in."

Lady Eastwick paused on the threshhold to take in his despondent posture, a far cry from that of less than an hour ago when he had been so sure of himself, basking in Christina's admiration. She had come to remonstrate with him on his unreasonable attitude toward Charlotte and Carlton Winstanley, but seeing him so unhappy she began to think better of it. Poor Edward, he was trying so hard.

As soon as he had seen who it was, he rose to his feet, drawing a weary hand through his hair. "I'm sorry, Mother. I don't know why I have to act like such a beast with Charlotte. It's just.... Well, I don't want Father to come home and find that everything is settled when he may not approve."

"Why wouldn't he approve, Edward?" Lady Eastwick allowed him to pull up a chair for her.

He shrugged. "I don't know. Probably he would, but he may have wanted something grander for her. Carlton Winstanley is acceptable, I know, but hardly a brilliant match. Besides, he's away at sea a great deal of the time."

"Your father and I are interested in seeing that our children marry happily, Edward. And though that often means avoiding a real *mésalliance,* it does not mean that they must marry into the aristocracy. You know, dear, you might depend on me to have some idea of what is proper for Charlotte."

Her words of reproof only made him sink deeper into his chair. "I do know, Mother. I don't really mean to set myself up as arbiter of all the children's destinies. It's just that I feel I should be doing something. Father would be doing something. I don't want him to come home and think I've made no effort to give the proper guidance."

Lady Eastwick sighed. "Edward, my love, what you must remember is that you aren't Eastwick's age, and haven't his experience. Any guidance you can give your brothers and sisters must stem from your empathy with them, not some high-flown idea of how your father would view the situation. Every parent knows that putting obstacles in a young man or woman's way is only the more likely to spur the least desirable behavior. Not that I least desire that Charlotte see as much as she wants of Carlton, but you will only have her dreaming instead of participating in a romance with him. Give her the opportunity to get to know him, and him to know her. They are a long way from a final decision, Edward, and they have such a short time before he leaves for his ship again."

"I've made a mess of everything, haven't I, Mother?"

"No, love, you haven't." She patted one of the tightly clenched hands. "You've made everything a great deal easier for me—except with the children. You can't be a father to them, Edward, but you can be a brother.

That's what they want. Don't try to be something you aren't. We were all quite happy with you the way you were."

Edward met her sympathetic eyes with an apologetic grimace. "I've been a bit confused...what with one thing and another. I'm sorry. I'll try to do better."

His mother rose and smiled at him. "Never forget that I'm proud of you, Edward, and that your father is, too. You don't need to live up to someone else's standards. If you live up to your own, you will do perfectly well."

Chapter Sixteen

Steyne found Theodosia in the Summer Parlor, where she had been deserted by the rest of the family but was working at a piece of embroidery for the dressing table in her room. Her brows rose questioningly as he entered through the doors from the terrace.

"We saw him digging," he informed her as he took the chair opposite hers. A slow smile spread across his face. "He's obviously been working very hard. There was a trench a good ten feet in both directions. A pity he couldn't have put his efforts to some more honorable endeavor."

"So you think there's no chance the treasure is buried at the boundary?"

"None at all. If he weren't so grasping, I think he would have come to that conclusion himself before now. And there's no chance that he's found it, since he's still digging."

Theodosia set her embroidery aside. "What was Thomas' reaction?"

"He wasn't particularly surprised, just disgusted." Steyne studied the long hands which rested on his thighs. "I tried to help him understand how a Heythrop could behave in such a manner."

"Thank you. You've been very kind to the children. Amy adores you."

"She's a sweetheart. In fact, they're all delightful— even Edward, when he comes down from his high-ropes. We had quite an interesting discussion about the American situation the other day."

Though she acknowledged this statement with a nod, Theodosia had obviously already switched her thoughts to another direction. "Do you think we should tell Edward and Lady Eastwick my theory about Arthur?"

"That's for you to decide." He grinned at her. "They, at least, are not likely to think you deranged."

"They might." But she returned his grin. "Tell me, where do you think the treasure is hidden?"

His reply was prompt. "In the house. The poem refers to its location at Seagrave Manor, and when Charton Court was built I would be willing to bet they made provision for it here. I think the plaque must be a clue. Would you take me to see it?"

"Certainly, but the house has been so thoroughly investigated by generations of Heythrops...."

"You can't expect it to be sitting on a mantel, my dear. Naturally it would be so well concealed that a chance discovery of it was impossible." Steyne rose and extended his hands to draw her to her feet. "Will you show it to me now?"

His hands were as reassuringly firm as they had ever been, and for a moment he didn't let go of hers, his eyes looking steadily into her wide brown gaze. Theodosia felt the breath catch in her throat and her fingers trembled slightly. Embarrassed, she would have withdrawn them if his grip had not been so firm; if the light in his eyes had not been so warm. When he spoke his voice was infinitely gentle.

"I know I've made a royal bungle of everything to do with you, Doe. I don't see how you can possibly forgive me, but I hope you will. There's no excuse I can offer for my arrogance. I can't even plead youth as an extenuating factor, since I was more than old enough to recognize what you were doing. Unfortunately, my prejudice against your father was so great that instead of respecting you for staying and being a dutiful daughter, I thought you stubborn and even lacking in sense. I can't think why, when I knew what courage it would take to tolerate his indifference. You will admit that he was indifferent to you, won't you?"

"Yes," she sighed. "He was everything you said, but he was still my father and I was only nineteen. Your suggestion that you could put pressure on him to force him to agree to our marriage was...appalling to me."

"As it should have been. Honestly, Doe, I find it difficult sometimes to believe I ever said that. My frustration at his total refusal to a match in every way unexceptionable—even advantageous—was monumental. It was tempting to want to see him humbled, I admit, and my influence with the bishop was such that I could have done it. I can't say that I wouldn't have, if you'd given me permission. Do you realize that during that one summer I was there he gave notice to a maidservant because she had an occasional fit and to another because she put an egg in the rice milk? And both of them well-known to be from families who desperately needed the small amount the girls made? This was a clergyman whose comfort came before his charity, and I fear it made me feel justified in bringing him to heel. I shouldn't have judged him; I know you tried not to. *Can* you forgive me, Doe?"

Theodosia let out a shuddering breath, lowered her eyes and raised them again. "Of course I can. In fact, I did a long time ago. You see," she explained guiltily, "I really understood then, and I secretly wanted you to do anything necessary to make my father agree. But I felt so wretched for thinking such a thing. It was almost as though I had inherited my father's selfishness and conceit. For a long time I worried that I was acting the martyr by staying with him—an even worse fault than selfishness—but after awhile I came to terms with both my obligations and my inclinations. I'm at peace with myself, Marc, and I want you to be, too."

If Theodosia meant this statement to be comforting,

Steyne found it far otherwise. Was she saying that she had ceased to love him? That even his renewed presence had failed to fan the flame that had once burned so vigorously? Was it possible that he alone remained in love? He hadn't even realized he was, at first, with the remnants of anger and hurt still clinging to him, but he knew now.

"Doe, I...." he began urgently, but there was a sweet, high voice chanting outside the Summer Parlor and Theodosia drew apart from him.

Amy tripped into the room singing, "Goosey, goosey, gander, Whither shall I wander? Upstairs and downstairs and in my lady's chamber." She smiled delightedly at finding the two of them there and asked, "Now why do you suppose a goose would wander about like that? I've never seen a goose in the house, have you?"

"No, dear," Theodosia replied, straight-faced.

"I should think not! Why, Mama would consider it the very worst sort of housekeeping to have a goose wandering about. Or a gander," Amy added, to be perfectly correct. "Lord Steyne doesn't have geese wandering about his house, does he?" Her eyes, full of youthful humor and curiosity, darted to his.

"Not when last I looked," he assured her. "All the geese at Kingswood are down by the pond."

"So are ours," she admitted, almost disappointed. "But that is not so unusual as the rest of the rhyme, really. Why would you find a cup of sack and a race of ginger in the lady's room?"

Theodosia, more familiar with Amy's analytical turn of mind than Steyne, attempted to give some reasonable explanation. "I shouldn't think it so farfetched to find a cup of wine there, but a ginger root.... Perhaps my lady had been making ginger wine, or thought to flavor her sack with the ginger."

The child delicately wrinkled her nose. "Ugh. That would be terrible. Mrs. Flowers makes her ginger wine with sugar, lemons, yeast, raisins and brandy, and of course ginger and water. Putting a piece of ginger root in a cup of wine would be ghastly."

"Yes, I'm afraid you're right," Theodosia admitted, "but it's all of a piece with geese wandering about the house."

Amy giggled. "I should like to see a gander wander into a lady's chamber. You may be sure there would be no end to the rumpus. Can't you just hear Charlotte calling for the footman? What fun! Perhaps I should...."

"Oh, no, you shouldn't, young lady," Steyne interposed, visions of geese strolling about Charton Court immediately coming to mind. "At least not until I've left, if you please. I should hate to trip over a goose in the middle of the night."

Ever alert, Amy regarded him curiously. "Do you wander about at night then, Lord Steyne?"

Steyne caught Theodosia's quizzing eyes on him and answered with a rueful grin, "Occasionally, though I've never found a cup of wine in my lady's chamber. Toothpolish, yes, but not even a trace of ginger."

"Well, of course everyone has toothpolish in her room," Amy said doubtfully. "I should think if you were looking for a glass of wine at night it would be best to look in the dining saloon. Fyfield always leaves a decanter there."

"I shall remember," he promised.

"Mama has gone to have a talk with Edward," Amy confided to them. "I think I shall go and cheer him up afterward."

"That's kind of you, dear," Theodosia said, "but Lord Steyne and I wished to talk to both of them so perhaps you could see Edward later. Are they in the office?"

"No, the library. Well, in that case I shall go to see the kittens." And she departed with a cheerful wave, chanting yet another rhyme about four and twenty tailors who were routed by a snail.

When she was no longer in hearing distance, Theodosia said, "Perhaps this would be a good time to tell them my theory. Edward is bound to be depressed."

"As you wish." It seemed to Steyne that she was avoiding a confrontation between them, but he could understand her concern. She had adopted the Heythrops as her own family and the care and solace of each of them was of paramount interest. He searched her face for any sign that she was willing to adopt him, too, but she was tidying her embroidery away into a workbox and when she had finished, she said simply, "Shall we go?"

They found Lady Eastwick about to leave the library, but apparently she and her son were entirely in charity with one another. Edward even managed to convey the impression to Theodosia that he was sorry for the way he had behaved earlier. But it was to Steyne that he turned to ask, "Have you found out anything more about my uncle digging?"

The excursion with Thomas to the estate boundary seemed a very long time ago, but Steyne marshaled his thoughts and explained, as briefly as possible, what they had learned that afternoon, both at Mr. Oldbury's and at the site of the digging. Lady Eastwick shook her head sorrowfully and Edward frowned. When the viscount had finished, he looked questioningly at Theodosia.

Theodosia was seated opposite Lady Eastwick in one of the comfortable leather chairs. "I almost hesitate to propose my theory to you. Lord Steyne thought I had quite lost my mind when I told him. Still, I think it can do no harm and might have a shred of merit."

Before she even explained her theory, Edward convinced himself that he would not laugh, no matter how ridiculous it was. However, by the time she had finished he was regarding her with bright-eyed wonder. "So you think it has to do with the Arthurian legend? How splendid! Just think, Mother, my name should have been Arthur. Well, if this proves to be the case—perhaps even if it doesn't—I shall have my first son named Arthur to renew the tradition."

His mother, exhibiting her endearing perplexed expression, turned to Steyne. "And you don't think Miss Tremere might be right, sir?"

The viscount allowed himself a glance at Theodosia before answering. "I think there is every chance that she is," he replied. "Just at first I thought she might be having a persistent nightmare, but after seeing the poem and the other documents I tend to believe the treasure and the tradition have something to do with Arthur. I was just asking her to show me the plaque, thinking that might give me some clue as to the solution. Miss Tremere thinks the figure might be that of a bear."

"By Jove, it might!" Edward exclaimed, all admiration. Suddenly he frowned. "Did it occur to you that perhaps the plaque itself is the treasure?"

Instinctively Theodosia turned to Steyne, who cocked his head thoughtfully and said, "It might be, but it's rather obvious and other than its legendary associations would have little intrinsic value."

"And there is the seventh earl's letter urging his father not to remove the treasure to a new location," Theodosia reminded him. "It seems senseless to think that he would move an item that is in plain view and has been for generations."

"Hmm, yes," Edward admitted. "On the other hand, think how much more significant the plaque is with these connotations! Keepers of the Trust. Do you think we are descended from Arthur?"

"Lord Steyne doesn't think he had any descendents," Theodosia said, smiling at Lady Eastwick, who, Theodosia felt sure, was already alarmed that her son would develop visions of grandeur if allowed to pursue this line. "I thought it might well have been an aide in battle to Arthur to whom he entrusted the 'spoils of battle' or the 'reward.' Perhaps the man was even killed in the line of duty and the treasure was bestowed on his family."

"Let's have a look at the plaque," Edward suggested.

Although that was precisely what Steyne wished to do, he had hoped for a chance to be alone with Theodosia when he did. Instead, all four of them made their way to the chapel, which was cool and only faintly lit by the late afternoon sun. The bronze plaque was located on the tower wall, close to the floor, so that it was necessary to light candles and hold them close to the wall, and even then the figure was not easily discernible. It might have been a bear, but it was partially melted from the Seagrave fire, and probably rather primitive to begin with. Steyne ran his fingers over the ancient carving and shook his head.

"Impossible to say. If this is the 'treasure' I'm afraid you're not likely to learn any more about the family secret. An expert on post-Roman Britain might be able to tell you something about its age and even the design but my own knowledge in that area is nonexistent. I've seen coins, of course, and even some of the finds at Bath, but I've never studied their significance."

"One of your forebears," Theodosia told Edward, "was fascinated by the location of the plaque and had it removed. The floor was taken up here, too, but nothing was found. Lord Steyne believes that the treasure is most likely in the house, since it was built after Seagrave was destroyed. The first earl's poem was undoubtedly meant to locate it there, and the same situation could not be duplicated at Charton Court. I wonder...."

She looked to Steyne, the germ of an idea beginning to form. "Do you suppose they attempted to duplicate the location on a theoretical level? I mean, rather than literally keeping it in a graveyard, they kept it with likenesses of those who were gone? Certainly the house is the most safe and secure location. Are there paintings of scenes of battle? Oh, my God!"

Her companions could read the dawning of revelation in her eyes, and Edward, replete with his family's history and every artifact at Charton Court, made the leap with her.

"The wooden medallions!"

"Yes, of course," Lady Eastwick murmured, catching their excitement. "There is a background scene of battle behind one of the men, an unidentified figure. But surely every wall in the house has been tapped. The medallions will have been, too."

Steyne dismissed this problem. "If the location was

chosen for its secrecy, you may be sure it will have been built so as not to reveal anything by a cursory inspection. Shall we investigate?"

The wooden medallions were located in the Long Gallery where the family assembled for dinner each evening, and were so familiar that the Heythrops had ceased to pay much attention to them. The room was almost entirely paneled in oak and the carved medallions ranged along the short section of wall between the two main doors which gave onto the room.

Lady Eastwick led the way straight to the most likely medallion at the farthest end: The head of a man was encircled within a larger square and the space between was filled with a minutely carved scene of battle below and two animallike figures above, facing one another. They might have been the artist's conception of a bear—if he'd never seen one.

"Actually, they look some nightmarish vision of a mad dog," Theodosia laughed.

Edward ran his fingers along the outside of the medallion but could feel nothing unusual. He pushed and pried and shook the area; the medallion remained intact. Thinking that perhaps a secret panel included more than just the one medallion, he proceeded to examine the entire area, looking for a concealed catch or some trick which would release the paneling. Everything remained precisely as it had for hundreds of years.

Exasperated, he stood back and looked to Steyne for help. The viscount tapped at each medallion and panel, listening intently for any difference in the sound they made. To Theodosia there seemed none, but Steyne finally turned around and said, "Only the medallion itself, I think, but it's almost impossible to tell. The difference in hollowness is minimal."

"Well, we'll just have to cut it out," Edward informed them.

His mother regarded him reprovingly. "The paneling is much too fine to be destroyed in any way, my dear. I'm certain that if this is where the treasure is stored, there is a way of releasing it without any damage. I know you're impatient to get to the truth of the matter but I cannot allow you to disfigure anything. In time we will learn the secret of opening it, but we should dress for dinner now. Heavens, we've already made incredible progress today, and I'm sure the children would love to join in finding how to open it."

"Dear Lord, Mother, don't tell the children about it while James is here! One of them is sure to let something slip. He'll be leaving soon. In fact, I thought he was leaving today." Edward hadn't considered the matter previously and looked to the viscount for some explanation.

Steyne gave a languid gesture. "James changed his mind again. I dare say he'll be ready to leave tomorrow, since he's had no success at his digging." He could not tell if this possibility affected Theodosia in any way, for she had turned to Lady Eastwick to comment that there might now be no need to use the spurious "treasure" after all. As the group disbursed to dress, he walked beside her and asked what she had meant.

"Lady Eastwick had her sister send an ancient belt buckle so that we would have tangible evidence of the summer's adventures. I was going to write some clues and have the children find it, in case we had no success with the real hunt."

"I see. How very foresighted of you, Doe." They had reached the upper landing and he placed a hand urgently on her arm. "Could we talk for a minute?"

Theodosia was about to agree when Amy bounded down the hall toward them. "Oh, Miss Tremere, you'll never guess what I've found! How do you do, Lord Steyne?" She dropped a curtsy and dimpled with pleasure as he bowed to her. "Thank you!"

"What is it you've found, dear?" Theodosia asked, her eyes dancing.

"Found? Oh, yes, of course. Do you remember the book you lent me on rare plants? Well, I am quite sure I have found one just like the picture in the book. I was playing with the kittens behind the stables when I saw it. Will you come and see it? I took it to the schoolroom. Would you mind if she came with me, Lord Steyne?"

"Not at all," he lied, smiling ruefully at Theodosia. He watched them walk down the hall hand in hand, Amy talking so fast that she almost had to skip to keep up with herself, until they disappeared around the corner. Theodosia did not look back at him. Although he was very fond of Amy, Steyne silently deplored her awkward propensity for interrupting at just the wrong moment.

With a sigh he entered his room and regarded with unalleviated gloom the evening clothes set out on his bed. He had worn them every night since he came to Charton Court and he made a firm resolve never again to travel so lightly.

Chapter Seventeen

Edward had hastened in his dressing so that he could arrive in the Long Gallery before it was time for the family to assemble. Feeling that he had no reason to worry about anyone coming upon him, he was poking at the medallion when his uncle entered the room. James so rarely joined them for a meal that he was the last person Edward had expected to see. An anguished flush suffused his face.

"Trying to absorb your ancestors' powers by rubbing them like a magic lamp, Edward?" his uncle asked sarcastically.

"No, no. I thought there was a bit of a scratch, don't you know? Probably someone has carelessly grazed it in carrying a tray through the room." Even to himself, this sounded a feeble excuse, and Edward tried again. "Or perhaps it has been there for a long time and I simply never noticed. I'm sure it's of no significance."

James would have been sure, too, if his nephew were not obviously trying so hard to explain himself. When the young man guiltily hastened away from the medallions, James began to wonder why all the mystery. He said nothing, but studied the rest of the family as they entered. Lady Eastwick, he noted, glanced toward the medallions but shifted her eyes when she saw that

James was in the room. No one else glanced at them, but it seemed to James that they made a concerted effort not to. His curiosity was piqued.

The conversation at dinner was mundane, but James sensed a suppressed excitement. He had a gambler's instincts and could almost smell the undercurrent of animation that, in opposing card players, would indicate a winning hand. Since James had spent the day uselessly digging at the boundary and had determined that any more effort would be wasted, his mind was already concentrated on the Heythrop family treasure. Added to this was his knowledge that the children, under the governess's leadership, were also hunting for the lost inheritance.

Could they possibly have found it? No, he thought not. Lady Charlotte sat at dinner completely bemused, but it was the dreamy sort of enchantment caused by love, not by a valuable discovery, James thought sardonically. Miss Tremere was as placidly entertaining as always, but Lady Eastwick was distracted. Steyne pointedly asked James if he could be ready to leave in the morning, as there were matters he should attend to in town.

That in itself was strange, James thought, as Steyne had shown not the least hurry the previous evening. James was convinced that it was an effort to get him away from Charton Court.

And there was Edward. During the meal he took little part in the discussion, his eyes often lingering unseeing on some innocuous object, his teeth unconsciously chewing on his lower lip.

Yes, decidedly something was afoot, and James had every intention of finding out what it was. The evening progressed almost as though it were a parody of a country house gathering—a little music, a little singing, a little polite conversation, some cards. And yet everyone watched him; circumspectly, of course, but they would glance in his direction as though trying to read his mind, to uncover any suspicions. At dinner he had agreed to leave the next day, which had obviously relieved his hospitable family, but he felt they still regarded him as a threat. The conviction grew on him that they knew he was hunting for the treasure—and they half expected that he might somehow find it before he left.

Now, if they were aware of his digging, they must be aware that he was not going to find it there, so they must think he could find it somewhere else. And the somewhere else had to be in the house—the Long Gallery, to be precise. Why else would Edward have acted so strangely? James determined to pay a visit there as soon as the household settled down for the night.

Several other people had come to the same conclusion. Edward was determined to be the one to unlock the secret compartment. It was a matter of pride with him, but as he was forced to admit to himself, it was also the excitement of the hunt, the challenge of the centuries-old mystery. Once he had discovered how to open the medallion, he would pretend that he hadn't and give the children a chance for the same sense of accomplishment. They had been working hard on their project with Miss Tremere and they deserved their reward. Perhaps the secret had once only been passed to the eldest son but Edward wanted his brothers and sisters to share the family legend. Not once did he bother to ask himself how his father would have viewed the situation. This time he knew he was right, but he also knew he had no intention of telling them until his Uncle James had left.

As Theodosia waited to accompany Charlotte to her room, Steyne approached her. He had said earlier that he wished to speak with her, and she expected him to suggest another meeting on the balcony, or in her chamber. Instead he asked, "Do you have the belt buckle Lady Eastwick procured for the children to find?"

"No. I'm to ask her for it when I need it."

"Will you do that now? I can come to your room to get it."

Charlotte had already finished bidding her mother,

brother and uncle good night. There was no opportunity to question him. Theodosia nodded.

She found him awaiting her in her room when she arrived there some little time later, having seen Charlotte to her room and then retraced her steps to Lady Eastwick's chamber in another wing. Fortunately her employer had not questioned her request, since Theodosia had no idea how she would have answered. Steyne rose as she entered.

"I haven't time to explain now, my dear," he said as she held it out to him, "but I will as soon as I can. Promise me you won't wander around tonight."

"Very well. I'm not really in the habit of wandering, you know."

Just for a moment he read anxiety in the wide brown eyes and he touched a finger to her cheek. "There's no danger, you know. James isn't desperate; he's merely greedy and amoral. I'll speak with you later."

Theodosia stared at the door after he had left. Actually she had little fear for Steyne's safety. He was James' superior in intellect, and probably strength as well. It was not fear for him which had shown in her eyes; it was for herself. Theodosia was indeed at peace with herself, or had thought she was. Years ago she had accepted that Steyne would hold no place in her life, though he always would in her heart. She had been able to bear this knowledge by rationally pointing out to herself that they were not well suited.

Both had a willfullness which caused them to grate on one another, and a stubbornness which did not allow for acceptance of the other's rigid determination. But in these last few days they had been reaching out, attempting to find new ground on which to meet, to compromise. They had, perhaps for the first time, begun to understand each other, and to admire what they understood.

Now, when Theodosia had begun to experience an aching longing to continue their companionship, he had deliberately terminated his visit, proposed that he and James leave for London in the morning. Oh, she could understand that he wanted James away from the family while they attempted to discover the medallion's secret, but he had not taken the chance to say even a few words to her about where they stood.

During the first part of his visit he had indicated that if she thought he was willing to take up where they left off, she was tragically mistaken. Then he had seemed to soften in his adamant stance, to accept her as she was and leave the anger and hurt behind. Was that all? Had he meant nothing when he called her "my sweet" the previous evening? He had thought she was having delusions and he had treated her gently, like a child. Had he not spoken of Amy as a "sweetheart"? But in his eyes, in his touch, Theodosia thought she had read something more.

A horrid thought occurred to her: What if he were already engaged to someone else? Would he have told her? At some point he should marry; he had thought *her* married. A shudder shook her narrow shoulders. It was possible that that was what he had to tell her, and not that he wished to renew their romance. Well, she would manage to handle it, no matter how devastating. Theodosia was an eminently practical young woman. But if she remembered, as she brushed her teeth, how he had sat and watched her a few nights previously, who can blame her?

To Steyne it was obvious that somehow James had a suspicion about the Long Gallery. He had not been there when James first entered, but he was familiar with the calculating look which James had worn for the remainder of the evening. It seemed perfectly possible to him that James had overheard some conversation, or observed them in the Long Gallery when they were not aware of his presence. Because Steyne knew that James would wait until the household had settled down for the night before he began prowling, Steyne had taken the precaution of slipping the footman a crown to patrol the main hall until he had the opportunity to do his own exploring.

When he left Theodosia's room, Steyne made his way through the dark corridors to Edward's. He knew that Edward was in the East Wing but he was not at all sure which suite he had, though the young man had indicated it to be in the rear. Steyne had no wish to tap at Lady Eastwick's door by mistake. Fortunately, as he was contemplating the various possibilities, Edward emerged stealthily from the farthest door. His surprise on being confronted by Steyne nearly caused him to drop his candle.

"Were you looking for me?" he asked, confused.

"Yes, but I wasn't sure which was your room." Steyne motioned toward his door. "Can we speak in private for a moment?"

Edward led the way and closed the door after them, impatient to be on with his search but unwilling to dismiss Steyne on some weak pretext. Though he offered the viscount a chair, Steyne remained standing.

"Edward, I'm convinced James intends to have one last crack at finding the treasure. He seems to know that it's in the Long Gallery."

A flush rose in Edward's pale cheeks. "You think he knows? I was tapping at the medallion when he came in before dinner. I never expected him! You know he's hardly eaten a meal with us since he came."

"Very true. Still," Steyne mused, "I think it would be a good idea to let him find it."

His host regarded him with astonishment, his jaw dropping ludicrously. "You cannot be serious!"

"Not until we've found and replaced it, of course." Steyne produced the Roman belt buckle which shone dully in the candlelight. "This is an artifact which Miss Tremere and your mother have arranged to allow the children to find, in the event the treasure eluded them. I propose that we see if we can locate the real one, remove it and put this in its place. It's of minimal value. I am hoping that James won't bother to take it, and that you needn't worry in future that he will pay the least heed to your family treasure."

"What if we can't find it?"

"Edward, my dear fellow," Steyne drawled, "if you and I can't find it, I'm sure James can't."

His companion laughed. "Then let's get on with it."

The footman, Parker, was still situated in the hall, seated in a porter's chair and reading the latest London paper. Edward stared at this unprecedented activity and Steyne explained as the footman hastily rose. "James isn't likely to come down while there's someone in the hall. If Parker sits here until we're through, I think we'll be uninterrupted."

The plan would not have occurred to Edward. He was not, after all, accustomed to worrying about being interrupted in his own home, but he could see its value and said, "If you will continue visible for another half hour or so, Parker, I would very much appreciate it."

Mystified, but willing, Parker returned to his reading as the two men entered the Long Gallery. Steyne lit a branch of candles and brought them close to the paneled wall. The series of wooden medallions was slightly below eye level with panels above and below. There were recurring patterns of shields and geometric designs, but no one detail stood out.

When Steyne stood back to view the overall effect, it was the simple oak leaf and acorn border which ran below that caught his eye. This border was too low to draw attention in the ordinary course of observation, hidden as it often was by assorted chairs and tables pushed back toward the wall. In height it was about a foot from the floor—precisely where the plaque was located in the chapel! The oak leaf insignia, too, appeared significant. Steyne had noticed that day when he and Thomas observed James digging, that all along the boundary of Charton Court lands there were oak trees planted at intervals of perhaps fifty feet. "Be guided by faith and our grant lands," he murmured. An effort had been made even here in the Long Gallery to adhere to the poem.

Edward had begun to poke at the medallion once again, but at Steyne's comment stood back to view the wall as the viscount was. "Do you think that's still important if the treasure is here in the house? I mean, what is there really in the chapel except the plaque?" When Steyne made no comment, but continued to stare at the lower panels, Edward had the uncomfortable feeling that he was missing something. The only really unusual thing about the plaque, of course, was how low it had been mounted on the wall, but at the same height here there was merely a pleasant carved border. He had not looked very closely at it, but now crouched to study the oak leaf and acorn border. Puzzled, he glanced up at Steyne.

"I noticed today that there were oak trees planted along the boundary where James was digging. Is that typical of the whole of the estate?" Steyne asked, not moving from his vantage point.

"Yes, they're all along the boundary. Oh, I see!" Edward exclaimed. "The height and the oak border. Rather a tenuous connection, but possible."

Choosing the section of border directly beneath the battlefield medallion he tapped and pressed to no effect until he discovered that one of the acorns turned. In his excitement he assumed that this would be the solution and jumped to his feet, reaching for the medallion. But nothing happened.

"The other acorns...." Steyne suggested.

Embarrassed by his eagerness, Edward crouched once again and found that, sure enough, all four of them turned. There was a clicking sound followed by a grating screech as the medallion swung back above his head. Edward stared at it as though hypnotized until Steyne handed him the branch of candles.

His hand shook as he held it to the small, lead-lined recess which was revealed. Within there rested a golden bowl on a base, gleaming in the flickering candlelight. How extraordinary to know that he was gazing on an item which had not been seen by anyone for several centuries!

Here, too, there was a battle scene, raised from the surface of the bowl. In the dancing light it was impossible to read the Latin inscription, but he ran his fingers lovingly over the surface. In an awed voice he said, "The illustrious treasure—found at last. My father will be delighted."

Since Edward was obviously lost in the wonder of it all, Steyne found it necessary to recall his attention to the present. "We had best remove it quickly and allow James his chance to discover the buckle. I would suggest for the time being that we place it in the writing room, so there's no chance of his seeing us leave here with it."

His mundane tone brought Edward abruptly back to earth. The very thought of James so much as setting eyes on the golden bowl made his blood heat uncomfortably. Steyne placed the buckle Lady Eastwick's sister had sent in the recess, while Edward cradled the bowl in his arms. The medallion snapped back into place with a satisfying click and Steyne extinguished all but his own candle, setting the candelabra back on the mantel where he had found it. Edward followed him into the writing room and reluctantly allowed the bowl to be placed inside a desk. Leaving the door slightly ajar, they retraced their footsteps to the hall where the footman was sleepily scratching his head.

"Did anyone come to the head of the stairs?" Steyne asked quietly.

Parker looked puzzled. "I thought someone was there—twice—but no one came down, my lord."

"Excellent." Steyne slipped a crown into his hand. "Thank you."

"That will be all," Edward informed the footman. "Good night, Parker."

At the head of the stairs the two men parted, each heading for his own room, but they had agreed to meet in the writing room in fifteen minutes. Steyne reached his own door without encountering James, and he stepped inside to wait. Only a few minutes passed before he heard a whisper of sound in the hall, nothing particularly distinguishable but enough to tell him that James had likely left his room. When a sufficient interval had passed he let himself out again and made his way to the writing room without the benefit of a candle. He found Edward there before him, bending over the desk to check that the golden bowl had not managed to disappear in his absence. Edward touched it with reverent hands but determinedly closed the desk after a moment, joining Steyne at the door where a gleam of candlelight could be seen through the crack.

By standing to the left of the door the two men were able to watch James as he duplicated Edward's earlier movements—pushing, poking, prying at the medallions. After awhile he stood back, hands on hips and head bent forward meditatively. He retained this posture for some time before abruptly raising his head to stare attentively at one section of the wall. James lit more candles and brought them over to study the first medallion and the paneling above and below it. Starting at the top, which he reached by standing on one of Lady Eastwick's finest tapestry-covered chairs, he searched every inch of the section. Eventually, almost an hour later, James reached the oak leaf and acorn trim.

There was a satisfied sigh as the first acorn turned under James' insistent fingers, and an almost gloating laugh floated to the two watchers as he worked the others and the medallion sprang back on its hinges. James reached greedily into the cavity and withdrew the "treasure." The candlelight shown on his face as he studied the bronze belt buckle with incredulity. Steyne's shoulders shook with suppressed mirth.

James was too incensed to care if the whole household heard him and exploded, "A damn belt buckle! I've ruined two pairs of boots for a damn belt buckle!" And he flung the offending item on the floor to claw around in the hole in hopes that he had missed something on his first attempt. There was nothing. He muttered a whole string of coarse oaths as he retrieved the artifact from the floor, shoved it in the cavity and slammed the medallion back in place. Edward hoped that he hadn't ruined the catch. Heedless of the dripping wax, James swung the branch of candles back onto the mantel and extinguished them with suppressed fury. Though he stomped from the room, he must have moderated his noise on reaching the hall, for they heard nothing further. In the darkness, Edward and Steyne grinned at each other.

"Perfect," Steyne proclaimed. "Shall we replace the bowl? Or better yet, why don't you take it to your room until James has gone?"

After all the excitement, Edward felt depressingly cast down. "But how would Uncle James have dared to steal the treasure? Surely he must have known that we would suspect him."

"James considers himself a law of his own." Steyne rested a hand comfortingly on Edward's shoulder. "Don't let his conduct distress you unduly, Edward. Every family has its rogues and scapegraces. James must have felt certain that you had not as yet actually found the treasure, and when you did.... Well, who is to say that it would still have been there? If you had opened the medallion and there was nothing in there, could you have sworn that James had taken it? After all, you didn't know what it was, if it would still be there after all these years. There would at least have been a reasonable doubt as to his guilt. And he did leave the buckle."

"Only because he considered it valueless," Edward said disgustedly. "I hope he leaves early in the morning and never returns."

Steyne laughed. "Both events are unlikely, my dear fellow. But after a wholly disappointing sojourn here, I doubt he'll be in a hurry to return."

The writing desk still stood open and Edward picked up the golden bowl as though it were fragile as an eggshell. He would be the first to really study the treasure after its long exile, to read the words that might offer a solution as to its origin. "Thank you, Lord Steyne, for all your assistance."

"I've thoroughly enjoyed myself," his companion assured him as they left the writing room. They silently made their way across the hall and parted at the head of the stairs, each to conclude the business most important to him at the moment.

Chapter Eighteen

Theodosia's door was locked. Steyne knew because he tried it before he knocked. In fact, he had to knock several times before she answered. Really, she had a wonderful capacity for sleeping at the most unlikely times, he decided. When she asked softly through the door who it was, he said, "Marc."

The door opened to a room in total darkness. She had struggled into a dressing gown, but had not taken the time to strike a flint and light a candle. Her hair was loose and rumpled, her eyes blinkingly sleepy. "Is everything all right?"

He nodded as he shut the door. "Everything is fine. Obviously I woke you. Would you rather we talked in the morning?"

"No, I don't mind. Just give me a moment to gather my thoughts together."

Standing there staring blankly at the buttons on his coat, she did look rather disoriented. Steyne set down his candle, making no attempt to light any others in the room. He went purposefully to the wash-hand stand and dipped a cloth in the now-cold water, rung it out and proceeded to rub it gently over her face as she stood with it patiently lifted, like a child. Her alertness was not visibly improved.

"How in heaven's name do you deal with the children in the middle of the night?" he asked with mock exasperation. There was only one way to clear her head, he decided, as he lifted her chin and leaned down to kiss her. And a light, passing kiss would hardly serve his purpose, of course. If he was to get her full attention, it had to be by arousing her interest or her wrath. His lips on hers were demanding.

Theodosia was instantly shaken from her drowsy trance, but it seemed wisest for a moment to appear otherwise. Her response to him might then be mistaken for a rather long-abandoned habit; she had been in the habit of responding quite admirably to him in the old days. If she was going to draw away from him—indignant, offended—she would have to do it soon. It hardly seemed worth the effort. Eventually he gathered her to him for an extravagant hug and then determinedly urged her to a chair.

"Now we can talk," he informed her, drawing another chair so close that he could, and did, hold her hand. "What would you like first—the story of the treasure or a declaration of love?"

Theodosia observed his delighted grin and shook her head mournfully. "What a romantic you are, Marc! Tell me about the treasure." When his brows rose, worried, unhappy, she explained, "I like to save the best for last, like a child."

"And my sister could never understand why I ate the turnips first. It will be so comforting to have someone who understands me."

Ignoring this juxtaposition of last on first, Theodosia folded her hands and asked, "What happened this evening?"

As concisely as possible he related the discovery, the substitution and James' search. Theodosia expressed appreciation that Edward had been the one to find the golden bowl but offered no comment on Steyne's part in the adventure.

He eyed her warily. "On the other hand, it may be difficult to live with someone who takes my few good qualities for granted. My sister always praised me lavishly for doing something useful."

"Your sister didn't mind spoiling you, Marc. Older sisters have a tendency to do that, I think." But her eyes were dancing. "I hope you know how grateful I am that you managed everything so well."

"Faint praise! And here I thought you would tell me how clever I am, how much you admire my resourcefulness, how...."

"All of that, certainly," she laughed, raising a hand as though to stop the flow of his self-congratulations. "I thought I would spare myself repetition by saving my admiration for your declaration of love!"

"Did you? Well, then, we should get on with it!" But he dropped his bantering tone immediately and took both her hands in a firm grip, his eyes wandering fondly over her animated face. "Oh, Lord, I hardly know where to begin. Should I apologize for my lack of understanding and my pigheaded behavior?"

"No."

"Good. It's very difficult for me to do that, but I'm sorry for all this wasted time and my part in it. And I'd like to wring my aunt's neck! Doe, if I had known when your father died, I would have come to you. I want you to believe that."

"I do," she said softly, pressing his hand.

"When I thought you had married someone else I was hurt and confused. I felt you hadn't given me a chance, but I confess I didn't blame myself until coming here. Of course I've been spoiled—all my life. I usually think I know what is best for other people and I have a tendency to tell them what to do. Believe me, it doesn't stem from disdain but from caring for them."

"I know."

He held her eyes intently. "If I've acted as though I didn't respect your judgment, I never meant to. No, I suppose that's not entirely true. When you were eighteen I did question your decision, but I can see now that you only did what you had to do, and I made it harder for you. I would like to leave that behind us. Is that possible?"

Theodosia nodded but an impish light gleamed in her eyes. "Marc, if you don't get around to making this declaration of love fairly soon, I am going to expire of anticipation."

"Oh, for God's sake, Doe! I love you! There, I've said it in all its simple elegance. I love you to distraction! (That's with a little more passion.) I want you to marry me. (That's the part that makes the passion acceptable!)" He had pulled her to her feet during this recital and now kissed her rather warmly. "That's to demonstrate the passion, the love, etc. Well, have you anything to say for yourself?"

"I am, of course, sensible of the honor you do me...."

"Not that!" he protested, unable to keep his lips from twitching. "A simple yes or no will do, my love."

"Well," she sighed, "if you won't allow me to respond to you properly, I suppose it will have to be a simple 'yes.' But it's very unfair of you, Marc."

"How can you say so?"

"Why, you haven't given me the opportunity to list all your admirable qualities in the course of my acceptance speech. I was going to drown you in rhetoric, just as you have been attempting to do. And, of course, I was going to tell you that I loved you, too."

"Do you?" he demanded, his lips close to hers.

She managed to murmur a shaky "yes" before she was unable to say anything further.

It was some time later, when she sat on his lap (two chairs seeming redundant), that he said, "I think, if it is acceptable to you and Lady Eastwick, that I will bring Ruth here to meet you. They were great friends and they could both use some companionship just now."

"Will you go up to London with James in the morning?"

"I should, but I'll stay if you wish it. I need only be gone three or four days."

Theodosia pondered this information. "Will that give

me a chance to keep my appointment with Mr. Oldbury for a drive?"

"Hussy! The only appointment you are going to keep with Mr. Oldbury is one that I will arrange in the morning for him to marry us." He regarded her with one quizzically raised brow. "If that is acceptable to you."

Her retort had not quite been formulated when the door burst open and Edward exclaimed, "I thought you would be here! When you weren't in your room this is the first place I thought to come!"

"We are going to be married," Theodosia said faintly, unable to rise from Steyne's lap since he refused to let her.

Edward did not appear to hear her. "It *does* have to do with Arthur! The Latin inscription is most definitely *Mons Badonicus,* Arthur's most famous battle, and the single word 'Arthur' is on the other side with a man carrying a shield! Imagine!"

With the greatest presence of mind, Steyne suggested, "I think on such an auspicious occasion you would be justified in waking your mother to tell her. And do close the door after yourself."

"Oh! Yes, of course."

When Edward had departed, with a sheepish grin and a mumbled, "Congratulations!" Theodosia sighed. "I shall miss the Heythrops. Have you ever seen such single-minded purpose?"

"Yes," he told her as he drew her back into his arms.

Epilogue

Theodosia stood by a window looking out over the rolling Kent landscape. The sun had set but the sky remained rainbow-hued near the horizon, casting an enchanting light over the lawns. She turned slowly as she heard the door open. "It's beautiful here, Marc. I wish we had arrived a little earlier so we could have wandered through the grounds."

"Tomorrow, my love. Any one of a thousand tomorrows." He joined her by the window and pointed to a distant body of water. "That's where I shall take you in the morning, if you like. You can skip stones there to your heart's content." He had begun to remove the pins from her hair, allowing it to cascade through his fingers. "Do you like to swing? There's a swing by the lake. I have always had it kept in good condition because Ruth enjoys it so much."

"Marc...." Theodosia paused as he kissed her and turned obediently so he could undo the fastenings at the back of her dress. "Ruth seemed very happy at Charton Court, don't you think? She was so kind to me. I...would have suggested that she come here with us, except for our being just married."

"Hmm."

Theodosia tingled to the touch of his warm hands on

her bare shoulders. "Marc? Did you think she seemed happier? I mean... being with Lady Eastwick and all."

"Much happier." He grinned at her averted face and continued to remove her clothing.

Unembarrassed, Theodosia stood before him disrobed, her eyes warm with love, but determined to discuss his sister. "She doesn't really like town life, I think, except for contact with serious people, people like those she knew with her husband, you know."

"Yes," he agreed, drawing her to him, "Ruth likes people with some purpose."

After awhile, Theodosia sighed contentedly, but drew back a pace to say, "It didn't sound as though there were very many people like that at her estate in the country. I don't mean they aren't *good* people! She spoke of them with real affection, but she needs someone to...."

"Yes, my dear, I know," he assured her as he began to remove his own apparel.

But Theodosia didn't think he understood. He spoke absently, the light in his eyes fired by desire, not by concern for his sister. Well, it was a stupid time to bring up the subject anyway, she told herself. And what did she know of the need for physical contact, except for these last few days? She could hardly be considered an expert on the subject of marital relations and she felt rather naive trying to discuss them with her husband on such a short experience. But what an enlightening, ecstatic experience! Frankly, she had never guessed the least part of it!

Still, to think of poor Ruth who had enjoyed this bliss with her husband for fifteen years, only to be bereaved, denied his presence, his love, his companionship... and this incredible physical sharing. How Theodosia ached for Ruth's sorrow. She could not help but compare it with her own joy.

"Marc, what I mean is...."

"Come here, Doe," he said gently, holding his arms open to her.

Nothing could keep her from him. How quickly the

body learned to crave this overwhelming sensation. His hands were so gentle, his lips so soft, and yet the fire they created raged through her until almost every other thought was banished. Almost.

"Marc love, we have so much...."

He was carrying her toward the bed, cradling her against him, her long brown hair falling on his arms and chest. "More than I had dared hope," he agreed, his voice husky. She could not see the quizzical tilt to his brows in the darkening room.

"Yes, well, when we have so much I was thinking of poor Ruth, so alone, you know."

"She's with the Heythrops. One can hardly consider that alone."

"No, of course not, but...." There was no use fighting the urgency now, Theodosia admitted to herself. You could not feel sympathy for even the most deserving creature on earth when in the grip of this delicious fervor.

Suddenly his touch ceased and he drew slightly apart from her. "But what?"

Theodosia was appalled that through her insistence on pursuing the subject she was now left suspended. Confused, her body a turmoil of need, she could not for a moment remember what he was asking.

He prompted her. "Ruth is not alone since she's with the Heythrops, but what?"

"Ruth?" Theodosia scoured her mind for what she had meant to say. Momentarily every thought had fled, dispersed by euphoria. "I...I don't remember. That is, I *will* remember but I can't seem to think just at present."

His hands had returned to her—thank heaven! The desire which had leveled began to mount again. And then, as though suddenly remembering something, he paused and said meditatively, "Perhaps you were going to say that you thought Ruth should remarry."

Remarry. Yes, that was it. Theodosia thought Ruth should remarry. Return to this state of bliss. Why must Marc move away from her when he spoke? He seemed to be awaiting her reply. "Yes, yes. That's it. I think Ruth should remarry." And she reached out to tug him tentatively toward her.

Although he allowed himself to be drawn to her, in fact lay pressed against her side, he obviously was not ready to abandon their dialogue. "It's all very well to say Ruth should remarry but eligible men aren't found on every road, Doe. You have to remember her age. And she was in London for months and thought the selection of gentlemen extremely meager. She can't just marry anyone to be married."

Theodosia put her arms about him. "I'm sure we can discuss it later."

"Oh, no," he replied, and there was the first hint of laughter in his voice. "You were the one who was so determined to pursue this line. And I am just as determined to prove to you that my passion for you does not outstrip my respect for your concerns. Now tell me, love, whom did you have in mind for Ruth to marry?"

"I'll tell you afterward, you unreasonable man," she groaned. "How *can* you talk at such a time?"

"Unreasonable? I promise you I am being the ultimate in reason, and sensibility as well. When my adorable, romantic wife shows a preference for discussing my relations to...."

His body was shaking with laughter against hers and she pummeled his chest lightly with her fists until he managed to control himself. "Wretched man! I'm sorry I brought up the subject at an inconvenient moment, but there really was something I wanted to say."

"I assure you I am all attention."

"But I don't want to say it now!" she protested, aggrieved. "Dear Marc, I am prepared to admit your perfect reason and sensibility, your consideration and fortitude, but I must also confess that you are the most attractive, lovable, enchanting, exciting man...."

"Say no more," he suggested gallantly.

* * *

"Marc?"

"Yes, my love?"

"I think Ruth and Mr. Oldbury were attracted to each other."

"Yes, I noticed."

"You did?" Theodosia raised herself on one elbow and stared at him indignantly. "You mean you let me go on all that time and you knew precisely what I wanted to say?"

"Of course. You married a gentleman, my sweet."

"Sometimes I wonder."